Falling, Freestyle

Never venture out of bounds without a buddy—preferably two.

Dara's past four incredible years have been lived to the fullest. Along with her best friends, Kane and Jack, she's left no local wilderness unexplored, no ski slope unchallenged. Yet lately she wonders why they've never seen her as more than a buddy with breasts. When—or if—either man will cross that unspoken line.

It's a line Kane eyes harder every day. Since high school, he and Jack have shared everything. A condo, vacations—and their best girl. Kane's ready to get serious about his wilderness school and outfitter business, and that includes putting down roots. Preferably with Dara.

Wary of the men who've recently been sniffing around Dara, Jack has a growing sense that he or Kane better make a move soon, or they're going to lose out on their perfect match. Question is, who does she prefer...and who's going to bring their easygoing trio to an end?

Overhearing the boys arguing over her, Dara's floored—and torn. Choose between them? No way. Drastic measures are called for, a plan for their annual holiday getaway that will clarify her feelings once and for all—or lose everything in a sexual storm of whiteout proportions.

Warning: Old friends turned lovers can get into the most trouble—exhibitionism, bondage, spanking. Anal sex, oral sex, unauthorized use of ski safety harnesses, icicles in the hot tub... The author apologizes in advance for any melted monitors.

Rising, Freestyle

Stuck between a rock-solid man and a hard place...

Melanie Dixon's body may have recovered from a horrific climbing accident, but her nerve is long gone. So is the natural enthusiasm for life she took for granted. Tired of being scared, beyond ready to conquer her fears, she pulls up stakes and moves to her brother's new hometown to start over. Her first step is the most terrifying—to tackle the wall at the local climbing center.

Derrick James is mesmerized by Melanie's dark beauty, and equally impressed with her climbing abilities and determination. Watching her retune rusty skills spurs a desire to partner with her—on and off the ropes. Melanie's a compelling mix of wit, sensuality and vulnerability, and it's his delicious task to convince her the scars on her body are no match for the heat rising between them.

Then a man from Melanie's past shows up, pushing their relationship to the edge. Nathan King wants photographs for a "where are they now" series, but his side agenda is more personal in nature. A proposal that brings her out of her sensual shell and onto a precarious sexual ledge. Where trust is crucial...and too easily shattered.

Warning: This book may cause heart-pounding, body-shaking adrenaline attacks—and that's before they leave the climbing gym. Contains blindfolds, ropes and a healthy dose of voyeurism. Go on—you know you like to watch.

Look for these titles by
Vivian Arend

Now Available:

Granite Lake Wolves
Wolf Signs
Wolf Flight
Wolf Games
Wolf Tracks
Wolf Line

Forces of Nature
Tidal Wave
Whirlpool

Turner Twins
Turn It On
Turn It Up

Pacific Passion
Stormchild
Stormy Seduction
Silent Storm

Six Pack Ranch
Rocky Mountain Heat
Rocky Mountain Haven
Rocky Mountain Desire

Bandicoot Cove
Paradise Found
Exotic Indulgence

Print Collections
Under the Northern Lights
Under the Midnight Sun
Breaking Waves
Storm Swept
Tropical Desires

Freestyle

Vivian Arend

SAMHAIN
PUBLISHING

Samhain Publishing, Ltd.
11821 Mason Montgomery Road, 4B
Cincinnati, OH 45249
www.samhainpublishing.com

Freestyle
Print ISBN: 978-1-60928-717-7
Falling, Freestyle Copyright © 2012 by Vivian Arend
Rising, Freestyle Copyright © 2012 by Vivian Arend

Editing by Anne Scott
Cover by Angela Waters

Falling, Freestyle, ISBN 978-1-60928-260-8
First Samhain Publishing, Ltd. electronic publication: November 2010
Rising, Freestyle, ISBN 978-1-60928-495-4
First Samhain Publishing, Ltd. electronic publication: July 2011
First Samhain Publishing, Ltd. print publication: June 2012

Contents

Falling, Freestyle

Dedication

For all those people who have a friends-to-lovers story. I think it's a great way to set up a lasting relationship.

And to my hubby, who's my friend first, last and everything in between.

Chapter One

Alpine Responsibility Code
Rule #1—Always stay in control...

The bright yellow safety marker passed behind them as Dara leaned back on the solid wood boards of the chairlift, easing her skis onto the rests. She relaxed and drew in a deep breath of icy air, turning her face toward the sun to soak in its warmth. Heat radiated off the bodies on either side of her. Jack and Kane—her best friends in their ski-crazy town.

"Which run do you two want to hit next?" Kane elbowed Dara in the ribs, his bright blue eyes flashing with amusement. Dark curls stuck out from the edges of his helmet to frame his boyish good looks. "You warmed up enough yet for something other than the bunny hills?"

The man was merciless. "Screw you. Just because I don't like starting the day with double black doesn't mean it's a bunny hill. And I kick your butt when we ski trees, so chill."

"She's got you there," Jack taunted. His blond hair was hidden under a woolen toque with long braided ties hanging down on either side of his face. Combined with the rest of his features, the image reminded her of ancient Viking barbarians—beautiful, strong.

Dangerous.

Kane winked at her. "Bull. I just like to watch the lines you take. It's the only chance I get to admire your incredible talent since I spend the rest of the time with you on my backside."

Dara laughed, tucking herself a little farther into the shelter of Jack's broad body as their chairlift crested the first major rise. He adjusted his position to completely shield her from the wind.

She was so grateful their local ski hill had a couple of triple chairs. The twelve-minute ride to the mountaintop was never as long, or as cold, when both her guys were there. The ride up was a chance to take a break from the wild downhill rush of swooshing through knee-deep powder, snow flying in her wake. She snuggled in tighter against Jack, nudging the walkie-talkie in his pocket out of her way. While his rule that they each carry one as a backup for if they ever got separated was smart, she didn't need it poking her in the back.

The chair rattled over another of the tall towers, setting them swinging slightly. They'd all arranged to play hooky from their evil day jobs to take advantage of the lesser crowds midweek. A bad day skiing beat a good day at work anytime. Kane made a satisfied noise, then turned his grin her direction, obviously as pleased as she was with their impromptu Wednesday getaway. "Your pick, Dara, which run will it be?"

"Diamond Drill. I want to hit the jump."

Jack swore. "Already? You don't need to prove anything to Kane. He's just being an ass, teasing you about being a bunny."

She had to laugh. "I know he's a shit, that's not why I want to do it." She wiggled her brows at him. "I think you're the one who's a bit of a chicken. That jump still freaks you out, doesn't it?"

Kane laid a gloved hand on her shoulder. "Don't you worry,

darling. You want to sail off into the wild blue yonder, I'll be there to catch you."

The banter continued back and forth until they reached the top of the lift. They slipped off and glided to the side where Jack and Dara waited for Kane to buckle on his snowboard. The first runs of the day were always magical. The cloud-free sky allowed the sun to flash blindingly bright off the fresh powder, individual snow crystals sparkling everywhere she looked. With clean uncut snow to track up, the thrill of exhilaration made being out of doors in the freezing weather worth it. Of course, getting to spend the day with her two best buds added to the pleasure.

Four years ago they'd found her struggling to bring her personal items into the apartment unit before a blizzard buried her. They had worked together to carry in all the boxes and bags stuffed into her ancient Volvo, ordered a pizza, and they'd been the three musketeers ever since.

Not only could they keep up with her on the slopes, they were a hoot in the ski lodge. After their time together, they had developed rituals and routines that made her smile. Simple things, like they always brought their own lunches, but splurged and shared the biggest plate of fries the cafeteria made. Hot chocolate from a thermos, and a cold brew or two when they got home. Yeah, life was good and Dara couldn't imagine any way it could possibly get better.

Well, except having the two of them actually notice she was a girl. That would be nice.

Dara glanced between them—Jack adjusting his goggles to cover his chocolate brown eyes, Kane waving lazily to another local sliding past. Yup—they were the best friends she'd ever had, and if there was a tiny piece inside her that longed for more, well...

15

There was too much at stake to risk changing their current state of affairs.

Kane whooped as he rose to his feet, propelling himself straight down the hill to pick up enough speed before cutting across the slope to the run they wanted to take. Dara smiled at Jack and they took off after him, their poles and skis making it easier to maneuver at the top of the run. Jack telemarked, with a ski and boot combination that left his heels unattached, forcing him to bend low on each turn. His strong legs moved rhythmically as he bounced between the upper moguls.

Dara was the ordinary one, with her freestyle skis and poles. She didn't have the stamina to spend the whole day doing lunges, like Jack would as he telemarked, and the one time she'd tried snowboarding she'd spent more time on her ass than on the hill.

Kane shrieked with laughter as he raced down the hill and Dara joined in, letting out her own cry of delight. She flew past Jack as she accelerated around the corner and headed toward the jump. The only time she'd seen Jack completely lose his eternal cool was the day he crashed, rolling limbs askew for a good twenty-five meters before coming to a stop at the base of a tree. Luckily nothing had been broken, but Jack still freaked every time she headed for it. She crouched in preparation, then extended her knees at the apex of the jump and let herself soar into the air. She flung her arms to the side to rotate herself in a three-hundred-sixty-degree circle. The dark green of the trees and the blue of the sky blurred together as she spun, the snow-covered ground a million miles away—for all of four seconds—before it rushed to meet her. She absorbed the impact of the landing, catching her balance with her legs wide apart.

Awesome. She let out a howl and Kane answered back from below. One more swoosh and she slid to a stop at his feet, spraying him with a wash of fine snow crystals.

"Holy crap, girl, that was the most height I've ever seen you get on that jump. Some day you might even be as good as me."

Dara punched Kane in the arm and they turned to watch Jack. He wove his way toward them, stopping with an extra bit of flair and coating them both with snow. "Okay, I'm officially pumped for our holiday. Three back-to-back days of skiing? Watching you two is going to put me into cardiac arrest."

Kane gestured down the hill. "Then go first so you don't have to see it, because it's only going to get better from here on."

They spent the next hour assaulting the fresh snow, the crowds slowly growing as people realized the weather had turned for the better. When they stomped into the lodge for lunch, Dara took a side trip for a bathroom break.

Yeah, Jack and Kane were the perfect ski partners, kayak buddies and best friends for watching movies and kicking back but...damn.

Dara stared into the mirror. Ordinary stared back. She was nothing like the women they dated. She was solid and plain, and tended to let other people speak for her far more often than she should. She even had a freaky dusting of freckles across her nose that made people who described her use words like "cute" and "wholesome".

Well, she doubted most people who were considered "cute" spent a day on the hill with her friends before returning home to a vibrator. The last in a long line of toys she'd burnt out in an attempt to tame all the wild fantasies streaking through her mind every time she thought about the guys.

And she was sure those "wholesome" girls would never daydream about what Jack and Kane looked like in the shower when they'd all head home after the day's excursions were done. The worst part was she didn't have to imagine much, not

17

after dozens of trips together where the guys both stripped to nothing but boxers when it got hot. To say nothing about the time they went swimming in the buff. Not that she'd been looking.

Much.

Ripped bodies, great attitudes. Kane and Jack had been best friends since forever...and that was the kicker. There was no way she wanted to screw up their friendship, not only with her, but with each other. The kind of loyalty they'd shared over the years was precious. Getting involved with either of them would be a recipe for disaster. She patted her face with water. Nope—she could satisfy herself with her fingers and her rubbery friends, and keep her relationship with the guys clean and clear.

Her pocket vibrated and she straightened with a jerk. It took her a second to figure out it was her walkie-talkie—the guys must be looking for her. She should have just told them to go ahead and grab the fries. The hard plastic slipped in her wet hands and she nearly dropped the thing. In her mad scramble to catch it, she hit *listen* instead of *talk*.

Jack's voice rose to her ears, and he sounded pissed off. "Shut up. This isn't the time or the place for this discussion. You really want to mess with what we've got?"

"You know as well as I do that someday she's going to find someone she likes, and we'll be out of luck. You want to sit around and wait until then?"

Dara listened for a minute before she realized the guys didn't know she was on the line. She reached for the call button when her name caught her ear.

"If Dara wanted to get involved with either of us, she would have done something by now."

What?

"You think so?" Kane's deep voice drawled. "I think since we're always together, there's not much chance for the girl to express interest in one of us. Like she's going to come on to me when you're around. She's too polite."

"Yeah, right."

Dara picked her jaw off the floor and glanced around the bathroom in shock, hoping no one else was listening. One stall door was closed, so she turned down the volume and held the receiver tight to her ear. She should turn it off, she really should, but she couldn't resist eavesdropping a little longer.

"What's the solution? You going to step back and let me show her who's the better guy?" Jack's husky voice sent a shiver racing over Dara's skin.

Kane laughed. "Here's where this conversation stalls every time. This is why neither of us is with Dara. We both think we'd be good with her, and that she'd be a good match for either of us."

Jack swore softly. "So why are we discussing this? The day we met her we agreed to keep our hands off."

"I'm saying maybe we need to change our rules. Frankly, I'm getting to the point I'd rather see her with you than with anyone else."

"Likewise, dickwad, but your timing sucks. With the ski trip we've got planned, I think we should just keep the status quo for now and change the dynamics when we get back. I'd hate to upset our getaway if...well if anything does happen. We've had this in—"

Loud crackling noise filled the speaker, nearly deafening Dara. Their voices faded, then cut out completely. One of the guys must have moved the receiver and accidentally clicked off the send button.

She leaned back on the wall and fought to catch her

19

breath. *Holy shit.* They were both interested in her. It was every woman's fantasy to have guys like Jack and Kane interested in her except...

There was no way on earth she could choose between them.

Every memory she had of Jack was wrapped up with thoughts of Kane. All the things she loved about Kane were connected by experiences with Jack.

Jack was her solid rock. Sturdy and dependable, even though he looked like he'd be at home pillaging a village. He fixed her shower, helped her with her computer and brought her chocolates when she got into a funk. They discussed books and movies, and somehow he instinctively knew when she needed a hug. His smile made her darkest day bright.

In comparison, Kane was her laughing buddy, rioting out with his loud mannerisms and boisterous good humour. He wasn't embarrassed to be caught sniffling during the chick flicks she forced them to watch. She never knew what to expect from the practical joker, except she trusted him to always be on her side.

As she made her way up the stairs to the cafeteria, her mind continued to race a million miles an hour, going down roads better not imagined. Like wondering again what Jack would be like in bed. Cautious? No, thorough, maybe forceful even. Kane, on the other hand, would be the type she could laugh with while they fooled around.

Damn. She shook her head and pushed through the cafeteria doors, clomping in her heavy boots toward their usual table. The swelling volume of voices drowned out her thoughts.

She should confess she'd heard their conversation, but what could she say without it being really awkward? In fact, doing anything about what she'd overheard seemed completely impossible.

If she knew which man she wanted to get involved with, it would be simpler. With her affections spread so evenly between them, that option was eliminated. In fact she couldn't imagine being with one and not the other.

Being with both of them? *Together.* Oh Lord, yes. As if she hadn't fantasized about that a million times as well.

Her face flushed hotter. The erotic books she'd read returned to her, and suddenly she wondered if she was brave enough to go through with the idea flashing through her brain. Their annual pre-Christmas ski trip away to another resort, just the three of them, was fast approaching. If she opened the door just a crack, what would they think of spending time getting to know her better—both of them?

Maybe if she introduced the concept of a ménage as a fantasy, asked them to help her out. She'd be able to see if there was a difference in the way her heart and body felt—see if she was more drawn to one than the other. In the meantime she'd be experiencing a dream come true.

If she could convince them to give it a try.

She stepped next to the table and they both turned their full attention her way. Darkness and light met her, in their eyes, their hair. Something inside her belly tingled with anticipation, and this time she let it build instead of beating it into submission.

Wanting them both wasn't wrong, she was sure of it. Wanting them both, together...that seemed more risqué.

"I thought you'd fallen in and drowned." Jack grinned and pushed the plate of fries toward her. "I saved some from the bottomless pit over there."

"I'm a growing boy. I need to keep my strength up." Kane slid to the side to give Dara room to join him. He had one leg on either side of the bench and as she nestled in she realized just how intimate the position was, her hip inches from his groin.

She choked down the fries, her gaze flicking from one to the other as they laughed and joked. Her guys, their faces glowing with health and energy. Drool-worthy Jack. Invigorating Kane. Daydream inducing—together or apart.

Something clicked inside and she took a deep breath.

They wanted to change the status quo? So be it, but she would be the one calling the shots. She had a few weeks to get everything in place, then come hell or high water she was going to make the most outrageous thing she'd ever dreamed of a reality.

She was going to seduce her best friends.

Chapter Two

Alpine Responsibility Code

Rule #2—Plan ahead...

Kane slammed his fist against the horn a couple of times. "What the hell is taking him so long?"

Dara sat on the bench seat beside him, her blonde hair pulled into two high pigtails. He forced his gaze away from where her sweater lay open at the top, one button too many open, leaving a gap that showed off the creamy upper swells of her breasts. One button too many, or seven buttons too few.

Ever since he'd mentioned to Jack he thought it was time to make a move on Dara, he'd found it more and more difficult to ignore her. The burning desire to treat her as more than one of the boys threatened to tear loose at any moment. Now that they were headed out for their long-weekend ski vacation, acting as if it was business as usual between them was going to kill him. Her light perfume filled the cab of the truck, and he rocked in place, attempting to adjust his half-hard cock without being too noticeable.

Jack stepped onto the sidewalk and Dara laughed. "He's traveling light, I see."

"Bloody fool."

Their friend carried a large cardboard apple box in his arms. Before Kane had left for work that morning, he and Jack had brought down their ski gear and backpacks from their apartment and stowed it all in the truck. They'd grabbed Dara's stuff from her place down the hall as well, so they could leave as soon as he and Dara got off work at noon. Kane couldn't imagine what Jack still needed to bring. He rattled his fingers on the wheel as Jack sauntered past the truck cab, flashing his hundred-proof smile at Dara as he headed to dump his box in the back.

Dara slipped off her boots as she waited, and Kane watched closely as she assumed her usual traveling position, legs curled half under her. The girl never kept her feet on the floor. It was part of her charm that like some pixie creature you could find her up on the counter, or wrapped around a chair. Dara didn't sit, she perched.

She wore his favourite winter outfit, the one that made him imagine all sorts of dirty things. Velvety smooth stockings of dark crimson covered her long legs, and he longed to touch her. To start at her ankles and run his palms all the way up and under her short flared skirt, the one that was barely respectable when she walked, but lost all semblance of propriety when she brought her knees up on the bench.

His cock pressed painfully against his zipper, and he slid his hips lower on the seat, adjusting the backrest as an excuse.

Jack jumped in, slamming the door on the freezing cold blast of air that followed him. Dara shivered and cuddled closer to Kane's side. Her warm body felt just right next to him. Damn if he was going to survive this weekend.

"We finally ready to roll? There's four hours ahead of us to the resort." Kane peeled out into the roadway fast enough to force their bodies against the backrest. Hell, that had sounded as if he was pissed, but he was mere seconds from begging Dara to sit on his lap and help ease his pain.

Jack snapped on his seat belt and threw his gloves onto the dash. "Drive on. Sorry I'm late, but I've got a great excuse."

"You won the lottery and you were making reservations for us to fly to Hawaii after the ski trip is over." Dara leaned on Kane's shoulder as she faced Jack. Kane casually lifted his arm and placed it along the back of the seat and she settled even closer, her head resting on his biceps. While she was in his arms under false pretenses, he would totally take it.

"How'd you guess?" Jack tweaked her nose and she laughed, her body shimmying against Kane's ribs.

"You have that look on your face. Spill." Dara poked Jack in the side, tickling him lightly.

Kane dragged his eyes off their interplay and focused on the road. They had a long way to go and staring at her was bound to get them stuck in a ditch.

"I got a call from the resort this morning after you left for work. Seems they had a bit of a reservation error."

"Fuck it. Now what? I booked our rooms ages ago." Kane gripped the wheel tighter. He couldn't take much more. Fighting his growing need to tell Dara he wanted her was making him cranky and crazy.

"Don't sweat it until I tell you the whole thing. The guy gave me some long-winded story about how someone mistyped digits and there's a family reunion—whatever. We can't have the adjoining rooms we asked for, but since it's not our fault they wanted to make it up to us."

That sounded more positive. "Complimentary drinks?"

"Better. The only other unit that was free for all of our booking dates is a private cabin—ski in/ski out."

"No shit?" This was either a gift from heaven, or one from hell.

"Seriously. Master bedroom in the loft with a king, a bedroom on the main floor with two queen beds. Full kitchen, a fireplace and a private hot tub on the balcony overlooking the ski hill."

Dara hadn't made a sound since Jack started describing the accommodation change. Kane squeezed her shoulders. "You going to be okay with that, sweets? You can have the loft to yourself, and Jacky-boy and I will close the bedroom door so you don't have to listen to him snore."

There was a slight hesitation before she laughed. "I've slept in the same tent as you guys too many times to fall for that load of bull. You're the one with the volume-control problem at night."

"Only when I'm horny."

Shit. He hadn't meant to let that slip out.

He glanced over and caught Jack shaking his head. "Right, because your dick is so heavy you can't sleep in any position but flat on your back."

Dara laughed out loud. "Play nice, boys. Jack, it sounds fabulous, but why were you late? I mean, he didn't charge you extra or anything, did he?"

"No, he reassured me everything was already paid in full, so unless we watch dirty movies or get room service, we're clear to go at checkout. I just decided if we were going to have a kitchen we should take advantage of it. I spent the last hour gathering treats."

Kane let out a whoop of delight. "Tell me you brought beer and nachos."

Dara's priorities were clear. "Ice cream? Chocolate?"

Jack grinned down at her. "Even better. Banana-split fixings—chocolate sauce, whipped cream, even a jar of those nasty cherries you love."

"The ones that are a million calories each? Score!"

She and Jack slapped hands in mid-air and she wiggled closer to give him a huge hug. Over her shoulder, Jack winked at Kane. A grumble of unease flicked through him. When Dara was going to have her own room, there had been a chance of getting through the long weekend without making a fool of himself. Now?

He was going to hit the slopes with a woody the size of his snowboard, constantly thinking of her nearby. Heck, he'd probably have to watch her wander the cabin in her PJs.

And the hot tub? Sheer torture.

"You okay to drive?" Dara shifted, tucking her feet under his right thigh.

"Of course, why?"

"You sighed like you'd had a hard morning or something. If you need a break, make sure you ask. I love driving your truck."

Jack laughed. "You know you're going to be fast asleep in under an hour."

"Am not. It's only noon."

Kane and Jack exchanged amused gazes over her head. "Bet you she's down in thirty minutes flat," Kane said.

"Guys..." Dara folded her arms. "I am not sleepy. I'm going to stay awake the whole trip this time."

"Okay, if you say so." Jack twisted his torso and snuggled her against him and a shot of jealousy streaked through Kane. "Why don't you stretch out? Kane doesn't mind."

No, Kane didn't mind, not one bit. Not even when those crimson covered legs pressed against his groin and he had to bite back a groan.

"So the box is full of food?" Anything to keep his mind off lowering a hand to fondle her thighs.

"Breakfast cereal, bagels, treats. We'll have to pick up fresh fruit and the ice cream, but with what we save on eating at the hill cafeteria, we can splurge a little. And, the pièce de résistance?" Jack dug into his pocket and held out chocolate bars.

Dana squealed with delight. "You remembered!"

"Have I ever forgotten?"

Kane waited as Dara unwrapped a 3 Musketeers chocolate bar and handed it to him. The tradition had begun before their first hiking trip years ago.

Kane lifted the candy in front of him, and the others met him, three hands resting together as if they were lofting swords.

"All for one..." he quipped.

"...and one for all." Dara bit into her chocolate bar, closed her eyes and moaned with pleasure. Kane jerked the wheel to the side to put them back in the middle of the lane. Shit, he was going to get them all killed if he didn't keep his mind on the road.

They settled into a comfortable silence, music filling the cab as they relaxed from their daily grind. He could do this. He could keep his mind off her legs resting innocently in his lap. He refused to think about sliding down the stockings and licking her skin from her ankles up to the warm honey between her thighs.

He had to resist. But once this weekend was over, all bets were off. It didn't make any sense for Jack and him to sit back and watch her go out with other men when one of them could be the right one for her. Until now his footloose and fancy-free lifestyle had suited him fine, but he'd always known a time would come when he'd want something more permanent.

No use in ignoring the draw between them anymore. He and Dara had tons in common, and from what he'd seen of the best long-term relationships, that was the most important factor. If they could spend the next fifty years hiking and canoeing and fooling around, he'd be happy as a clam.

At least he knew they were compatible in the first areas, and somehow he thought they'd be just fine in the sack as well. Dara wore her sensuality like everything else she did. Honest, pure. She wasn't an innocent, but pure as in what you see is what you get.

Even now she settled closer against Jack, the asshole's ever-present grin stretching wider when she twisted to lean on him, her head resting on his chest. He cradled her close and she let out a long, slow sigh of contentment.

She wiggled her hips lower as she settled, and her skirt rode higher. Kane gritted his teeth together. He could see the junction of her thighs now, her legs slightly separated as she curled up drowsily.

Kane shot Jack a dirty look. Jack raised his brows and deliberately draped his arm around Dara a little more intimately. She was already slipping off into dreamland—woman never could keep her eyes open when they drove anywhere. Within minutes she was purring, her breath escaping in a low rumble of sleep that twisted something inside his gut. Okay, he wanted her body, but there was definitely something more to their relationship. Once it became a relationship.

"You okay driving?" Jack stroked back a strand of Dara's hair from where it had escaped her elastics.

Kane glared at him. "What kind of dumbass question is

that?"

Jack snickered evilly. "Just thinking if you had half the boner I've got right now, I'd hate to have to shift."

"You know, talking about it isn't going to make it go away. I'll live."

They sat in silence for miles. The skiing was going to be fantastic, the weather forecast fabulous. But the thoughts running through his brain on an endless loop included a king-sized bed and a hot tub on the deck.

So much for a relaxing après-ski time. He was in for a fight to keep his hands off her.

"Wake up, sweetie, we're almost there."

Dara stretched and yawned, her mind slow to come out of the fog. "Shit—don't tell me I fell asleep again."

She squirmed to sit up and found herself pinned by two sets of strong hands.

"Slow down, or you're going to hit something important." Kane lifted her feet from his lap and she flushed.

"Sorry."

He waved a hand in her direction. "I was okay until you started practicing your drop kick."

Under her, Jack's firm chest shifted. "And your right hand is fine, but watch how much pressure you put on the left. I'll have trouble keeping up with you two as it is without a handicap."

Dara paused in confusion until she realized she wasn't leaning on his thigh like she'd imagined. She pulled away quickly, curled into a ball and spun on the seat as she looked for somewhere safe to place her limbs.

She glanced at Jack. He stared back wordlessly. There was a little extra twist to his smile and she licked her lips involuntarily. Ever since Jack had announced the change in rooming for their trip, she'd been nervous. It had taken a dozen phone calls and wad of money to arrange for the "complimentary upgrade" to their rooming situation. When she'd finally thought it through, she'd realized there was no way she could seduce them if they had kept their original booking. She could afford the private cabin, just, and it would be money well spent if in the long run it helped her make a decision.

Everything was perfectly in place for her to work on them both. She'd planned on using the road travel time to her advantage—start flirting a little.

She slammed her feet into her boots and followed Jack out the door, tugging her coat back on. She was worse than a child. Couldn't even stay awake for a couple of crucial hours. Fine. As soon as they hit the room, she was turning up the *oomph* and making her move.

Yet by the time they signed in, grabbed the key and drove over to their accommodations, her already unsteady nerves failed her. She wandered into the cabin, dumped her armload of gear on the couch and slipped onto the balcony. The rest of the cabins and townhouse units spread out along the base of the hill sparkled with Christmas lights, the section of the slope wired for night skiing a brilliant streak of white against the darkness of the hillside. Music floated to her ears from either the bar or the restaurant at the lodge. She grabbed the railing and took a deep breath. Somehow she had to find the strength she needed to make this holiday more than just a nice getaway with her buddies.

She was tired of nice. It was time for fabulous and sexy and smoking hot. It was time to figure out the future.

The glass door *swooshed* open behind her. Kane came and stood by her side. He leaned his elbows on the railing and peered out at the vista. "Damn good view. Much nicer than from any of the hotel rooms."

Dara bit her lip. Kane would be the perfect one to approach first.

"Did you see that?" She reached past him to point out the main swimming pool just visible to the left. The move made her lean against him, brushing her breasts casually against his arm. He didn't react beyond a slight tightening in his body, but he didn't pull away, and she took that as a good sign.

He cleared his throat.

"Did you see what's on this balcony?" Kane placed his hands on her shoulders and twisted her on the spot to face the four-man hot tub gracing the enormous deck. "I don't see any reason why we need to go to the pool when we've got a private one right here. That thing is going to feel awesome when we finish making tracks for the day."

Dara stared at the steaming pool and sudden inspiration hit. She shrugged out of her coat and tossed it on one of the deck chairs. The only way she could do this was to rush forward at full steam.

"Did we get everything in from the truck?" she asked.

"What's that?" Kane seemed distracted. "The gear? Umm, yeah, Jack went back for the last load. Dara, what are you doing?"

She'd already toed off her boots, and as she pulled her sweater over her head she heard his rapid intake of air. One quick snap and unzip, and her skirt fell away. She turned to face him, keeping her chin high. "I'm going for a dip. You coming?"

He looked like he'd swallowed his tongue. His eyes widened

as she tucked her fingers into the top of her tights and wiggled them past her hips. When she stood upright clad only in her bra, panties and a deep flush, he covered his face with his hand.

"Dara...shit, woman, you're killing me."

The tightness in his voice—was that because he wanted her or because the thought of seeing her naked was like watching one of his sisters strip? Only one way to know for sure. Dara unclipped her bra, slipped off her panties and tossed both on top of the rest of her things.

She took a step closer. His erratic breaths shook his frame and when she touched the waistband of his jeans he jerked in surprise.

"Are you coming swimming with me?"

Kane's throat jerked, then he reached for her. A gentle touch, tentative and light, as he brushed his palms along her upper arms. "What are you doing, Dara?"

Freezing? Waiting to see if she was going to be totally humiliated? The indoor/outdoor carpet beneath her feet was covered with a thin layer of frost, and the cold night air made her nipples tighten to hard aching nubs. She leaned forward and lifted her face to him, leaning against his warmth and strength, trying to get away from the chill in the air. She saw it, the moment he decided. He leaned closer and their lips touched.

The door behind them screeched open and the usually calm and sedate Jack roared out, "What the hell is going on?"

Chapter Three

Alpine Responsibility Code
Rule #3—Be prepared for surprises...

It was not a sight he'd been prepared to see—Dara stark naked not even five minutes after arriving at the cabin. Jack snatched a towel from beside the hot tub and wrapped it around her. He'd dreamed for years about having her gorgeous body fully revealed for his enjoyment, but never like that. Not in the arms of another man, not even his best friend's.

"Whose fucked-up idea was this?" Shit, the feel of her in his arms, knowing that underneath the fluffy fabric she was nude, did crazy things to his brain. Jack carried her into the cabin and plunked her down on the couch amidst the bags dumped there.

She glared at him as she clutched the towel, her face as crimson as the tights dangling from the chair on the balcony. She opened her mouth to say something when Kane beat her to it.

"She just wanted to go for a swim, Jack. No harm, no foul." Kane dragged his hand through his rumpled hair and shook his head. "She just was in kind of a hurry, I guess. Forgot her suit. We've skinny-dipped before."

Dara swore at him. "Kane, you're a chicken shit."

Her legs disappeared under her as she curled up on the couch. She stared at the coffee table like there was something of vital importance written on its surface.

"Dara? What's going on?" Jack dropped to his knees in front of her to be able to look into her eyes. His control was a tentative thing at best.

She paused before twisting to dig into her backpack. As she scrambled through her things, the towel loosened and the upper circle of one pale nipple slipped into view. His whole body reacted. Whatever she was up to was going to have far-reaching consequences. He'd seen Kane's expression and felt the lust raging though his own body. She was seconds away from finding out exactly what happens when you poke a guy too hard.

She held out a book to him before rearranging the towel to cover her assets.

"*The Count of Monte Cristo*? What the...?"

She growled at him. "No, it's a fake cover, you ass. You guys are always teasing me about how I've been reading that book forever and never done. Well, take a closer look, because it's not written by Alexandre Dumas."

Jack carefully peeled back the edge. Kane stepped forward to peer over his shoulder as he revealed a cover with three naked bodies on it.

Kane swore. "Porn? You've been reading porn in front of us for years?"

"It's not porn, it's erotic romance. And that's what's going on. My sex life up to now has consisted of pretty vanilla sex. I'm curious and I just thought if you guys were interested we could..." She swallowed hard before lifting her chin resolutely. "I thought we could try a few things."

God almighty. Jack rose in a rush and turned his back on her. The scent of her perfume was having a terrible effect on his libido, and the image of her face along with his and Kane's on the bodies tangled together on the cover of that book—

His cock pressed against his jeans in a state of urgency.

"I'm sorry, I should have said something first, only I was afraid I'd lose my nerve and so I just acted without thinking. If you're not interested, that's fine. Forget I even—"

"Not interested?" Kane kicked off his shoes, letting them fly across the room to slam into the front door of the cabin. "Holy *shit*, Dara, one minute you strip in front of me, the next you suggest your two best friends get involved with you sexually? And then you have the balls to turn around and say forget it?"

She snorted. "Yeah, me and my balls. I've got tons of those."

Jack needed to get this whole situation back under control. It was too close to exploding into something that could tear their friendship apart, and he was sure that wasn't what Dara had intended.

But he wasn't sure she'd intended for her suggestion to be anything other than a one-time fling either.

He had already decided once this weekend was over he would slowly bring their relationship to a new level. They were good friends, and he'd always looked out for her, careful never to cross the line sexually. Oh, he'd seen her glimmers of interest toward him, but he'd also caught her checking Kane out with the same expression at times.

Jack wanted her. In his bed, in his life—in his future—and he would do whatever it took to make that a reality.

Including, it seemed, share her.

He returned to her side and cautiously sat beside her on

the couch. His body weight made the cushions shift and she leaned against him involuntarily. When she would have scrambled away, he placed an arm around her shoulders and trapped her.

"Just slow down, sweetie. You've put both Kane's and my brain in a bit of bind. We're not saying no to anything."

"You're not?" She whispered the words, her body tense in his embrace.

"We're not saying yes right off either."

"Jack..." Kane warned.

He looked up at his best friend. They'd never fooled around with the same woman before, at least not at the same time. And this wasn't just any woman; it was someone they both cared deeply about. Kane tended to be a lot more private about his sexual practices than Jack had ever expected, maybe from growing up in a house full of women. Still, knowing that Kane desired Dara and cared for her—if he couldn't have Dara to himself right now, sharing her with Kane while they dealt with this mess seemed the best way out of a bad situation.

"If there are kinky sexual experiences Dara wants to try, you prefer she experiment with us or some nameless guys off the street?"

Dara hit him in the chest. "Yeah, right. Like I'm going to put out an ad in the paper for a threesome, Jack. I'm not an idiot."

"A threesome?" The flash of lightning her words produced short-circuited his logic center. Every time she spoke she upped the ante. *Fuck this.* She wanted to have a discussion about them getting it on? Welcome to reality. He picked her up and plopped her into his lap. She squealed for a second, then gripped the top of the towel so hard her knuckles went white. He stroked a finger across her smooth skin above her hands,

37

wondering what she would taste like.

He could barely wait to find out.

"No, you are not an idiot. But you've managed to freak me out. Sweetheart, we've never kissed beyond platonic busses on the cheek and you're talking about sex. That does things to a guy."

She wiggled slightly and there was no way she could miss one of the things that it did to him. His cock was at full strength, pinned behind the taut fabric of his jeans. The curve of her ass pressed down on him and her eyes opened wide as she realized what she sat on. "Fuck."

"Hell yeah, fuck." Jack wrapped his arms around her and held her close, breathing in the scent of her skin. She whimpered as he brushed his lips against the pulse pounding in the vee of her throat. He was going to explode just from the thoughts filling his head.

A ménage. With Dara. *God damn.*

"Jack, I'm sorry. I didn't mean to mess up our holiday. I just care a lot about—"

He covered her mouth with his to silence her. With her lips open to speak, their tongues met instantly and in a flash her taste filled him. Sweet, with a twist of cinnamon from her gum, the lingering taste of chocolate. He kissed her, leaning back on the couch and dragging her with him so her slight weight pressed on him more fully. She dug her fingers into his hair and suddenly it wasn't enough. He crushed her closer, the top of the towel sneaking down to her waist as their tongues tangled together. God, the woman could kiss. She took his mouth like she took to the hills, full out, full speed—caution be damned.

The sounds escaping her registered like early warning signs. Little gasps as he nipped at her lips, a long drawn-out moan as he kissed his way down her throat. A whispered plea when he rearranged her on his lap without taking his mouth from her skin. She straddled his hips, the heat of her core resting on top of his erection and damn if he didn't want to strip them both and let her ride him.

Go slow.

His brain shouted it, but his body protested vehemently. He rocked his hips instinctively, rubbing against her center and they both swore.

Fuck going slow. He grabbed her hips and ground her over him, sucking one nipple then the other into his mouth. The sweet tips felt amazing as he rolled them under his tongue, her hands clutching his head to trap him in place.

Closer and higher his climax approached, the tightness in his balls flashing to pain. Moisture from her sex coated the ridge of fabric barely containing his erection, the heat of her cream bleeding through to taunt him. She gave a little cry and called out his name, rolling her hips over him slower as he grunted with his release.

Jesus, Mary and Joseph, what the hell had just happened?

The balcony doors clicked shut as they broke apart, gasping for air.

"Well." Dara bit her bottom lip.

Jack panted a few times, waiting for a sign some blood had returned to his brain. He reached up and swiped his thumb over the swollen surface she'd nipped. He could kiss her for hours. Someday, if he had his way, he would. "Bit more than a 'well'. Shit, woman, I came in my jeans."

She glanced down at their groins, a grin covering her face. "Not quite the first time I'd imagined, but I enjoyed it."

"You're just happy you made me lose control." He collapsed back on the couch, his ears still ringing from his climax. Zero points for style, but he didn't really give a fuck at the moment.

Shit...he needed a minute. Responding any further before his brain went back online was a bad idea. He cupped the back of her neck and drew her against him. Dara sighed softly, nuzzling closer. They sat in silence until the pounding beat of their hearts slowed.

She sat up and the brightness of her smile melted most of his lingering apprehension away. "You don't hate me for putting you on the spot?"

"Of course I don't hate you. You're our best friend and you want to have sex with us? If you'd asked us over coffee or something, that could have made it a little easier, but we might not have believed you were serious. All in all, Kane and I are tough. We'll survive being asked for sexual favours." He glanced toward the balcony. Kane sat on the railing, staring at the ski resort. While there was nothing he wanted more than to keep Dara in his arms—and his bed—all weekend long, that wasn't what she'd asked for.

Until the weekend was over, he had no right to demand her to himself.

He swept his gaze down her torso, admiring her breasts and the smooth skin of her belly inches away from him. Her eyes sparkled, and her cheeks were flushed. "You're fucking gorgeous."

"Such a poet." She bit her lip again, glancing out at Kane.

Fuck. Jack hesitated for a second. She was certainly aware of Kane's location at all times. He gave up. "You're going to need to go to him."

Her head snapped around. "You...don't mind?"

"Hell, yeah, but it's kind of hard to have a ménage with only two people." He loosened his grip on her hips, stroking the soft skin under his hands, rubbing his thumbs back and forth lightly. "Dara, if you're sure this is something you want to try, I'm honoured you trust us that much. At anytime if you want to stop, that's all you have to say. You understand me?"

She nodded, leaning into him, her head resting on his shoulder as she hugged him close. "You're my best friends, Jack. I trust you both completely."

As he skimmed his hand over her bare back, caressing her skin and feeling her shiver under his touch, he wondered. She was trusting them with everything—not just her body, but her heart—and that gift was the most precious thing he could imagine.

He stood, lowering her slowly to the floor. When she fumbled with the towel covering her, he reached out and helped her secure it, his fingers slowing as he brushed the rounded tops of her breasts.

She stared at him for a full minute before she turned to join Kane on the balcony.

He watched her walk away, her hips swaying easily from side to side, and he wondered how in the world he could possibly share her for the next three nights and not be changed.

"Kane?"

He continued to stare away from her as she waited. *Temperamental ass.* Fine. She knew how to handle Kane when he was in a mood. She grabbed him by the back of the collar and pulled hard. He slipped off the railing to land in a puddle at her feet.

"Fuck it, Dara, what was that for?"

She glared at him. "I wanted to apologize for springing this idea of mine on you, and it's too freaking cold to stand here in my bare feet while you pout."

"I do not pout, and damn right you should apologize."

She stuck out her lower lip. "Did I offend your delicate feelings with my wicked proposal?"

He leered at her as he rose to his feet. "Hell no, I was just trying to figure out how you managed to avoid suggesting it a long time ago. Two righteous studs at your beck and call for years, and it took you this long to finally come to your senses?"

She shivered, and he scooped her up, carried her to the hot tub and placed her carefully on the rim.

"Are you going to swim with me?" she asked again. The bottoms of her feet tingled as she lowered them into the heated water and a groan of pleasure escaped her lips.

Kane stared into the cabin. "I think I'm going to skip it right now."

Dara leaned over to see what Kane was looking at. Inside the living room Jack gestured madly at Kane. She laughed out loud. "You getting his sign language or shall I interpret?"

"Fucker." Kane yanked open the door. "What?"

"Kiss her already."

Kane gave Jack the finger and shut the door in his face. Dara fought her giggles as she settled farther into the water, leaning back in the molded plastic of the hot tub. Kane sauntered over slowly and stared down at her. She watched his face, watched his gaze as it traveled over her body, lingering on her breasts. The water was no obstruction to his vision and he seemed to like what he saw.

"You sure you don't want to join me?" Crap, was that her voice? Breathless, sultry. Kane pulled one of the deck chairs closer and sat beside her, his arms resting along the top of the hot tub.

"All things considered, I think I should stay out here for

now."

Dara deliberately stretched, arching her breasts higher. "So…?"

Kane sucked in a deep breath. "You sure know how to make a holiday special, don't you, girl?"

"You mad at me, Kane?"

He played with her hair, twirling her nearest pigtail around his finger again and again. "Not mad, just thinking things through. I'm sure Jack already asked if you were sure you wanted a ménage, and I'm not going to insult you by asking again."

Dara turned and knelt on the seat, raising her torso slightly above the level of the water as she faced him. "Again, so…what you going to do?"

He traced a finger down her nose, along the side of her throat. He carried on the motion until his fingertip scraped her bare nipple. She let go of the little cry of need begging to escape.

When he lifted his gaze to meet hers, she knew everything was fine. He was in—all the way—and he'd do everything to make this good for her. Just like the time he taught her how to mountain bike rails, or the kayak-rolling lessons. All the way, all-out effort, all the time.

The ache between her thighs increased. She snaked out her arms and clasped his neck and pulled their lips together.

He wrapped his fingers around the back of her head to control the kiss, keeping it soft and gentle. Barely a whisper—his lips over her skin, against her throat, over her eyes. He didn't ravish her mouth, but stroked and teased with his tongue until she shook with need.

He slid a hand down her body to cup one breast, and she moaned. A delicate touch, his fingers against her nipple, stroking and drawing the tip to a tight point. All the while he kissed her, their tongues meshing and exploring. Why had she never taken the chance and done this before? He pinched forefinger and thumb together lightly, and she squeaked with pleasure. The hard surface of the hot tub against her belly annoyed her. She tried to rise higher but he held her in place, drawing her as close to him as possible with the barrier between them, her naked wet breasts pressed against his chest.

She tore her mouth from his. "Please..." She wasn't sure what she was begging for.

"Oh, sweetheart." Kane leaned his forehead against hers. "We gotta take it slow. Trust me, I'll make love to you, and we can check out all the naughty things in your book to your heart's content, but I'm not taking you this instant."

"Bastard." *Fine.* She tried to regain his lips, but he pressed his finger against them. She growled and muttered against the single digit. "Why not?"

Kane cleared his throat. "Because I'm an old-fashioned kind of guy? One step at a time."

"I'll totally let you run the bases before you hit a home run with me."

"Fuck." He closed his eyes. "Bloody hell. You got any condoms, woman?"

"In my bag." Her heart beat like crazy. Was he really going to make a move?

He laughed. "In the same bag as the dirty book? Very appropriate."

Another kiss, his arms dragging her hard against him. This time he wasn't as gentle. His teeth bit into her bottom lip, sending a sharp tingle all the way down to pulse in her clit.

By the time he reached into the water and plucked her out

she was half-crazy with need. The ache between her thighs grew by the second, her climax with Jack a distant memory. Kane carried her dripping-wet body into the cabin and stormed his way into the back bedroom.

"You kids going somewhere?" Jack lay on the second bed wearing nothing but a pair of boxers. Dara clung tightly to Kane's neck.

"Grab a towel and throw it on the bed for me, will you?" Kane growled.

Jack put down the book in his hand and darted out of the room. Dara noticed the cover and laughed. "You jerk—that's my book."

He paused on his way back to drape a towel around her and kiss her nose. "Consider it research. I didn't want to miss out on any kinky activities you were hoping for."

Kane shouldered past Jack and laid her on the bed. The steamy look in his eyes made the goose bumps on her skin disappear as she flushed with heat. He dried her carefully, taking extra time over her breasts and between her legs.

Jack sat on the bed next to her, using his fingertips to join the gentle exploration of her body. "You have no idea how good it feels to be able to finally touch you."

Dara sucked in air, desperate to maintain her composure and keep things light. "I would never have guessed."

"You're our friend first and foremost, Dara," Kane said. "We don't want to fuck that up."

She struggled onto her elbows, blushing slightly under the combined stares of the two most important men in her life. This was it. This was the moment she had to get right to make the ménage work and set the tone for the future. For if she picked one of them, and not the other. Something to keep it light, and keep them together as friends.

"You're not going to mess anything up. Come on, guys, we're all grownups. I don't see why we can't enjoy another aspect to our relationship and still kick each other's butts on the ski hill. Or wherever else we want to go together."

Kane nodded, his dark curls falling around his face as he looked her over slowly. "Friends, and more. You're right, we can do this."

"You can do me, you mean." The guys laughed. Kane stripped off his shirt and Dara hummed with approval as she admired the chiseled muscles before her. A faint trail of hair began at his belly button and led south. "Oh yes, very nice."

She reached out to help him with the snap on his jeans and found herself blocked by Jack. He eased her back on the bed, pinning her wrists above her head.

"Starting right now, we're in charge. You want the two of us in your bed? You got it. But you get us, not some idea of who you want us to be. You comfortable with that?"

Her nipples hardened to rocks. She wiggled slightly, testing his hold and something thrilled inside when she discovered she couldn't move. Okay, this was hot. Hotter than she'd expected.

Kane and Jack exchanged glances. "She likes a little restraint?" Kane asked.

Jack nodded. "Looks that way. You want to get her legs?"

"Hey guys, *she's* right here, listening to you...holy—"

Kane pulled her knees up and to the side. With no further preamble, he dropped his head between her legs, and suddenly she couldn't breathe. Her heart raced as he licked her slit, circling the tender area with his tongue. The tight grip he had on her ankles kept her spread wide to him. Rather than being embarrassed, she found the sensation exquisite—mind-boggling even.

Jack leaned over her, carefully checking her response. "You okay with this?"

Dara was sure she responded, but the actual words she said escaped her—a "yes", and maybe a little pleading thrown in for good measure.

He grinned down at her. "That sounds like you're more than fine. Get ready, here we come."

His lips met hers, fleeting but bold, before he worked his way down to her breasts and enveloped one aching peak with his mouth. He suckled, an uneven, erratic draw on the tip that contrasted sharply with the rhythmic pressure Kane maintained between her legs. The tingling fire in her core expanded, spreading fingers of desire through her belly. The flames fanned out to make her skin hypersensitive to each touch of their mouths, and another orgasm rapidly approached.

As her eyes closed, the sounds in the room grew louder. Soft mutters, moans and groans. Music carried in from the still-open door of the balcony. Somewhere in the cabin a fan turned, the constant flicker matching the beat of her heart.

Kane licked harder, releasing her ankles to open her more fully to his touch. He pressed a finger into her sheath and she hissed.

"Yes. Oh hell, more."

Wet heat touched her clit, his tongue flicking the tender nub and her head shot up. Jack captured her mouth and pressed her back to the mattress, swallowing her cries. Kane added another finger, pumping slowly, massaging the sensitive spot deep inside. Sensory overload approached like a freight train, and she let herself go, knowing they would catch her.

Bright white pleasure rolled over her and she relaxed, letting her body respond as it wished. Her sex clutched Kane's fingers and he swore softly, stroking slower until her hips stopped rocking. He disappeared and she opened her eyes to stare into Jack's dark brown orbs.

"Wow." She wiggled her wrists. He still held her trapped.

"You're beautiful when you come. I had no idea it was going to be so hot seeing you two together."

"Why do you think I went out on the balcony?" Kane stepped back next to the bed, clad only in his boxer briefs. "I was about to explode from watching you guys on the couch."

He crawled on top of Dara and nuzzled her neck. His lips touched the lobe of her ear and he licked it before whispering softly, "I want you. Will you take me?"

Jack released her wrists and she grabbed on tight to Kane, wrapping her legs around his body and urging his groin closer to hers. The thick ridge of his cock pressed against her sex and she rocked into him.

"Is that a yes?"

"Hell, yeah." She watched in anticipation as he lifted up to strip off the last bit of fabric remaining on his body. He ripped open a wrapper and covered himself, then she couldn't see anymore because Jack turned her face toward his.

"I'm going to watch."

Oh God. Totally new sensations dragged through her brain. This was not just her having sex with Kane. It was she and Kane having sex with Jack there. Watching.

The tip of Kane's cock pressed against her, easing through the moisture built up by her orgasm. He was hot and hard, and he stretched her as he worked his way fully into her passage.

"Fuck, you're tight. So bloody tight." Kane pumped again and again, and Dara opened her knees as far as she could to help.

"You're a little bigger...*Jesus*...than my toys and it's been a while. Oh, that's fabulous. So good..." It was hard to concentrate, hard to think with the wonderful sensations pouring through her. Dara stared into Jack's face, his gaze fixed on where Kane was now buried in her body.

"That's the hottest thing I've ever seen." Jack shook his head before turning back to her. "Gorgeous woman."

Kane thrust harder. He filled her to bursting, every nerve taut and stretched and ready to shatter again in no time flat. He adjusted his angle and his groin rubbed against her clit, and it was all she could do to not scream. Every pass drove her need higher, made her call out for more. Dara turned her gaze back to Kane. Seeing the expression in his eyes made her entire body shake with an adrenaline rush. That was her friend making the flaming-hot pleasure rise. A twist of a smile on the corner of his mouth, his eyes rolling back in his head before he grimaced.

"Gotta...slow...down."

Dara thrashed her head wildly. The last thing she wanted right now was for him to falter. "No, please..."

She lifted her legs again and dug her heels into his butt cheeks to try and force him to resume his pace.

"Christ, Dara. I'm not going to last. Give me a break." A drop of sweat trickled down his temple and she groaned in frustration. This was probably one of those man things, but right now she didn't care if he blew quickly. She was so close. So close the fidgety sensation in her clit was ready to overtake her whole body. Bliss slammed through her with each penetration.

"Don't stop. It's not a freaking contest. Just a little more. Little more, oh, please." One last push to drive her over the edge, that's all she needed. She arched hard into Kane, striving to find the spark.

Jack snuck his hands between them, clasped her nipples

49

and pinched. An explosion ripped through her—the detonation hard and full-body impacting. Tight contractions squeezed Kane where she held him in her depths, and his pace faltered, body wavering over her.

"Fuck, what did you do? *Fuck...*" Kane lost it, slamming into her one last time, his cock jerking as he spilled into the condom. His arms gave out and he covered her with his body. Dara sucked for air, the aftershocks continuing to race through her system. She tangled her fingers in his hair and lifted his head off her shoulder, thrilled to see the way his blue eyes glowed at her.

She purred with contentment. The wild rush of being intimate with Kane for the first time eased as she slipped into a pleasure-filled haze. "Okay, that was more incredible than I ever imagined. I mean...wow."

Kane kissed her briefly before rolling off and groaning out his agreement. "It's not even six p.m. and I feel like I put in a full day boarding."

The bed shifted and the distinctive sound of a condom being opened hit Dara's ears. Her heartbeat increased as she sat up to watch Jack finish rolling on the latex before lifting his heated gaze to her.

"Turn over and get on your knees."

Kane disappeared as she obeyed Jack's command. That's clearly what it was, and her fading tingle of desire returned in a shot. She rolled slowly to her belly, his hands on her bare hips to lift her. Dara glanced over her shoulder, mesmerized to watch his turgid cock move closer as he settled in place. The front of his thighs brushed her, the coarse hairs scraping erotically over sensitive skin. Jack rocked between her legs a couple of times, coating himself in her juices. She whimpered as the movement nudged her clit.

"You ready?" Before she could answer, he lined himself up and slid home with one push. Her breath vanished and she collapsed to her elbows, ass high in the air.

"Holy shit." The different angle, even so soon after the orgasm with Kane, set off a line of small quakes deep inside. Jack retreated, dragging his cock through her tender passage. His girth stretched her, consumed her. He pressed on her upper back, forcing her shoulders to the mattress. He locked her in position before plunging in again, this time deeper than before.

"Oh my God, it's too much..." Dara whispered as Jack held her hips steady and thrust repetitively, his groin snapping tight to her butt.

"Not too much. You—damn it, you feel so good around me." Jack surged in hard, but his words were soft. His voice trickled along her spine like the brush of an erotic feather. "Seeing you in front of me like this, so willing, so giving. Welcoming me in, surrounding me. You're gorgeous."

"Jack is right, you are gorgeous." Kane had returned and lay beside her. He smoothed a strand of hair from her face. "Your cheeks are flushed, your eyes sparkling."

She licked her dry lips and Kane met her, kissing her steadily as Jack powered into her body. Jack rubbed his thumbs against her, pressing into the muscles of her ass, his fingers hard on her skin. "Shit, I'm not going to last either. Watching you two before, and now seeing..."

Jack groaned, long and loud. It was such a primitive sound, so unlike her orderly and pristine friend, she shook as her desire ratcheted up a notch. Dara was beyond caring how much longer Jack could last. Another climax beckoned and she raced to meet it. Kane's mouth controlled her, his tongue thrusting into her mouth in time with Jack's possession swirled up a maelstrom, and she was lost.

As her core attempted to lock Jack in place with a series of rhythmic compressions, her breasts, her clit—all of her including her mind—flickered between pleasure and pain. It was too much, and at the same time not nearly enough. She squeezed her eyes tight and let the sensations ride her, just as Jack rode her, forcing her hips back to impale her on his cock.

The reverberations of Jack's shout as he came echoed off the walls. All she had the energy for was a long happy sigh before relaxing completely into a puddle on the mattress.

Chapter Four

Alpine Responsibility Code
Rule #4—Know your own limits...

Kane was going mad.

They left Dara snoozing while they unpacked and organized the cabin. Jack did his usual bit of magic getting supper going before burying his nose in her camouflaged book. Other than the occasional grunt and snort of laughter from him, the room grew quiet. Too quiet. The fire crackled, the soft and peaceful sound nowhere near enough to drown out the taunting voices rising in Kane's brain. He busied himself, hauling his portable speakers in from the truck. Even the steady pulse of his favourite songs failed to lighten his increasingly dark mood.

All mention of what they'd done with Dara seemed strictly off limits until he couldn't stand it any longer. Supper was nearly ready, and they'd have to wake her soon. Kane gave the spaghetti sauce one final stir before plopping down on the couch opposite Jack.

"I thought we were going to wait. We were going to let Dara know both of us were interested in her after this trip was over." Jack raised his brows but kept reading the fake classic. Bloody bastard. "You caved damn fast."

Jack put the book aside and leaned back in his chair. "Considering the ménage was Dara's idea, I don't think I caved. I went along with her offer, like any gentleman would."

Right. "Like you weren't instantly all over her when she offered."

"Yeah, well, I claim temporary insanity. I'd have to be a saint to not act when offered what I've been craving for years. What I didn't expect, or want, is you in the picture. Still, I stand by what I said. If she's looking for kink, it's going to be with us and not some asses off the street. Doesn't that make sense?"

"Yes, but this totally changes everything."

Jack sighed. "I'm trying not to think too hard about that. It's true, when this holiday is over, we'll have to figure out what the hell is the next step." Jack rose and peeked down the hall. "We need to wake her in a minute. Funny how she can sleep through anything."

Kane grumbled with frustration. "We're really going to give her a ménage?"

His friend pivoted on the spot and examined him closely. "What's the matter? What aren't you saying? I thought what happened earlier proved you were good with this. In spite of claiming I caved fast, I didn't see you turning down the sex."

The gaping pit in Kane's belly grew to monstrous proportions. He struggled to articulate the discomfort that had started in the back bedroom.

Ah, fuck it, this was his best friend. If he couldn't be straight-up honest with Jack, he was in deeper shit than he thought.

"Sex with Dara is not the problem, but have you ever been involved in a real ménage before? Because an hour ago, that was me having sex with her, then you having sex with her. Kind of like glorified porn where it's live action and we know the performers."

A sharp laugh burst from Jack. "I doubt Dara would appreciate being considered a porn star, but what's your point?"

Damn it. Having to spell it out made his worries seem more and more stupid. "Forget it. I shouldn't have said anything."

"Don't be an asshole, Kane. We've got three days ahead to handle being insanely intimate, having sex with our best friend who we both want for much more than a fling. Things are going to be fucked up enough without you having some deep, dark secret hanging over our heads. Now spill."

"That's the issue. The insanely intimate part. I'm not into guys."

Jack choked. "What the hell are you taking about?"

"You don't turn me on. I'm not into the slash shit I hear about, okay? I mean, there's nothing wrong with it, but it's not my thing." As soon as Kane let the words burst out, Jack relaxed, a bit of a smirk crossing his face.

"*Jesus*, is that all? We've been friends since grade school. I've seen you naked more often than anyone I know and I've never once hit on you. Relax. I'm completely heterosexual, and so are you."

"Just wanted to make sure, because—I have read a few of those books..." The confession stuck in his throat. Jack held back his laughter and Kane didn't know if he should thank him for it, or punch him.

"You've read erotic romance?"

Kane sighed. "On my phone. There was a reading program included with my latest upgrade and I started downloading freebies off the web. One was this really hot book and..."

"And it was one of Dara's naughty type. Oh the hidden

depths of your soul. Shit, I wonder what other revelations I'm going to discover this weekend? Dara's reading smut behind a fake cover, you're not sending a million text messages but getting into kink. All of a sudden my reading habits seem so pedestrian."

"Don't be an ass."

"Don't be an idiot." Jack stepped around him to drain the noodles. "You know I'm not into guys. Dara's the only one I want, and since what *she* wants right now is a ménage, I can handle your ham and eggs on the bed. She can enjoy them, because I'm not going to."

Kane sat heavily in his chair, relief spreading slowly through his limbs. His fears didn't disappear completely, but at least Jack knew his discomfort. That should make it easier, shouldn't it? "Okay."

A hearty guffaw bounced back. "You're so damn amusing."

He gave Jack the finger. "Screw off. I wasn't the one staring at your dick earlier."

Jack paused in opening the kitchen cabinets. "No, but maybe you should try it."

"Shut the fuck up." Kane whirled a throw cushion at Jack, who deflected it easily and fixed Kane in place with a penetrating stare.

"I'm serious. Usually when I'm watching that kind of action, and it's my cock in the woman, my mind has already gone numb. It was a serious turn-on being able to appreciate sex without my balls dictating what my brain registered."

Kane dropped his head into his hands and groaned loudly. "I don't need this. You're making my brain crazy."

The room quieted for a moment before Jack spoke, all trace of teasing gone from his voice. "Kane. This is uncharted territory for all of us. If we're going to make sure Dara's comfortable with everything we do over the next couple days, you're going to have to buy in one hundred percent. Don't go borrowing trouble. You might discover you enjoy watching Dara and me have sex. Pleasure is pleasure, no matter what the twist. I promise I won't touch you if that's going to make it better—"

"It will—"

"Shut. Up." Jack leaned back on the kitchen counter, his arms folded in front of him. "You need to open your mind. Sex isn't all about missionary position and blowjobs."

"I've never had any complaints in the bedroom."

"I'm sure you haven't. Neither have I, but I doubt what we're doing is carbon copy."

Oh man, there was a huge understatement. "Damn right. I put on my headphones as soon as I know you've got a woman in your room. I've never been into voyeurism."

Jack flashed his deadly smile. "Looks like you and Dara are both in for an education, aren't you?"

What the hell have I gotten myself into? Kane dragged a hand through his hair and let out a deep breath. "Fine. So for the rest of it, how are we going to do this?"

"Keep it fun, keep it light. Everything we do is intended to make Dara's fantasy a reality. We've got a ton of skiing to do every day with the evenings wide open for play. I don't think we need an agenda beyond that."

The book lay on the table between them and Kane gestured toward it as he rose to his feet. "You enjoying that?"

"Just speed-reading for now. Looks like it's got all the classic moves, although remember how Dara responded to being restrained? The book's got a little more along that line."

"Damn. Fine, I'm okay with that, although it's not my typical bedroom ploy."

"I can handle it." A fairly smug expression crossed Jack's face.

Kane stared at him. "No shit? Really?"

Jack wiggled his brows. "You should leave your headphones off a little more often."

"Arghhh..." The images racing through his brain did nothing to ease the ache in his groin. Just thinking about Dara soft and submissive under him made him hard. Maybe he wasn't being completely truthful to Jack about what he liked in the bedroom, but he'd never gotten into ropes and shit.

His friend laughed. "I think you should read chapter seven. I'm pretty sure you could get into what's in there better." Jack slapped him on the shoulder and the weight lifted a little more. "I'll put the rest of dinner together. You go get Sleeping Beauty up and bring her here. The night is still young, and I think we should enjoy every minute of it."

Kane strolled slowly toward the bedroom, his good humour returning rapidly. What the hell had he been worried about? Jack was his best friend and Dara his constant sidekick for the past four years. Heck, she'd sat with him when he got blood work done. She'd helped clean his bedroom. If that hadn't scared her away, and she still wanted this with him and Jack, he could suck up his concerns.

He stood in the doorway for a second, loving how she lay spread-eagle over the entire mattress. She was an admitted bed hog. When they shared a tent, they usually pinned her between them to stop her from stealing all the available space. He sat slowly on the edge of the bed, not wanting to frighten her. She rolled toward him and stretched lazily.

"Umm, something smells fabulous." Her blonde hair had

escaped the pigtails completely and lay unruly on the pillow. The soft tresses framed her face, and he couldn't resist leaning over and pressing a kiss to her lips.

She latched on, her arms holding him close. When she let his lips go, she moved to tenderly cup his face in her hands.

"You ready for dinner?" Kane kissed her nose and pulled her upright with him.

"Very ready. I can't believe I slept again. I'm not narcoleptic or something, am I?"

He laughed. "No, you've been working full-time and you're on a holiday. It's fine to let go and take it easy. Besides..." He stood her on her feet and thrilled as he smoothed his hands over her soft skin once more. "We worked you over pretty hard. We want you to have enough strength for the rest of the holiday."

She flushed. "Oh, don't worry. I'll be up for the double-black-diamond runs first thing tomorrow morning. Give me a second to get dressed and..."

Dara looked around pointedly and he swore. He'd been so distracted by his conversation with Jack, he'd left her bag in the main room. "Shit—I'll go grab your clothes for you."

She lifted her chin. "Either that or you strip as well. I'm not into being the only one naked in the room."

Her arms were crossed and there was the most adorable pout on her face. Kane paused for a minute. He remembered Jack's comment that she might like to be controlled. Maybe...he could make her fantasy continue.

Kane slipped back to the living room. Jack gave him a questioning look, but he simply headed to the couch and dug into Dara's bag. *Hallelujah.* Matching bra and panties in the top pocket. He pulled them out and a slim makeup bag followed, snagged on the bra strap. With a quick grab, he caught it before it could fall to the floor. He turned to replace it when the shape of the object inside made him pause.

Holy shit.

Jack came to his side. "Kane? Are you going through Dara's bag? That's dangerous. Women have killed for less—"

Kane held the now-open cosmetic bag and let the dildo show. The anatomically correct, life-sized cock made of some sort of purple-and-yellow-striped rubbery material. It was all he could do to not drop the thing back in her bag and race away.

"Fuck—I wonder if it glows in the dark." Jack took the bag from him and peered intently at the thing.

"There's a whole side to our girl I'd never dreamed of," Kane muttered.

Dara's voice rang from the back room. "You going to China to buy me new clothes, or what?"

Kane snatched up the frilly underthings he'd found and turned to go.

"Hey, aren't you taking her bag with you?" Jack waved the fake cock in his hand and suddenly it was funny as shit. Kane shook his head as he laughed out loud, walking back to the bedroom. Jack called after him with an evil tone in his voice. "Your funeral."

Dara sat on the bed, the top sheet pulled across her body like a shield. "What the hell took you so long? I'm starving."

"You could have come out and joined us." Kane passed over the dainty bits of lace and she took them, hand extended as if she expected more. "That's enough. You won't be naked, and it's not cold. Jack's got the fireplace going."

She opened her mouth to protest. He was sure something rude about his mental capacity was ready to fly when she surprised him. She stood and let the blanket fall, her pale skin shining under the soft light from the bedside lamp.

His mouth watered.

Her full breasts stared him in the eye as she passed back her bra. "Maybe you should help me put this on."

She pivoted on the spot, her tight buttocks shifting slightly. He responded like a moth to a flame. One step brought him close enough to cup her ass cheek as he leaned against her warm skin.

"You're full of tricks, aren't you?" The scent of her perfume filled his brain and all thoughts of leaving the room vanished.

"Only if you want to play."

He smoothed his hands over the crests of her hipbones, drifting upward an inch at a time until he cupped her breasts. Kane drew in a deep breath, his nose buried in her hair, the tight peaks of her nipples stabbing his palms. He nibbled on her neck and earlobe, massaged her breasts and her heartbeat accelerated under his caress.

Her stomach growled, long and loud, and they both laughed.

"How sexy." Kane pressed a final kiss to her neck then fastened her bra, helping her settle the straps on her shoulders. He leaned her forward, gritting his teeth as her ass pressed against his groin. Ignoring the contact as best he could, he repositioned her breasts in the bra cups before guiding her upright.

Dara laughed. "Oh my God, Kane, I've never met a guy who knew how to do that."

"I love cleavage, and you've got the build for it." He knelt at her feet and held the panties for her. She braced herself on his shoulder, fingers firm against his muscles as she stepped in. He slipped the tiny piece of fabric up her legs, arranging the thin straps over the smooth rise of her hips. "You know I've got four sisters. Nothing was sacred when I was growing up. The things those girls talked about when I was around would have scarred a lesser man."

He rose and held out his hand to her.

She hesitated. "Kane..."

It wasn't something he would force, but he didn't think she'd want to skip even a single experience they offered. "If you want me to grab your clothes, I will. Think about this first—are you really uncomfortable or just turned on? You are simply beautiful, and I'd love to enjoy looking at you throughout dinner. It's your choice. It's all your choice, all weekend. But I think you should trust me."

She licked her lips and his cock reacted, pressing hard against his jeans. Dara slowly lowered her hand into his and together they walked to the dining room.

Chapter Five

Alpine Responsibility Code

Rule #5—Safety restraints must be used at all times...

Dara stood erect, her breasts like some kind of missile system. Cocked and fully loaded, they aimed forward, barely contained by the wisp of fabric on her skin. It was the sexiest thing she owned and she felt more naked in it than if Kane had insisted she come to dinner in the nude.

She'd packed the scanty lingerie with uncertainty. Heck, she'd bought it during her mad planning session for this getaway, trying to think of what the guys might find attractive. It wasn't her usual attire—having a string up her butt was not what she'd choose to wear most days. Besides, it was scary how much the shop had charged for mere inches of material.

It was all worth it when she saw the expression in Jack's eyes as Kane led her around the corner. His hands skittered over the utensils he was placing on the table.

"Oh sweet thing. Where have you been all my life?" He gave her one of his exaggerated winks.

Suddenly she was comfortable again. These were her buds, her "cuddle in the dark because there's a lightning storm outside the tent" friends.

Her lovers as of an hour ago.

There was nothing to fear from them, not even clad in the most come-hither outfit in the world.

Kane seated her carefully, taking the chair on her right. Jack sat on her left and they all filled their plates with the pasta and aromatic sauce.

Jack placed a piece of bread on her plate and she wrinkled her nose. "Garlic bread?"

Kane pointed with his knife. "He made Caesar salad too. We're all goners, so you'd better eat some in self-defense."

"Garlic breath. Ugh. I guess we're not planning on doing anything else tonight."

The expression in Jack's eyes shot down that idea immediately. Dara took a deep breath and turned her attention to the table. She couldn't maintain his gaze, not yet. Not when he seemed to look straight through her and see what she really wanted.

Which wouldn't be so bad if she knew herself.

Their lovemaking before supper had made it clear she was physically compatible with both the guys. Now she needed to concentrate on her real agenda. Who did she want the most, not just in the bedroom? Who did she have the best chance at forever with?

She reached for her fork and stopped in surprise. "Umm, Jack? The food looks great, but you forgot to give me any utensils."

"Didn't forget."

Okay, now he was getting annoying. She pointed beside her plate. "Hello, nothing to eat with."

His fingers encircled her wrist and tugged her arm toward him. Jack laid a thin black strap over her skin and smoothed the Velcro fasteners together. The band formed a loop around her wrist, like a sports-watch strap. A longer section, with a locking clip, extended five inches toward the floor. She stared at him in confusion, attempting to pull her hand back. He closed his fingers over the strap and trapped her in place.

Oh my God.

Kane cursed. "You just happened to have handcuffs in your luggage?"

Jack shook his head. "Safety harnesses from my skis."

Dara's head spun a little as her heart rate increased in a rush. Pure adrenaline shot into her veins and morphed into desire. The tiny scrap of lace between her legs grew instantly soaked. Jack's pupils dilated as he steadily returned her gaze. He waited, his hand supporting hers and she knew he'd felt her tremble. She waited, willing the blood pounding through her limbs to slow enough she could stay vertical.

"Dara?"

Jack held out his other hand, a second restraint dangling from his fingers. His unspoken question hung in the air. Did she want this?

Hell, yes.

Slow, unsteady, she lifted her arm and offered her wrist. Kane swore quietly. Jack pressed a kiss to her palm, his gaze locked on hers. "Good girl."

He fastened the second strap, then rose to his feet. She kept her gaze fixed on the table, sensing him walk behind her. Waiting for his touch. A hand landed gently on her shoulder and she shivered. He kissed her nape, brushing back her hair to whisper in her ear.

"There's a flush over your whole body right now. Like a glow, lighting your skin. It's going to make you more sensitive.

Make every touch so much richer."

He drew the back of a finger down her throat and over the upper swell of her breast. The way Kane had arranged her breasts in the supporting cups had forced the edge of her areolas to be visible at the top of the wispy fabric. Jack caressed, butterfly soft, along the dividing line between skin and material, and she swore her heart would explode.

His palms came to rest on her arms, slipping downward until he reached her wrists. Carefully he brought her hands together behind her back, looping the extra material around her lightly. The click of the clips locking together echoed in her ears louder than the blood roaring past.

A moan escaped. She was on fire.

Jack slid a finger inside the strap loops, testing the fit. "They aren't tight, but you let me know the instant you want them off, understand?"

She nodded, unable to speak. If she truly wanted to escape she could slip free. It was the thought of being restrained that carried her into the fantasy.

Jack knelt and cupped her chin in his hand. He pressed his mouth to hers, his tongue stroking her lips—soft, teasing. When he drew back she would have followed and he brushed his knuckles past her cheek in a tender caress. "Later. Now we eat."

Dara breathed out slowly as Jack regained his seat. She jumped lightly when a hand touched her right shoulder, Kane seeking her attention. His expression made her whimper, just a small sound of desire escaping as the hunger visible on his face twisted her insides.

"You have no idea what you are doing to me." Kane's words drove the need in her core even higher.

She caught a flash of his blue eyes before he kissed her as

well, rough and thorough. Sucking the air from her lungs, his fingers tangled in her hair to hold their mouths together. She lost track of where she was, forgetting even that they were in front of Jack. The haze of excitement enveloping her grew until she attempted to clasp him back, and her arms wouldn't budge.

Another burst of lust shot through her. Oh my God, the restraints. Whatever else happened this weekend, she was already more turned on than she'd been in her life.

A loud rumble from her belly broke through, and she laughed when Kane's stomach answered back. They separated, only inches apart, grinning at each other.

"We'd better feed the bears before they escape."

Jack lifted his wine glass in the air. "To us."

Kane lifted his own glass and saluted Dara with it before touching it to her lips and tipping it slightly. She took a tiny sip before he pulled it away, the rich flavour bolting across her sensitive taste buds.

How she was supposed to eat when she could barely breathe?

Jack twirled his fork in the pasta on her plate and offered it to her. She wrapped her lips around his fork, vividly aware of each individual tine against her tongue as her senses went into overdrive. Each mouthful became more and more erotic as Jack and Kane took turns feeding her. A bite of pasta, a tidbit of bread. A sip of the wine—but it wasn't the alcohol that made her blood hum.

She tugged lightly at her bonds, just to savour the thrill that shot through her. Okay, she was officially kinky. If this was day one, she could hardly wait to see what Jack could come up with as the weekend progressed.

The sexual tension in the room grew as the food disappeared. Jack watched Dara and Kane closely for any indication the situation was too much. He stretched his legs and adjusted in his chair, attempting to find a more comfortable position. Relieving the ache in his groin was fucking impossible, not with his cock rock hard, and he refused to rush again. Dara had caught him by surprise earlier, and he'd reacted poorly. He really should have had better control. His plea of temporary insanity to Kane wasn't far off the mark. There was no way he would let that happen again, especially now that he had Kane to worry about as well as Dara.

It would take a delicate balancing act to make them all come out at the other end of the weekend unscathed.

There was a touch of a glassy haze in Dara's eyes, and her breathing increased in tempo. Every time she tugged her restraints her pulse leapt, the throb visible in her neck. A hard pulse at the base of his cock answered back. Discovering she really did get off on being submissive thrilled him, but that wasn't the only thing she'd asked for.

A ménage. Jack glanced at Kane. His friend gave Dara another sip of wine, reaching with his finger to catch a drip of crimson liquid clinging to the corner of her lips. Raw possessiveness flashed for a second and he beat it down ruthlessly.

It was time for the next step. "Did you have enough to eat?"

Kane and Dara stopped their quiet conversation. Two sets of eyes turned on him, desire and lust painted on both their faces.

"Yes." Confessional soft. Trepidation and longing in the tone.

He stood and helped Dara to her feet. She swayed slightly and he wrapped an arm around her, pressing her against his body for support. She nodded then leaned her head against his chest.

"I'm full and I'm..." She blew out a long slow stream of air.

"Horny?"

She lifted her head to look him in the eye as she laughed. "Pervert. Yes. Oh my God, Jack, I'm dying here. How can I feel so aroused when no one is even touching me?"

"Don't try to figure it out, just enjoy." He walked her slowly toward the fireplace, keeping her tight against his side. Kane pushed back his chair and rotated to watch them.

A wash of heat from the fire hit them, the rosy glow of the flames highlighting her skin and making her even more beautiful. She wasn't movie-star pretty, but healthy and rosy, and he couldn't wait to taste her everywhere.

"How do your arms feel?"

She wiggled her fingers. There was plenty of room for movement; it was more the psychological aspect he was worried about. "Fine. You know I'm never going to be able to look at your skis without remembering this."

He grinned. "That's the idea."

Waiting any longer was out of the question. He cupped her face in his hands and kissed her. The flavours of dinner, of the wine and the pasta, lingered on her tongue, but the predominant taste was her. Jack savoured the moment. Enjoyed how she participated fully, meeting his tongue with her own. The way she leaned closer, joining in the kiss. Jack eased back and stared at her in admiration. Her breasts welled up, damn near overflowing the bra cups, and he had to stop himself from reaching out to rip the fabric away.

Stay in control. Stay in fucking control.

Even restrained she was a firecracker. She was probably

the type to fight just to see if he'd really take charge, and then willingly let him take the lead. God, he loved that type of woman. Had suspected she might have that streak in her, but to see it...

He sucked in air and concentrated. Next step.

"It's time. We're going to give you the next dose of your fantasy. Any requests?"

Her voice quivered lightly. "Requests?"

"This is all about you, sweetie. About what you want, only I'm going to say no more actual sex tonight. You took both of us earlier, and I don't want you too sore to ski."

Kane laughed. "I'd never thought of that as a way to slow her down."

Dara flipped her hair back, her eyes lit with mischief. "Only damn way you can beat me on the slopes."

The tension in the room rose a notch as she stared intently at Kane. Jack laughed quietly. Her devious mind was working overtime and it looked like his buddy was going to get it. "Dara, honey? You got something you want from Kane?"

The goofy smile on Kane's face froze in place as she nodded. "I want to give him a blowjob."

Kane jerked back in his chair, on the verge of tipping over. "Hell, Dara."

"What? The big words scare you? I want to suck you off, taste you, give you head. Ever since I saw..." She dropped her bold posture, biting her lower lip as she glanced away from Kane and Jack paused.

"You been peeking on Kane and his women, or what?"

A flush of embarrassment coloured her face but she nodded. "I didn't mean to, but, yeah. She complained he was too big. Which he is, from what I could tell earlier today but still..."

Jack nodded. "What about me? While you're sucking him off, what shall I do?"

She glanced at him coyly from under her lids. "Whatever you want. You decide."

Pleasure raced through his entire system. Sweet mercy—no other request could have made him react any stronger. His heart pounded like a drum and he turned away.

To hide his response, he grabbed a cushion from the couch and threw it to the floor by Dara's feet. With his help she knelt, the crackle of the fire in the background, the music from the speakers filling the room with a hushed expectancy. Jack stepped back, mesmerized by how fabulous she looked, virtually naked, waiting. Hands behind her back, breasts thrust forward. Lips wet from licking them.

Kane groaned. "You're serious?"

"Please." She tugged the restraints again and Jack gritted his teeth. Moisture at the juncture of her limbs glistened in the soft light of the fire. She was so wet it had soaked through her excuse for a pair of panties and coated her thighs.

Kane glanced in his direction. The inner struggle his friend fought was clear, and Jack was almost sure Kane was going to refuse when he finally rose to his feet.

"Damn, Dara. I'm going to admit I'm over my head here. If you want this, if you're really sure..."

Her lashes fluttered but her chin went up. "I'm sure. Please."

Kane squatted before her and took her lips, kissing her, tangling his fingers in her hair. Pressing kisses to her cheeks and her neck. Then he stood and opened his zipper, reached in and pulled out his cock. Dara moaned as he stroked a few

71

times, his length already fully engorged and ready for her. He held the base and directed the tip toward her mouth, her hands still locked behind her.

"Lick it." The gravelly tone in Kane's voice was completely unlike him.

When Dara's tongue darted out to touch the ruddy head of Kane's dick, Jack closed his eyes briefly in self-defense. The sheer eroticism of watching—he'd never expected to experience this much pleasure. It was true what he'd told Kane earlier. The pressure in his balls rose, but not as urgent as if it was him standing before her. He waited patiently, one hand rubbing his own cock through his jeans. The rigid length pressed against the fabric and he longed to strip off his clothes.

Kane threaded the fingers of his free hand into her pale hair, pulling it away from her cheek and clearing Jack's view.

"Fuck." Kane groaned. His head fell back as Dara opened her lips and sucked the tip of his cock into her mouth. Her tongue flicked out, adding moisture to the surface, and he guided her deeper on every pass. Her lips stretched around his girth as he rocked his hips a bit farther each time until her nose nestled in the curls at his groin.

Her bright eyes stared up at him and Kane stroked her cheek. "You good?"

She nodded slightly and he withdrew, her cheeks hollowing as she sucked. Kane pressed in again and again, supporting her head and fucking into her mouth gently at first, then with increasing force. Jack watched Dara's body closely for any signs of discomfort, but she leaned eagerly into the thrusts.

It was better than any porn he'd ever seen. Fuck, it was better than some sex he'd personally experienced. Jack stripped off his clothes, completely ignored by the others as they continued their erotic dance. Jack stroked his cock, thrusting into his fist in rhythm with Kane's motions.

The wet sounds of sucking, the continual mutters and groans from Kane's lips, echoed in the room. "So close. Damn, I'm so close, Dara. If you don't want to swallow, you got to let me—*fuck.*"

Her throat convulsed and Kane arched his back, his cock buried deep in her mouth. The two of them locked together, his body shaking, face screwed up in a grimace of extreme pleasure. Jack moved quickly and dropped his knees behind Dara, catching her body against his as she wavered unsteadily, her hands trapped between them. He wrapped one hand around her torso, shoving aside her bra to cup her breast. His other hand slipped between her legs, under the tiny triangle of fabric and into the wet heat of her slit.

She hummed, her mouth still full of Kane's cock, but her hips thrust against him, seeking his touch. She shook in his arms, reaction to the whole situation obviously overwhelming her.

"It's okay, sweetheart, I've got you." He stroked upward, drawing moisture over the tight nub of her clitoris. Kane stepped away, and Dara let him go, her head falling back to rest on Jack's shoulder. He teased her, fingers light over her clit, and she shivered then laughed.

Kane sat in front of them where he'd collapsed. He stroked a hand up her torso to clasp her other breast. "What's so funny?"

Dara rotated her hands until her fingers cupped Jack's balls and cock. "Holy fuck, woman, not too tight."

"Just keep doing what you're doing. Oh damn, that feels good, Jack."

One finger he pressed into her, then two, the heel of his hand continuing to stimulate her clit. Dara panted lightly, her

73

hips rocking forward in an even rhythm to fuck herself on his fingers.

"Not enough. More."

Another finger slid next to his—and he met Kane's eyes over her shoulder. His friend shrugged and grinned, leaning over to suckle her breast through the thin fabric of the bra.

Dara let out a long moan. "Yes, oh yes, that's good."

She panted lightly, the tiny whimpers driving Jack insane. She maintained a steady pulse with her fingers over his dick, and he bit down on her neck, laving the mark he left behind. He pressed kisses upward to behind her ear, sucking the lobe into his mouth then swirling his tongue around the sensitive tissue. He could eat her alive, every inch of her, and not have enough.

The tight pressure in his balls and cock made him lightheaded, and he'd never wanted more to be deep inside a woman. He fought for the strength to keep his promise of no more sex. The touch of her hands on him was enough and his release edged closer.

"Holy shit." Dara straightened, her body tightened and she came. Her sex tightened around his fingers, a long low keen of delight escaped her lips. She shook in his grasp, head writhing from side to side until the shaking diminished. Jack swore as his climax hit, strands of semen spurting from his cock to coat her lower back and buttocks. The sticky moisture smeared between them, her fingers wiggling against him and drawing out his pleasure.

Stars floated before his eyes.

Kane's hand withdrew and he pulled Dara forward to cradle her against his body. Jack shook off his own lingering stupor to undo the straps from her wrists, the *rippp* of the Velcro loud in the room, carrying above the harsh sound of their erratic breathing.

Holy shit was right. She'd reacted so beautifully, he was still in a cold sweat from all the possibilities flashing through his mind. If he had his way, he'd pick her up, carry her to the master bedroom, tie her to the bed and start all over. But that would hardly be fair, not to her, not to Kane.

The battle between the bonds of friendship and the desires in his belly was fierce, but short. Tonight, he'd put aside his remaining hungers, but he needed some space if he wasn't going to act on his yearnings.

Jack rubbed her wrists tenderly, massaging her arms and lifting them around Kane's neck. "Why don't you take her to the shower? Have a nice hot one, then head to bed. Tomorrow is going to come early, and we've got a reputation to maintain of setting the first tracks of the day."

Dara twisted in Kane's arms, confusion on her face. "What about you?"

He smiled reassuringly. "Shower's too small for three. You guys go ahead."

Kane stood and jostled her for second, attempting to balance with his open jeans and still carry her.

"Put me down, you idiot, you're going to hurt something."

"Sack of potatoes…"

Dara slapped playfully at Kane as he wiggled until he could flip her over his shoulder. She squealed, Kane laughed, and something warm and tender lit in Jack's belly in spite of the acid bite of jealousy. They were friends—at the root of it all they knew how to care for each other.

He watched Kane walk down the hall, Dara bouncing on his shoulder. She lifted herself up, happy face smiling as she blew Jack a kiss before disappearing from sight into the bathroom.

Jack hauled himself off the floor to collapse on the couch. As the sound of the shower clicked on in the distance, he stared into the fire. Tonight had done nothing but offer more convincing evidence that he truly wanted to be with Dara.

And proof that sharing her was going to be the hardest thing he'd ever done.

Chapter Six

Alpine Responsibility Code
Rule #6—You must have sufficient physical dexterity to safely ride all lifts...

The distant sound of Kane's slightly off-key singing woke her. Either that or it was the violent shaking of the mattress as Jack threw himself beside her, wrapped his arms around her and tickled. Dara squirmed, attempting to wiggle free.

"Damn it, Jack, stop." The quilt was toasty warm from Kane's body and she didn't want to lose the lazy sensation in her limbs. She'd forgotten how much she loved sharing a bed. No cold toes, cuddles all night long. Relaxed from their shower the previous night, she'd crawled into Kane's arms and promptly fallen asleep. Waking in the night and rolling to find a warm body to snuggle against had been a little bit of heaven.

Still half-asleep, she lost the battle with Jack. Somehow he managed to pin her under his heavy body and she gave up, temporarily. She mock-glared up at his beautiful smile. "Jerk."

"Hmm, good morning, sunshine. I see you're bright and chipper today. Ready for a hearty breakfast? Porridge, eggs, kippers..."

Her stomach rolled. "Good Lord, that sounds disgusting."

Jack grinned at her. "How about a chocolate banana smoothie instead?"

"Now you're talking." One of his legs nestled between hers and she savoured the weight of him against her body. Except for one thing.

"Think you can ease off my bladder there, big guy? I'm going to have an accident."

Jack laughed and rolled, finishing with her on top of him. He nuzzled against her neck and cradled her close. "Sorry."

"No worries. How long until the first chair starts?"

"An hour."

"An hour? Sheesh, Jack, why'd you wake me so early?"

He tugged her against himself, naked except for a pair of plain boxers. "I need a little one-on-one time."

His lips were gentle against her throat and the caress felt fabulous. "Where's Kane?" she asked.

"In the shower."

She dragged her fingers through his hair, loving the soft brush against her fingers. "You didn't join us last night."

He was quiet for a moment, his gaze scanning her face intently. "Wasn't sure how well we'd sleep with three people in a bed. Besides, you and Kane were wrapped up together pretty tight."

She pressed down on his chest, leaning away from him. "You watched us?"

"Just making sure you were all right. Last night—was everything okay with you?"

Was she okay? Even now the thought of the previous evening made her wet. There was certainly no problem with physical compatibility between either her and Kane, or her and Jack. "I loved it."

His face softened, the concern written there easing.

Dara rested her head on his chest and listened to his heartbeat. Yesterday had opened her eyes to a side of Jack she'd never seen before. He'd always been her protector. Last night had taken the level of trust she had in him to a new level. Being restrained had been wicked-hot, made so much better by the knowledge she had absolutely nothing to fear. Not with Jack guarding even as he guided her through the experience. She hadn't realized how much giving control over to another person would turn her on. Reading about it in her books was nothing compared to the reality.

She could get to like it. A lot.

Jack twisted them slightly, resting on his side, pulling his knee up while keeping her leg draped over his. The position opened her, the bottom edge of the oversized T-shirt she wore as a sleep shirt sliding toward her waist. The soft brush of his fingers over her hip and the swell of her butt sent a shiver up her spine.

He kissed along her jaw, over her cheek and up to her ear. "I can't stop thinking about you. I need to know how you taste," he whispered.

His hand continued to glide in slow even circles on her body, never moving any closer to her core. Dara threaded her fingers into his hair and pulled their mouths together, licking at his lips even as she opened her legs invitingly.

Jack laughed softly against her mouth. "You're a demanding little creature, aren't you?"

"Hmm, sometimes."

"Me too." He leaned back, putting space between their upper bodies. "Place your hand on my chest."

His whole tone changed. It wasn't cruel or harsh, but it was definitely an order. She dragged her fingers down his throat

79

until she felt the muscular ridges of his chest. Her palm absorbed the heat radiating out from his bare skin. She traced small circles on his skin, relishing the opportunity to explore him so intimately.

His gaze trapped hers. "Don't move."

Dara smiled and pressed her open hand to his skin and froze it there. He stared into her eyes, observing, evaluating. Her pulse kicked up a notch as the endless circles he'd been making on her hip changed and he slid his fingers under the edge of her panties. It was the work of a moment to tug them to the side. A finger parted her already wet curls—just being with him had made her needy. Made her ready, and when he slid two fingers deep into her sex, she moaned aloud.

All motion stopped.

His voice whispered tantalizingly over her skin. "I'm sorry. I forgot to warn you. No noises either. Understand?"

She blinked and squeezed her lips together.

"Good girl." He slid his fingers in and out a few times, nicking her clitoris with his thumb on every thrust. Dara concentrated hard to remain still, to not pump her hips toward his hand to add to the intensity.

Suddenly his fingers left her and she bit back her protest. She was nowhere near done. Empty, aching. He brought his hand up to his nose and breathed deeply, moisture glistening on his fingers.

Her heart skipped a beat.

"Fabulous. I wonder if you're as sweet as I think you'll be?" Jack flipped his hand around and brushed his fingertips against her lips, the scent of her arousal strong in her nostrils as he painted her lips with her own cream.

Then he kissed her. Nibbles and licks, tiny bites to her

lower lip before dragging it into his mouth and lapping all traces of moisture away. A heavy pulse beat in her core, along with a throbbing desire to be filled, but she remembered to stay still in spite of the temptation to rub against him. As he kissed her, he returned his hand to cup her mound, holding her firmly, but without enough pressure for her to reach a climax.

She was painfully close from only his kisses.

His tongue thrust into her mouth and she suckled it happily, imagining it plunging instead into her heated core. Wishing there was something filling her up. The kiss went on and on, and all the while she was conscious this was *Jack* she was kissing—her friend, her confidant. He held a piece of her heart, and now he seemed to have found the key to her body.

He drew back, breathless, eyes dark with desire, pupils dilated. He stared at her for a long moment before speaking. "You are very sweet. Thank you for sharing with me."

When he moved to separate them, she shivered with dismay. Oh my God, no, that wasn't it, was it? Dara opened her mouth to protest, then paused. He smiled. "You can talk."

"You're not going to stop, are you?" Damn, was that her voice? That whining child?

He examined her face, and she wondered if it revealed exactly how hot he'd made her. How close to the edge he'd brought her with a very simple touch. "Anticipation will make the rewards ahead even sweeter, Dara. I choose to wait. Can you?"

The sexual heat raging inside made her want to scream no and demand he bring her to a climax. The woman in her wanted to please him. She'd loved being restrained last night at his suggestion; perhaps this was something else he could teach her.

She lowered her eyes and took a deep breath. "Yes."

Jack lifted her chin and forced her to look at him. He shook his head gently, tenderness in his gaze. "I don't want you cowering before me or hiding your eyes. I may like to call the shots, but you are my equal in all ways. You can always say no. Understood?"

A smile broke free. That's the Jack she knew, looking out for her even as he whipped her world into a frenzy. A shot of mischief skipped through her and she rolled on top, catching him by surprise.

"Understood." She leaned closer and kissed him hard, ignoring the urge to grind her sex against his rock-solid abdomen.

He sat up with her in his arms and tousled her hair. "Come on, sweetheart, it's time to get ready for the day."

When he pushed her toward the bathroom, she went with a final kiss to his cheek, a smile lingering on her lips.

An hour later Dara was still smiling.

"How many runs you think we can we track up before we lose the fresh powder?" She flipped her goggles onto the brim of her helmet. The sun dazzled her eyes, crystals catching and reflecting back on every turn. There weren't many skiers out yet, not this early on a Friday.

"If we keep heading higher, we'll be good for the whole morning." Kane and Jack bumped fists then slid forward to wait their turn for the chair.

"Remember there's only double chairs on the top half of the hill." Dara didn't want to be separated from either of them. She leaned her hip casually against Jack's side and he snuck a kiss from her. The cold air contrasted with the warmth of his mouth and made her lips tingle. She hadn't intended on doing anything physical with the guys while they were on the hill, but they had other plans. They couldn't seem to keep their hands off her. Every time they stopped she got pulled against one or the other of them and kissed thoroughly.

All the attention was making her feel a trifle giddy.

"Don't worry, we'll keep you warm." Kane wiggled his brows at her as they settled on the chair and lowered the safety bar.

"Let me hold your poles," Jack offered, and she handed them over. She twisted on the seat, trying to get comfortable for the long ride up. She leaned on Jack, his right arm that rested along the back of the chair the perfect height to support her head.

Kane pulled off one glove and stuffed it in his pocket. "Lift her leg for me, will you, Jack?"

"What are you doing— Oh my God, are you insane?" Dara found herself spread-eagle, her left leg hitched overtop of Jack's, her right resting on Kane's knee. Jack had snuck his right ski under hers and somehow pulled their limbs into a tangle without losing their skis in the process. "Bastard. You know the rule. Drinks for the rest of the trip are on you if they have to stop the chair so we can get off."

Jack whispered in her ear. "Oh, I don't think we need to stop the lift for at least one of us to get off. Ready to finish what we started this morning?"

Oh damn. "You're not serious..."

Kane reached for her. "I love your ski pants. I was telling Jack earlier that seeing you in those things always gives me a hard-on."

"They're just backcountry overalls— Hey, no way!"

Kane paused, his hand under her coat as he played with her zipper. "You want me to stop, I will, but there's no need. The fifteen-minute ride to the top is long enough for a bit of fun."

Dara sealed her lips as she scanned the slopes below. They were right out in the open, the dangling chair in full view of anyone who happened to ski past and look up. Of course, there were so few skiers out she doubted anyone would bother looking to see what was happening—they'd be more intent on the uncut snow before them.

The sheer naughtiness of what Kane proposed sent an extra thrill through her. This was part of what she'd asked for in her excuse, wasn't it? Sexual experiences she would never have thought of? It was also part of finding out what the guys were like when they weren't simply being buddies to her. Dara took a deep breath and deliberately relaxed back against Jack. "Go for it."

Kane smirked as he leaned over to kiss her. He tugged at her zipper and she sucked in her belly. Her bibbed overalls were designed with one zipper set that reached from waist to the top of the bib, and a second set that slid downward. She supposed if she were a guy she could have used the lower escape hatch as a quick-release method. She'd never dreamed of this possibility.

Kane adjusted the zippers until her pants were open just enough to allow him to sneak his hand under her long johns and into her panties. He stroked through her curls and she jerked at his touch.

"Shit...your fingers are cold!"

Behind her Jack shifted and she twisted her neck to look at him. "Kiss me," he demanded, taking her mouth with his.

Erotic overload in three, two, one... Jack had turned her on in the morning without giving her release. All the attention and kisses for the past hour had been more than enough to keep her motor running on high, and now, between Jack's lips and the teasing rub of Kane's thumb against her clit, she was ready to have a meltdown. Kane's cool forefinger slipped into her sheath and she cried out. Jack swallowed the sound and thrust his tongue into her mouth. The whole encounter seemed too fabulous to be true. The chair continued its ascent, the wheels overhead on the long support arm squeaking every time they rolled past a tower. Cold air snuck in with Kane's hand, adding a layer of tension and unfamiliarity to the situation.

Kane added a second finger, the additional stretch drawing her closer to the edge of orgasm. He changed the angle of his hand and a violent rush of pleasure overtook her. She squeezed her eyes shut and groaned. "Oh my—yes, right there. Don't stop—don't...ohhhh."

"Sweet spot?" Jack asked, his warm breath tickling her ear.

"Seems that way." Kane voiced his approval. "Right about...here."

Bright spots floated before her closed eyes and she panted for breath. She'd been longing for this since Jack had left her aching this morning. "Screw...the play...by...play. Kane, please. A little more."

He pressed on her clit on the next pass, repeating whatever mysterious trick he played internally, and it was enough to set her off. She leaned back and enjoyed every second of her orgasm, letting her guys support and hold her up. Her passage clutched Kane's fingers, a sharp streak of pleasure racing from her core over her entire body. He stroked her labia softly as he withdrew his fingers, circling her wet slit again and again until the tremors ceased.

She was glad Kane had figured out how to adjust her zippers back to their proper places because she had no muscles to deal with it herself. In fact, if she didn't pull it together quick she was in danger of buying drinks. The way she felt, managing not to fall the instant her skis hit the slope was long odds.

"God, you're gorgeous when you come." She opened her eyes to see Kane pop his fingers into his mouth and moan with approval. *Holy shit.* He licked his fingers clean, his gaze never leaving her face.

Dara licked her own lips. Kane was a dirty boy and she absolutely loved it. "Holy...damn that was good."

They grinned at each other like fools until the chair wobbled again and Dara finally clued into their surrounding. They were five towers from the top of the hill, now within easy visibility of the lift operator in the safety booth.

"Watch yourself for a second." Jack lifted her thigh and twisted his ski under the chair, returning her leg to the normal straightforward and side-by-side position with its partner. He handed back her poles and lifted the safety bar. "And we're ready for the next run."

Kane leaned past her to speak to Jack. "You wanna do her next trip?"

"You're not serious." Dara flipped her gaze back and forth between the two of them, examining their faces carefully. She should have been embarrassed, but the sexual hormones racing through her bloodstream made it tough to feel anything other than euphoric.

Jack nudged her shoulder. "I think we can keep you entertained, on and off the hill."

Dara focused forward intently, attempting to regain strength in her still-trembling limbs. She was not about to trip and fall flat on her face like some bunny-hill skier. Holy shit...what had she unleashed?

Kane grabbed the edge of his board as he caught air off the

jump Dara had discovered on their previous run. His mood was lighter than he expected, in spite of the rumble of need in his belly that grew larger by the second. If the erotic images flashing through his brain didn't ease up, he was going to end up on an emergency stretcher. His cock was hard enough to wax and use as a snowboard.

The snow conditions had never been better, but for the first time ever on a ski fling he found the day dragging. Normally, they'd ski until they were running on fumes, grab a quick lunch then power it out until the final second possible on the hill.

Yet today all he could think about was getting Dara naked in the damn hot tub. Or bending her over the couch and driving his cock into her from behind. Screw the skiing; he wanted to be spending time with her. In her. Now that the craving he'd had for her body had been released, like some Pandora's box, there was no place to hide all his dirty fantasies away.

Even the knowledge Jack would be in the picture didn't freak him out as much as it should. Last night, when Dara had sucked his cock, it was Jack who had ended up saving them both from what could have become a bad situation. There was no way Kane could have reacted fast enough to catch Dara when she wavered, not when she'd virtually sucked his brains out through the end of his dick.

Jack's timely catch had made a potentially bad situation redeemable. If the anxiety he felt having a guy in the room meant fooling around with Dara was safer, he'd just deal with his discomfort.

The sun dipped behind the mountain and the temperature dropped noticeably as they finished their run. Dara yawned hugely, covering her mouth with the back of her glove, and Jack laughed.

"You ready to call it quits?"

She stuck her tongue out at him. "Not until you do. I'm not winning the wimp award the first day out."

Kane cleared his throat. "Last run for me. Let's angle over to the—"

"You're kidding." Dara narrowed her eyes at him. "You? You never give up first. We usually have to haul your ass off the hill and hide your equipment so you don't disappear in the middle of the night."

Colour rose in her cheeks as he stared at her intently. Something in his face must have shown what boiled inside him. He leaned over to whisper against her ear. "I'm not planning on sneaking anywhere tonight that doesn't involve you. And the only place my equipment is going to hide is deep inside your pussy."

Her mouth hung open for a second before she glanced at Jack. "I think I've had enough skiing for the day as well."

Sexual tension shot skyward. By the time they reached the cabin and placed their gear in the storage locker outside the door, their need was a tangible weight. They tumbled inside, shrugging off ski coats, scrambling to remove their heavy boots. Kane dragged Dara against him, one hand on her lower back to press her stomach into his erection to make sure she knew exactly how much he needed her. She pushed off her suspenders, Jack grabbed the bottom of her long sleeved shirt, and faster than Kane thought possible, she was naked from the waist up.

Screw finesse, he needed her now.

He took her breasts into his hands, cupping the weight of them and admiring the red nipples as they puckered tight.

"All day long I've been imagining this." He sucked one nipple into his mouth, twirling his tongue around the point. Dara arched against him, locking her fingers in his hair and holding him close. He struggled out of his own clothes, tearing off his shirt then returning to the warm temptation of her skin.

The noises she made drove him insane. Each purr of pleasure from her lips, each sharp cry as he nipped, all of it teased him and brought him to the point of no return.

Jack joined in as well. Stripped to just his boxers, he pressed her from behind, kissing her neck, and she moaned out her delight.

"I want...oh God, I want whatever you want to give me."

Kane managed to tug her overalls past her hips and knelt to bury his face in her crotch. She was wet, her curls slick with moisture as he used one hand to open her to his tongue. He had barely a moment to dip into her warmth before Jack interrupted.

"We need to move. Dara, I want your mouth on me and I can't wait any longer." His voice was a growl, primitive and harsh, and Kane couldn't argue. He couldn't wait either.

He scooped her up and carried her to the couch. Along the way Jack tugged the overalls past her ankles and suddenly there was nothing but her naked skin everywhere and goddamn if he wasn't about to explode.

The soft leather of the couch beckoned and the images from earlier in the day leapt to mind. Kane twirled her, connecting her back to his front, his erection lying in the valley between her cheeks. He rocked his hips and it felt so fucking good he was ready to lose it.

Dara whimpered lightly and he loosened his grip. "Sorry, I—"

"Don't stop. Come on, Kane, I want this."

That was all he needed to hear for the slight edge of restraint he still had to break.

He pressed her over the back of the couch, bending her at the waist. She shot her arms out to catch herself, braced on the seat of the sofa. Her feet dangled off the floor, the soft smooth skin of her ass shining in the glow of the subtle lighting. He dropped to his knees and nipped one cheek.

"Fuck." She squirmed and he moved quickly to pin her in place with one hand.

"Uh-uh, you're not going anywhere. Here's a fantasy I bet you've never experienced. I'm going to fuck you from behind, Jack's going to fuck your mouth. Two guys at one time—you want it?"

"Yes." No hesitation. She looked at him over her shoulder, wiggling back against his hand. "Hurry."

Jack laughed as he moved in front of her. "Bossy chick."

"Isn't she?"

His friend squatted and lifted Dara's chin, gazing into her eyes. "Maybe she was a bad girl today and she's actually looking for a little punishment."

In a split second the tension in the room was completely transformed.

Dara sputtered before whispering her response. "Anything."

Kane blinked in shock. He was still hotter than a fire, but suddenly he was uncertain, glancing at Jack for direction. His friend's eyes almost glowed with lust. "Spank her," Jack ordered.

Kane opened his mouth, but nothing came out. His hand already rested on her ass, the pleasure of the touching her naked skin making his dick so hard he was having difficulty seeing straight. And Jack wanted him to spank her?

"Do it," Jack growled.

Kane jerked upright at the command. He rubbed Dara's

ass, circling gently. He waited until she relaxed, the tension in her body easing off a tiny bit before raising his hand and bringing it back down. The sharp ring of the smack of his palm against her skin echoed in the room. Her moan of pleasure rang louder still. The pink tinge to her skin increased and he smoothed the heated section slowly.

"You okay?" Jack brushed back the hair falling over her cheek.

She wiggled and sighed. "Yup."

Kane smacked her other cheek and she squealed, a little hitch in her voice.

Jack stood and motioned to Kane. "How 'bout you?"

It wasn't his normal kink, but damn if seeing how much it thrilled Dara didn't make this work. "Oh yeah."

He spanked her again and again, careful to place each strike in a new spot, careful to temper the strength of the blow. Dara rocked back into him, as if welcoming the sensation. Kane brushed his fingers past her slit, and her juices soaked him instantly.

"Oh hell, you do like that, don't you?"

"Hmmm." Dara's words slurred as she spoke. "Now fuck me. I need you inside."

No arguments from him. Kane grabbed his cock, ready to line up and thrust in when Jack shoved a condom into his hand.

Shit. His brain really was missing in action. It took a second to cover himself and move behind her, the pretty pink of her ass cheeks driving his lust higher. The tip of his cock lodged within her wet opening, he looked up to see Jack already in position in front of her.

"Ready for us?" Jack asked.

"Do it." Passion deepened her voice, dragging at his senses.

Jack held his cock by the base and pressed the engorged head against her lips. She lapped at him before opening wide. As Jack slid forward, Kane copied the motion, rocking to work his way into her tight passage. He clasped her hips, his fingers digging into the muscles to get a firmer grip. Once he was totally seated, his groin flush with her butt, he paused, enjoying the sensation of being deep within her body. Then the need to move overwhelmed him, and he drew back, stopping with the head of his cock clinging to her opening.

One hard thrust after another followed, the demand to drive into her increasing until he felt nothing but the tight squeeze around him.

Jack groaned and Kane dragged his gaze from where his cock disappeared into Dara's body. Jack held her head carefully, supporting her even as he buried his shaft between her lips. His cock glistened with saliva, and if the tension in his muscles was any indicator, his friend was nearing climax. Kane's own impending explosion threatened, his balls tight to his body.

He was not going over without taking Dara with him. He reached under her body and found her clit.

A muffled cry broke from her lips, blocked by Jack's cock.

There was more than enough moisture to smooth his fingertips over the rigid nub. Rubbing harder as he plunged deep, her gasps turned into a long steady squeal around Jack's dick. Her passage convulsed, squeezing his shaft, dragging his own climax from him as he locked them together with a final drive. His cock jerked, semen flooding the condom until he wondered if he was ever going to stop.

Jack shouted, lost control and came. Dara swallowed eagerly, liquid spilling from her lips. Kane watched in fascination. In his brain-dead fog, it took a while to register that Jack had been right. A little voyeurism wasn't a bad thing. Time blurred for a few minutes before Kane found the muscle to pull from her body. Suddenly Jack was there, cradling Dara against him as he made his way to the balcony.

Kane stumbled ahead to pull open the doors, and moments later they were relaxed in the hot tub, three boneless heaps.

Dara wiggled until she was draped over them both, one arm wrapped around his neck, her hips still resting in Jack's lap. "Oh wow, that was fabulous."

Jack laughed. "You're going to have to speak up, I can't hear past this ringing in my ears."

Kane had to agree. He couldn't even convince his tongue to work to tell Dara... He glanced down at her in his arms. He wasn't sure what he wanted to tell her, but the satisfied glow in his body was nothing on what grew in his heart.

It was just as he'd suspected—they were compatible in and out of bed. Only, while the spanking had been interesting, that appeared to be more in Jack's line of sexual play. And if this weekend was the time to impress Dara, and try to head toward a forever with her, he needed to not just blindly follow anymore. Not Jack's lead, not his dick's. He needed to make sure what he had to offer Dara got laid on the table as well, and he wanted it to fit with her fantasies.

It appeared he had a little speed-reading to do, from her personal fantasy book.

Chapter Seven

Alpine Responsibility Code

Rule #7—Showboating is allowed within designated areas only…

"You're not serious." Dara stared at Jack in shock.

"I'm not? Hmm, I thought I was."

"But—"

"And wear this. I love this top." He handed her the undershirt she'd originally brought to wear to sleep in. It was old and worn soft. It was also paper thin.

Dara pulled the garment over her head, that slight thrill of obeying his orders enough of a rush to make her forget to argue. When the fabric brushed her bare skin, she had to bite her lip to stop a moan from escaping.

She'd pretty much been in a constant state of arousal for the past two days. This morning she'd opened her eyes to find Jack wrapped around her in the big master bed, stroking her body to a feverish pitch. They slipped into making love before she finished waking up, her desire building hot and fast. It didn't take long before his forceful thrusts made her climax so hard she'd screamed loud enough to wake Kane in the room below them.

The last thing she remembered the previous night, she'd

been cuddled between her two guys, eating popcorn and watching a video until her eyes refused to stay open. Kane must have disappeared sometime after that. It was almost like an elaborate game of keep away, only she was the ball and they were taking turns tossing her between each other.

Jack growled, a low husky sound, regaining her attention and making her belly quiver with anticipation.

"That's what I thought. Your nipples show through your shirt." Jack dragged a finger down the swell of her breast. His fingertip caught the edge of her nipple as it tightened and he smiled. "Very lovely."

He pulled up the suspenders of her bibbed ski pants and adjusted the strap lengths as she fought for composure.

"Jack, Dara. Hurry up. Aren't you guys ready yet? The hill opens in ten minutes." Kane wandered into the master bedroom and jerked to a stop, a lecherous expression drifting across his face. "Holy crap. Dara, you look hot."

She stood a little straighter. *Incredible.* She was surrounded by Neanderthals. "Damn it, Kane, tell Jack I can't ski like this."

He shrugged. "I don't see why not. You're going to wear a coat, right?"

"Yeah, but—I'm not wearing a bra."

Kane grinned. "That, I noticed. Nice one, Jack. I like how you've got her ski pants arranged. Kind of looks like one of those old fashioned corsets holding up her boobs. God, you've got the most fucking gorgeous tits, Dara."

She crossed her arms and covered herself. "Thanks so much, oh caveman."

He wiggled his brows. "I told you before I'm a breast man. Look, it's up to you, but so what if you're not wearing a bra?"

"Hello, boobs hanging loose."

"Again, so? Don't try to bullshit me and say that teeny thing you wore the other night supported you more than this. You're not jumping on a trampoline or anything—let the girls be free."

She shook her head. "You've been watching way too much television."

Kane pulled her close. He crushed her breasts against his torso and kissed her senseless. She wrapped her arms around his neck and dove in for all she was worth. Kissing Kane was rapidly becoming an addiction. He had a way of teasing with his lips and tongue that set every nerve on fire. The way he smoothed his fingers along her jaw made her feel all feminine and cared for. They stood for an eternity and yet it was only a moment before Jack cleared his throat and brought them back to earth.

Kane let her go, the dark expression in his eyes promising so much even as he turned her to face Jack. Again she was consumed, kisses and caresses raining down. If it wasn't one of them, it was the other. Touching her. Holding her, caring for her. It all felt very right.

And she was no further in being able to choose between them than when she started.

Kane skidded to a stop beside the lift lineup and waited for Jack and Dara to join him.

"I love that run. Simply love it. Can we go again?" Dara's cheeks were rosy and her enthusiasm poured out like sunshine.

Kane swallowed around the knot forming in his throat and forced out a laugh. "Of course."

Jack stretched his legs, kneeling in a lunge. "Good Lord, guys, now I know you're trying to kill me. Those moguls are big enough to disappear between. I'm calling *pax*. I want to do some easier runs through the trees."

Kane nodded. "No worries. You want to meet up in the cafeteria for some lunch today? My treat?"

"Fries?" Dara grinned at them both.

"Sounds perfect," Jack agreed. "You got your walkie-talkies? We can touch base once we're done a few runs and arrange to meet."

Jack stood and slid next to Dara. She offered her lips without any prompting, and Kane thought how much things had changed in just a couple days. How had they spent so many years together without getting involved? Kissing her seemed as natural as breathing, holding her just as right. They waved Jack off and turned to stand in line for their turn on the lift.

It was time to add a little fun to their day, Kane-style. "So, you enjoying your trip to Big White?"

Dara smiled at him. "Very much."

"How long you here for?" A furrow appeared between her brows. He hurried on, knowing she'd catch on soon enough. "I'm here until Sunday. Sure hope the ski conditions hold."

Her eyes widened as she figured out what he was doing and he fought to hide his grin. "Oh, I got here a few days ago myself. Yeah, the conditions are great."

"Have you found a favourite run yet?"

"There's a super one to the right of the chair, if you like them hard."

Kane took a deliberate ogle down her body before looking her in the eye. "I know how I like them. Do you like them hard?"

Someone behind them snickered as they slipped into position for the chair to pick them up. Dara spoke softly. "You're such a perv."

"You wanna play some more?" he whispered back.

The look she turned on him was pure Dara. "Come here often?"

The entire ride up they exchanged sexually loaded innuendo until she was squirming in place. "Shit, Kane, you need to stop. I'm already hanging out the front of my ski pants, I don't need to have a wet crotch as well."

"People will just think you fall down a lot."

She hit him on the arm. "How dare you insult me? I don't fall down."

"Well, there was that one time I seem to remember you doing a few spectacular wipeouts. Your first day on a snowboard."

She laughed. "Oh my God, I'd forgotten you were there to see that. Good thing I'm flexible, or I would have snapped something for sure."

He caught her eye and let the heat he felt for her simmer to the surface. "I think I'd like to see just how flexible you can be."

Dara stared at his mouth, her pink tongue slipping out to peek between her lips and leave behind a shimmer of moisture. "Hmmm, that sounds—intriguing. But that would require you to catch me first, and I somehow don't think you're fast enough."

They'd reached the top of the lift, slipping off the chair and heading toward the run they'd done earlier. Kane had to stop to fasten on his second boot. As he fumbled for the buckles, she stuck out her tongue and saucily wiggled her ass before poling hard and heading for the trees.

By the time he caught up to her, they were already a third of the way down the hill. He cut her off and laughed as she shouted, pulling out of his path. He herded her closer and closer to the trees, keeping an eye out for other skiers. The run was fairly empty—only expert skiers would take this route in the first place and the closer it got to lunch the fewer bodies remained.

She turned to the right and he paced her, coming in low on her side and forcing her back to the left. Small trails disappeared into the bush, and he saw the moment she made her break, turning sharply and disappearing from the main run. He followed her, staying on a higher trail so he could track her direction. They descended farther, Dara laughing the entire time until she pulled to a stop on top of a small rise hidden in the trees. She leaned over her poles, panting hard.

"Okay, I give up. You win."

Kane glanced around quickly as he released one foot from his board. He maneuvered her back toward the nearest birch tree tucked in amidst all the fir and spruce.

"What are you doing? Kane, are you insane?" She was still laughing as he crowded her body with his. Her skis extended backward on either side of the tree, and he braced himself between her legs, rocking his groin against her core. Dara grinned her approval. "Oh hello, not insane."

She ripped off her helmet and dropped it mindlessly to the snow before fumbling with his chinstrap. The instant it was loose, she shoved his helmet off as well, letting it crash and roll away as she dug her fingers into his hair and hauled his lips against hers.

God, she tasted good. Sunshine and fresh air and all Dara. Sweet and alive and he lifted her up slightly to get a better grip on her ass. He thrust his hips, rocking his erection hard against her body, her legs and skis dangling in mid-air. He didn't care how heavy it was to hold her up, could only think of the violent need in his groin to slip into her warmth again.

She yanked his mouth from hers, a gasp escaping her lips. "Jesus, Kane, why'd you start this out here? I'm going to die if you don't fuck me."

Sweet mercy. "Oh, I can so do that."

He lowered her, frantically scrambling through his pockets to find the condom he'd hidden away that morning in the hopes of just such an event. Dara wiggled, struggling to keep her balance as she unzipped and rearranged her clothing.

"Damn it, Kane, I can't..."

He paused in the process of hauling out his cock. She'd managed to open her zippers but her long underwear stood between him and paradise.

"You like those undies, sweetheart?" *Screw it.* If she did, he'd buy her new ones. He dropped to one knee, snagged the fabric in his fingers and, with one harsh pull, ripped the crotch open.

"Thank you. Hurry." She stole the condom from between his teeth where he'd placed it for safekeeping, and shredded the plastic wrapper. He stood still as she reached down to cover him. Her warm hands surrounded him, and he hissed, holding back from coming at the mere touch of her fingers.

"Hurry, hurry, hurry—" Dara leaned against the tree and opened as wide as she could, tilting her hips forward.

In an instant he nudged at her core with his cock. After the icy air surrounding him, her scalding heat welcomed him in. He squatted slightly to find the right angle, lined up and drove in with one hard motion.

She gave a cry of delight and clutched his shoulders. "Oh

yes, Kane..."

With one wild thrust after another he plunged into her, their heated gasps filling the air with a cloud of fog. The faint noises of the forest and skiers swooshing by in the distance faded away, overwhelmed by the incredible gasps of pleasure from her lips. Wet sounds from where their bodies joined carried up to him, adding to the pleasure rocking his mind. Inside Dara, playing games and laughing, even as he loved her. He wanted this forever.

The heat of their bodies almost crackled in the air. When she grabbed him by the head and pulled their lips together, moaning with her release, he let go, driving his cock as deep as possible as he poured into the condom.

They stood, pinned together like some frozen butterfly specimen, waiting for his brain to resume functioning. He was locked into a half crouch, and if he moved the wrong way, he was likely to end up flat on his ass with his dick hanging out. He dropped his head to her shoulder and sucked for air.

"That...holy moly...that was fucking marvelous."

He laughed in response. "You're a dirty girl, Dara. I love it."

She cupped his cheek in her hand. He savoured the sensation for a moment before they parted and worked to put everything back in place.

Kane caught her looking at him with an amused expression on her face. "What?"

She gestured toward his slowly deflating cock as he dealt with the condom and tucked himself away. "Cold air is supposed to make that thing smaller, not bigger. Oh, and good job on being a boy scout."

He caught her close for another moment, striving to enjoy every second, every touch.

"The payback for following the motto of 'Be prepared' has never been sweeter."

The cafeteria was packed and Dara looked around in confusion, hoping to spot one of the guys. Kane's head stuck out above the other customers waiting in the food line, and she headed his direction.

"Dara."

Off in the corner, Jack waved a hand, and she wove her way to his side. They were in the farthest corner of the room facing the bank of windows overlooking the ski hill. Jack cleared a space on the bench and patted the wood beside him.

"Come here, I have something for you."

She climbed over, dumped her helmet and gloves on the table and stared at him expectantly. He wrapped a hand around her neck and drew her close enough to kiss. Soft, mouth to mouth without demanding anything else. His tongue nicked her upper lip as they parted and she smiled. "Why, thank you, that was so sweet."

The boarder dudes on the other side of the table grinned before carrying on with their conversation. With her back to the main room, the rumble of voices in her ears smeared into a wash of white noise and it was like being alone. Her. Jack. The trio of guys across from them rambling about the gnarly jump they'd found on one of the side runs.

Jack leaned closer and nibbled her earlobe. A thrill shivered through her and her nipples tightened, rubbing against the thin fabric of her undershirt. Good lord, she was becoming a nymphomaniac. She'd just had sex with Kane in the trees and she was already panting hot for Jack. This weekend was supposed to be helping her decide between them, and so far the only thing she'd been able to decide was that both of them were excellent in—and out of—bed.

"Unzip your jacket." His voice tickled in her ear as heat built in her belly. Warmth spread as she lifted her hands slowly to obey his command. She glanced out the windows, taking a clandestine glance at the guys opposite them, wondering if they would notice what she was wearing. Or not wearing.

"Look at me," he commanded.

She stared into his eyes. His chocolate brown orbs mesmerized her as she inched the fastener on her coat downward. The sound of each zipper tooth releasing rang impossibly loud in the room. How could it be so clear over the rumble of hundreds of people talking and laughing simultaneously?

How could her heart beat louder still?

Jack's gaze lowered, skimming the edges of her jacket and lingering where she knew her nipples stuck up like headlights on high beam. "Very nice. Take your jacket off completely when I tell you to."

Dara remained visually locked with him. "But..."

He cupped her cheek and kissed her again, sweeping his tongue into her mouth this time. She melted a little and her resistance failed. As long as he was there to watch over her, she had no trouble with being a little...risqué...in public.

Jack rested his forehead against hers and whispered softly. "Kane and I spoke while you were in the washroom. So, you only met him today, did you? Hussy."

Oh my God. "He told you about us fooling around on the hill?"

"Of course. And it looks like your *new* friend might come over to our table as well. Want to keep playing?"

Jack role-playing? "Do you want to?"

He shrugged. "If it makes you feel good, I'm all for it. This is all about your fantasies."

She sucked in a gasp. He'd snuck his hand inside her coat and now tormented the aching tip of one nipple. Small smooth circles with his thumb teased the hard nub and she bit her lips together.

"Dara? Is that you?"

Jack withdrew his hand and turned to face Kane. She played along. "Hi."

He nodded toward the seat. "That spot taken?"

She shook her head and he plopped his tray down.

Jack nudged her shoulder. "You going to introduce me?"

Dara glanced between the two of them, watching them eye each other like strange dogs vying for territory instead of the best friends she knew them to be. "Jack, this is Kane, he's who I skied with on my last couple of runs. Kane, this is my..."

"Partner. Good to meet you, Kane." Jack thrust out his hand and the two shook, Dara trapped between them. Jack's inner arm brushed her chest, and her already hypersensitive skin drove her need up another notch.

"Same. You're a lucky dog, Jack. Your girl's a great skier. I enjoyed myself with her very much." His tone implied more than just a run down the slope and Dara flushed furiously. This was seriously twisted—how turned on she was getting. Her ruined underwear had no chance of containing the moisture flooding her passage as she considered the sexual overtones swelling around them.

Jack raised a brow. "You did? Well, Dara's full of tricks. Aren't you, sweetheart?" He turned her to nestle her back to his front, both of them sitting astride the bench and facing Kane.

Jack brushed his lips against the side of her neck and she instinctively leaned to open room for him. He took advantage of her vulnerable position to slip her coat from her shoulders.

Kane stared greedily. Her breasts were displayed like an exotic smorgasbord. Dara concentrated on moving enough air into her lungs to stop from passing out. She grew light-headed. She'd never felt this desired before in her life. Jack's hands rested possessively on her hips and she ached to have him touching bare skin.

Kane cleared his throat, dragging his gaze back up to hers before looking over her shoulder at Jack. "She's a very special lady."

"Definitely. And a hungry one. Dara, you mind if I leave you for a minute? I need to pick up some things for our lunch."

Dara shook her head, slightly dazed. Somewhere along the line she'd lost track of what was going on. Clarity returned in a rush as Jack slid her forward, closer to Kane. "You seem like a decent guy. She told me what happened, you know."

Kane jerked back. "She told you—?"

"I'm the one who suggested she needed to find someone she liked. Dara enjoys things a little on the wild side. Maybe you want to join us later in our room." Jack stood and kissed her cheek, pausing to whisper in her ear. "You should see the faces of the guys across the table right now. They're listening intently and I think one of them is ready to explode. I'm going to go get us some lunch. While I'm gone, follow Kane's lead." He dragged his fingers through her hair and kissed her one last time, lingering, passionate. He stared intently at Kane, nodded once, then left them alone.

Alone, except for an audience of three who held their breath as Dara peeked at Kane from under her lashes. When in the hell had her guys learned how to act like this? It was like some kind of elaborate hoax, yet they were playing it improv.

Kane cleared his throat. "He knows?"

Dara nodded.

"Good. That's an interesting proposition he just made. You think I should take him up on it?"

Her skin flushed red-hot as he winked the eye on the side away from their watchers. Her mouth was bone dry and she struggled to unstick her tongue from the roof of her mouth. She was as good as naked from the waist up, with the see-through shirt allowing her nipples to peek through. She quickly checked the main area of the cafeteria. It was one thing to pull a stunt like this in front of adults, but she didn't want to freak out any families or kids.

The setting was perfect. No one could see what was going on, tucked into the corner like they were. Well, no one except Kane—and three very quiet young men fiddling with their food. They weren't even pretending to hold a conversation anymore, far more intent on the drama before them.

So be it—she officially got off on being watched and thought a sexpot. Dara squirmed, hoping the seam of her ski pants would provide a little relief against her throbbing clit. She spoke softly. "What do you want to do?"

Kane locked his fingers in her hair, an erotic echo of Jack's movement only moments earlier. With infinite slowness he leaned toward her. "I want to come back to your room and fuck you again."

The audible gasps from across the table slid into white noise as he took her mouth under his. By the time he pulled away, her mind swirled with a mix of passion and confusion. What must the snowboarders think? And could she get any more turned on? Her sex ached to be filled, by Kane, by Jack. Heck she wanted both of them, right now. Hard, pounding into her.

She whimpered. Out of the corner of her eye, she saw one of the boarders rise to his feet, adjust himself quickly and race from the table.

Kane held her chin, his forefingers and thumb cradling her delicately but firmly enough she couldn't move without making a scene. "You need some more of what I gave you on the hill?"

Dara ducked her head and mumbled.

He laughed. "That's not an answer. I want to hear the words. Did you enjoy what we did? My cock in your pussy? Fucking against the tree like animals?"

Her breasts heaved as she panted for breath. "I loved it."

His gaze caught on her chest. Kane reached out to pinch one nipple between his fingers, rubbing the rigid peak where it speared the fabric. "Nice, but not as nice as if you were naked, those tits bare for my mouth. Or your boyfriend's. Jack, right?"

She nodded.

"What about both of us at the same time? Sucking and biting, one on each side?"

"Please..." The images flashing through her brain had nothing to do with cafeterias or ski slopes, and everything to do with being touched by both her guys. Filled by them, again and again, until she couldn't move.

Kane growled in frustration as he glanced around them. He stared for a moment across the table at the boarders. "You guys mind switching sides? We need a little more privacy than this bench allows."

They shook their heads wordlessly and rose to their feet. One of them ogled her shamelessly, his gaze eating her up, and damn if she didn't get even hotter. Kane tugged her against his body, his erection hard against her hip as he guided her around to the far side of the table.

"Kane. This isn't a good idea. People will see my—"

He pressed her down until her back was flat against the bench. Far overhead was the solid wood framing of the open timbers of the roof. Nearer to her left, the edge of the long row table hung inches above her head. Under the table, on the bench she and Kane had just vacated, she watched as the boarders took a seat. One cupped his groin, rubbing himself with a harsh rhythm.

She was completely hidden by the table, tucked away in the corner of the room with an exterior wall at her head and one on her right. Kane's body blocked her from the view of anyone at his back. They could have been alone, except for the continued audience of the boarders.

Kane massaged her breasts, pulling her attention back to him. "No one can see anything. In fact, let's just pretend there's no one here but you and me."

Oh my God, he was messing with her zipper again. He tugged the crotch of her ski pants open, totally ignoring the guys on the opposite side of the table. He slipped his fingers along her soaking wet slit. She covered her mouth with both hands to contain the noises threatening to escape.

"It's too bad there's no one here. Because I think you'd love to have someone watch me do this." He buried his fingers in her pussy and her hips involuntarily rose to meet him. The instant pressure in the core nudged her closer to yet another release, most of it from the sheer wickedness of what they were doing.

"If I had another condom I would fuck you here and now. On this bench. And your drenched pussy tells me that's exactly what you want, isn't it?"

He thrust into her again, his thumb riding her clit hard enough stars formed before her eyes. She was so close to coming, so close—

His pocket rang and he swore violently, fumbling with his coat one-handed, his fingers still buried in her pussy.

"Kane here."

Every breath she took shook her violently and she rocked as best she could against his hand, trying to reach that final bump to push her over. He withdrew his fingers with a long sigh. "I'm on holidays. This had better be a huge emergency, Derrick."

Damn. *No.* She reached for her crotch. She had to come. It was a physical need now. She slipped her fingers into her own body and pushed the heel of her hand onto her clit. Kane grasped her wrist and pulled it away from her body, preventing her from masturbating. The moisture clinging to her fingertips cooled as the air met it. He spoke briefly to his client before hanging up and tossing his cell to the table in disgust.

"Derrick owes me big-time. I have to go for a while and baby-sit a customer through a booking issue. We're not done." Kane leaned over and sucked her fingers into his mouth, cleaning them one by one before zipping her up. Regret and longing covered his face. "I'll join you as soon as I can."

He picked up his drink from the table and chugged it back, his throat moving rhythmically and Dara swallowed in time. Her entire body buzzed with adrenaline. She didn't think she could move if she tried.

"Kane? Where's Dara?"

Dara struggled to a sitting position. Jack stood with a filled tray, his gaze darting between her and Kane. She snatched her coat off the table and covered herself. Her cheeks flamed, her body even hotter.

Kane rose to his feet and grabbed his things. "Emergency work call. Glad you're back. She's a pistol. I thought I was going to have to rip her clothes off again, or tie her up."

"Oh, we can do that later." Jack growled softly. He put down the tray and handed Kane a piece of paper. "When you can make it."

Kane took a few steps away from the table before glancing back at Dara. He licked his fingers, the ones he'd had buried deep in her body and she shivered. She really was going to die.

Jack sat next to her and kissed her cheek gently. Such a chaste touch after the porn-ranked actions of the past half hour. He pushed a plate of fries her direction before eyeing the boarders seated across from them. "Time to hit the slopes, boys. Conditions are good out there."

"You won't believe—"

"Move along."

Dara bit her lip and fixed her gaze on the table as the two guys left without another word. Canadians were so polite. They'd watch, but they wouldn't say anything.

A new group claimed the vacant bench—a mom and dad with their two kids. Dara made sure she was properly covered, then she and Jack ate in silence, her blood pounding through her hard enough she felt breathless. An afternoon of skiing still ahead?

She would never survive.

Chapter Eight

Alpine Responsibility Code

Rule #8—Before merging, always look uphill and yield to others...

"I can't believe you made me do that."

They slipped back into their cabin. Jack held the door for Dara as she rumbled at him.

"Made you? Oh boy, we need to talk about willing accomplices and other things." He peeled off her coat and paused to admire her breasts. "God, I'm a genius. You're just dying for me to put my mouth on you, aren't you?"

Dara whimpered and nodded, reaching up to plump her breasts, tugging her own nipples.

He grabbed her wrists. "Hey, hey, slow down. There's no need to rush."

"You're not the one suffering here," she complained. "Kane had me on the edge of an orgasm before he left."

Jack snickered evilly and splayed his fingers against her lower back, rocking her against his erection. "Oh, I'm in pain, believe me."

He tried to keep it light, joking far more than he usually would, but he *was* fucking suffering. Not only were his balls blue from wanting her so badly, the urge to kick Kane out of the picture rose all the time. He didn't like the sentiments he'd been experiencing toward his best friend. It was a hard contradiction—being turned on watching Kane and Dara together, and yet feeling jealous he wasn't the one in charge.

The door flung open behind them and Kane stormed in. "Where is she?" His eyes lit on Dara and his frantic expression calmed. He shook his head sorrowfully. "Fuck it, that went a little farther than I intended. I'm sorry, Dara."

She grabbed him by the collar and hauled him closer. "Damn right, and now you're going to pay."

A rush of lust and a flash of rage hit simultaneously. Jack forced himself to step back as he stripped off his ski coat. Dara was up to something, and she deserved the right to play this one out as she desired. She lifted her chin and her gaze darted between him and his friend. There was none of her usual submissive softness in her stance, just an all-out sensual burn that threatened to ignite the entire room.

"I want you naked, Kane." Her voice husky, yet firm, made the hair on the back of his neck stand upright. His anger eased—Jack might not enjoy being dominated himself, but watching Dara lord it over Kane was a serious turn-on.

Kane nodded slowly and moved into the living room to comply. She turned her steely gaze in Jack's direction and he raised a brow at her. Did she really think she could order him around as well?

"Kane and I are going in the hot tub to fuck like bunnies. You want to come?"

All his tension dissipated as he laughed and flicked open the button on his pants. Dara knew just the right thing to say.

"Oh, I want to come more than you can imagine." Her gaze dropped to his waistline to watch intently, even as she removed her clothing. When she pulled off her snow pants and he saw the tufts of her curls through the ripped long johns he groaned. "Holy crap, Kane, you *did* rip her clothes off."

"Necessity is the mother of invention."

Soon the only item remaining on her body was the undershirt he'd given her that morning. The smooth skin of her ass peeked out from under the tails as she pivoted in front of him to check out Kane's progress. His best friend sported a boner to rival his own as he stood patiently waiting for Dara's lead.

Jack had to admit he was impressed—Kane didn't hide himself as Dara strolled around him, one hand trailing over his skin.

"You were taunting me... You knew I couldn't say anything in public so I think you owe me one. Or two."

Kane grasped her fingers, trapping her palm against his ridged abdomen. "Damn climbing center. Derrick's all balls and no brain. He could have waited until I got home to ask his questions but no...I didn't mean to make you crazy."

Dara leaned closer, glaring at him. Her threatening pose held for all of ten seconds before her face broke out into her usual brilliant smile. "Yes, you did, and I loved every minute of it."

She took a deep breath and closed her eyes for a moment. "Guys, you are seriously rocking it in the 'give Dara her fantasies' department. But I've still got a request and I'm not sure how you're going to take it."

Jack leaned back on the wall, giving her a little space. "Try us."

Dara took a deep breath. "I can't complain about anything you've done, except—it's pretty much been a lot of one-on-one stuff. I..."

Her cheeks were rosier than they'd been when they came in from the cold.

Kane tugged her back against his body and she purred. He slipped his hand over her belly, fingers wide as he nestled her against his naked skin. "You want us together?"

She hesitated, then nodded slowly. "Does that make me some kind of super-kinky girl? I get so damn hot when I read about it, and maybe the whole experience is one of those 'better in fantasy than reality', but..."

Jack paced closer, his cock aching hard. Even though he wanted to rush ahead, she needed them to slow down a little. They'd been racing through everything for the past couple days, and while they'd stopped to watch movies and eat, they hadn't really talked about their actions.

Frankly, Jack had been deliberately avoiding any discussions. He didn't want to talk about what they were doing, because that would mean acknowledging he was enjoying the whole situation way too much. Enjoying it, while simultaneously hating it. The more time passed, the more he'd held himself back, forcing himself to not call all the shots.

Taking a backseat in the bedroom wasn't sitting well. He loved being with Dara more intimately, and other than occasionally wanting to rip Kane's throat out, things were okay with his best bud. Heck, it was great that Kane had asked him to join in the little game in the cafeteria—and he was happy Dara had gotten a thrill out of it, but it wasn't his style.

But these were his issues to deal with and this wasn't about him. It was supposed to be about Dara, and her needs and fantasies. He'd been too busy dreaming about how things could be in the future, when it was only the two of them, that he'd steered clear of the one thing she'd really asked for.

Time to grow a set and put his ego aside.

Dara trembled under Kane's hands. He stroked her gently, easing her back and nuzzling her neck. "You ever have anal sex?"

"Yes. Not for a while, but I tried it."

"Did you like it?"

Dara nodded again, guilt written on her face.

Ah, shit.

"Dara, look at me." Jack tugged her to the couch and sat her on his lap. He luxuriated in the soft skin under his hands. She cupped his face and dragged her fingers through his hair, scratching his scalp with his fingers and sending a shot of pure lust to his groin. "You don't have to be embarrassed about liking something that gives you pleasure. Anal sex, oral sex—"

"Fooling around in public?"

"Did that bother you so much? I thought you enjoyed it."

"I did, and that's the trouble. I shouldn't feel as hot and needy as I do from making a spectacle of myself."

Jack schooled his expression. She didn't need him laughing right now, but damn, if she and Kane weren't two peas in a pod. "I'll say it again, anything that gives you pleasure and doesn't harm another—why should you feel guilty?"

She wrinkled her nose. "Because I spent too many years being told to be a good girl?"

He shook his head. "If you hurt someone, go ahead and feel guilty. But you didn't, so enjoy the horniness it caused. And if you want to take both Kane and me on at once, I'm game. We'll go slow, and see if we can match your fantasies. I don't think there would be so many stories written about it if there wasn't an inkling of truth in them. In fact, the thought makes me hot as anything."

Dara turned to look at Kane. "What about you?"

He laughed as he moved to kneel at their side, and the sex-charged tone changed the tension in the room, as if he'd lit a stick of sexual dynamite.

"If you're asking if I'm up for it, I think you can tell my answer." Kane wrapped her hand around his cock and rocked his hips slowly.

Dara touched her other hand to his cheek. He nuzzled her fingers for a moment, kissing them softly. His tongue darted out and he licked her, his face shining with mischief. Dara laughed.

Kane winked. "I thought I heard something about fucking like bunnies in the hot tub. It's getting cold in here. Shall we move the party to a warmer climate?"

Jack opened the balcony door, gliding ahead to pull the cover off the hot tub. Kane cradled her, his fingers caressing and teasing her skin as he brought her to the side of the pool.

Dara clung to his neck as he lowered her in, drawing his mouth against hers. As their tongues tangled a sense of déjà vu washed over her. It felt so right, so proper to be in Kane's arms. A splash splattered heated droplets on her back seconds before Jack pressed his lips to her neck and bit down lightly.

Having him there was just as proper as Kane.

They twisted her between them, raining kisses on her face. Kane slipped into the water to add his hands and body to the erotic teasing. Her mind fogged as pleasure built within her—the fires stoked higher and higher with every brush of their fingertips. Every caress of their lips. Kane raised her slightly, his fingers exploring and teasing her sex. The chilled winter air floated over her wet breasts and her nipples hardened, a second before Jack latched onto one and sucked the peak into the heat of his mouth.

Another drag of his tongue over the tip. Another circle

around her clit by Kane. She teetered on edge, waiting for the moment her body would follow her mind—it was already gone, lost in the pleasures her men provided.

Kane teased a finger down the crease of her ass, pausing to circle her anus. When he dipped his fingertip into the nerve-sensitive area she let out a moan. Jack seemed to take that as an order to increase his assault and suckled harder, one hand cupping a breast, one slipping down to rub her slit. She leaned helplessly on Kane and let the wave break over her.

"That's a girl. Let go, we've got you." Kane whispered in her ear, his hands gentle, his tone caring. Tears sprang to her eyes in spite of the pleasure drenching her soul.

She panted to regain her equilibrium. It was suddenly too much, too intimate. The long hard length of Kane's body behind her, the tender touch of Jack before her, the heated expression on his face as he ate her up with his gaze.

Dara struggled to her feet and pulled away from them to sit on the edge of the tub, fanning her face and blowing hard.

Kane grinned at her. "Getting a little overheated, are you?"

A nod was all she could answer. She stared at him, the cut muscles of his abdomen glistening in the faint lights reflecting from the hill. The moisture clinging to his skin defined each ridge, each slope, and she wanted to run her tongue along them, consume him in one sitting.

A sharp crack rang out and she snapped her head to the right. Jack stood on a deck chair, a gleaming icicle in his hand. He reached overhead and added another foot-long spear to his collection, then another. He spoke over his shoulder.

"I think we can do something about the heat, sweetheart."

Oh God. The shiver racing over her skin had nothing to do with the temperature outside. She was so hot that melting with desire became a distinct possibility. Jack turned his brilliant smile on her as he climbed back into the hot tub, his collection of icy instruments of torture laid out in a row on the decking.

"Do you mind if I try one?" Kane reached past her to pick one up, the tip glistening with a droplet as the heat rising from the tub hit it.

"More than enough for us both, my good man."

Dara laughed at Jack's atrocious British accent. "You two are— Oh my..."

The words stuck in her throat. Kane slid the wet tip of his icicle down her torso with deliberate intent to drive her mad. He leaned over and sucked her nipple into his mouth, lashing it again and again with his tongue until it ached, fiery hot. When he stepped back and drew circles around the feverish tip, she thought the pleasure of it would set off an orgasm.

"That looks like fun. My turn." Jack copied Kane's actions and the pulse of desire shot from her breast to her sex, and she slipped a hand down to her aching clit.

"What do you mean 'your turn'? If you hadn't noticed, she's got two."

Jack laughed softly. "So she does." He glanced at Kane for a second. "You okay with this?"

Kane nodded. "For Dara? Piece of cake."

She forced her eyes to remain open to take in every second of their united attack. Jack wrapped an arm around her hips to lock her in position while Kane smoothed a hand up her thigh. His fingers inched closer to her needy sex, then she couldn't see anything, or feel anything, but their mouths on her body.

She squeaked as Kane nipped the side of her breast then soothed the spot with the softening icicle. Flashes of heat and icy cold followed, all over her body. Her breasts, her ribs. Kane's finger finally reached her slit and she purred with satisfaction as he slid a digit into her.

"Yes. Oh, that feels so good." She looked down and tensed. "Hang on a minute. Kane, you're not really going to—?"

Jack grasped her hips tighter and kissed away her protest, locking his lips over hers. His tongue thrust into her mouth but she knew what was coming. Anticipating the moment—this was either the stupidest thing she'd ever done or the wildest.

Icy coldness brushed the sides of her labia. Kane swirled the tip of a new icicle between the layers of her sex, and melting water poured off her heated flesh. He stooped and replaced the cold with the heat of his mouth, driving his tongue into her sopping-wet depths and lapping eagerly. Hot, then cold, again and again. All the while Jack kissed her, made love to her mouth, locking his fingers in her hair and dragged their mouths together. Kane pushed the now blunt end of the ice into her and she cried out. Jack released her lips, staring down as Kane fucked her with the icicle.

"That is so incredibly hot."

Dara bit her lip and squirmed. "Hot? I think we need to shove an icicle up your butt if you think it's hot."

Kane stopped with the frozen shaft buried in her body. He leaned forward slowly, maintaining intimate eye contact, and gave her clit a deliberate lick. "Up the butt, hey? We can arrange that if you'd like."

Oh sweet Jesus, what had she done?

He suckled her clit with increasingly harder pulses, once again moving the icicle. Her body had melted the shaft away so there was barely enough to touch her passage. Kane abandoned the chunk of ice and simply ate hungrily at her sex. The discarded pieces of ice swirled on the water's surface as they rapidly melted away.

"Shove over, Kane." Jack cracked a new icicle in two,

119

drawing the edges over her body, rotating it to melt the sharper sections into a new smooth-tipped surface. He stood for a moment and held it out to her. "Suck on the tip."

Dara opened her mouth and let him slip it in. It was freezing against her tongue, flavourless. She would have far preferred to take his cock, or Kane's, into her mouth. Her saliva moistened it and made the surface slick.

He pulled it from her mouth with a *pop*. Kane increased the motions of his tongue against her clit as he twisted to the side to allow Jack more room. Jack pressed the ice back into her sex and she instantly came. Rocking hard, a quivering mass on the side of the hot tub. Jack's strong arm supported her upright as she shook with her release.

Jack waited until she stilled before pulling her back into the water, arranging her over top of his body like a blanket. She breathed out a heavy sigh.

"That was incredible."

"We're not finished," Kane warned.

Guilt rushed her. "You guys must be dying."

Jack dropped a soothing kiss on her forehead. "We're not done, but relax for a minute. Trust us?"

"Of course."

He cupped her neck, massaging her shoulders, the tight sections of her upper body easing under his caress. Kane massaged her legs, pulling them into his lap as she sprawled belly down in the pool. Incredible attention, complete tenderness. She was going to break into tears at the emotions flowing through her.

Her best friends. Her lovers. How was she supposed to choose just one of them to go forward with after this weekend?

Kane lowered her legs and sat next to Jack, reaching over

his friend's torso to cup her cheek. "We don't need to do anything more tonight. You skied like a banshee all day, and we've fooled around tons."

Jack nodded his agreement. "Why don't I go and make us dinner. We can rent a movie, have a few drinks. Just relax."

Dara opened her mouth to protest. Kane spoke first. "I know it's our last night here, but that doesn't mean there's an agenda."

But there was. She squirmed off them to stand in the middle of the tub. Her gaze darted back and forth between them. Light Jack, dark Kane. Both smiling at her, both with heartfelt emotion showing in their eyes. Caring...even love?

Maybe she'd made the biggest mistake ever in even starting this weekend. Maybe when they went home she'd find their friendship would take a long time to repair. She didn't know at all what tomorrow would bring. She was only certain of one thing.

She'd regret it forever if she didn't take this opportunity to love them both.

"I want you. Please?"

Jack and Kane stood simultaneously. They didn't look at each other, simply rose and held out their hands. She took Kane's in her right, and Jack's in her left, and let them lead her from the hot tub back into the house.

Kane stripped the blankets off the king-sized bed. Jack wrapped her briefly in a towel to catch the most of the moisture, then turned to start the gas fire across from them. The heat reached out and traced her skin. She sat on the bed and the heat from their gazes wrapped around her, even hotter.

They tumbled over her, hands touching, more and more intimate. Lips on her breasts, lips on her sex. Jack flipped her to her belly and laved from her slit to the star of her anus, and she moaned. His tongue pressed at the muscle. A tingling sensation raced through every inch and made her core ache with the need to be filled.

Kane tugged her to his side, his cock pressed to her thigh. "You need to ride me, okay? Jack's going to take your ass."

She smiled, wanting to chase a way a little of the seriousness. "You're not an ass man?"

He shook his head. "Breasts all the way." He cupped her neck and drew their mouths closer. "I want to be able to look you in the eye when we make love. I want to see every bit of what you're feeling. Know every bit of what you're thinking. I need to be there, with you, for every second."

Her heart expanded and she kissed him, rolling him to his back and straddling his hips. He'd already donned a condom, so she rocked against his hard length, his shaft brushing her erect clit and making her want this even more. The tip of his cock breached her passage and they paused for a second before she settled, his shaft deep in her body.

Kane's eyes rolled up in his head for a moment before he grinned at her. "Oh yeah. Now lean forward and kiss me while Jack gets you ready."

Her heart fluttered as she obeyed. She liked anal sex, but with Kane stretching her full, this was going to be an entirely new experience. Not to mention she was doing this with them. Kane, and Jack, who even now trailed his fingers softly up and down her crease until she relaxed under his touch.

"I'll go slow," Jack promised again.

Dara wiggled back, trying to find a little more pressure from Jack's fingers and Kane groaned. "Not too slow, or you'll be a one-man show. I can only last so long."

Jack slicked her up with the lube, teasing the nerve-sensitive area until she was begging for him to do more. One finger. Two. By the time he pressed three into her, the burning pressure carried as a steady pulse in her blood. Kane held her hips up and pressed in a few times, his cock igniting pleasure points deep inside as Jack teased her beyond belief.

"Now. I'm ready."

"You need a litt—"

"Now!" Dara jammed herself back on his fingers. Wanting more. Wanting it all. Jack withdrew his hand and suddenly the hard tip of his cock was against her. Kane cupped her face and watched closely. She breathed out slowly as Jack pressed in, the flared head of his cock spreading her in two until he got past the tight outer muscle. He stopped and she screwed up her face.

"You okay?" Kane whispered.

"Not enough. Make him move, make him—"

"Do it, Jack," Kane ordered.

Jack rocked slightly, the lube between them easing his way but the fire... Oh my God, she was going to go up in flames and he wasn't even halfway in.

"I don't want to hurt you, sweetheart."

She groaned in frustration. "It doesn't hurt. It feels good."

Jack grunted, continuing his slow progression until his groin hit her ass. He rested his sweaty forehead on her back and groaned. "Thank God, because this is fucking incredible."

Dara blew out a long breath and all three of them paused. Kane nuzzled her neck. "You ready for the triple chair?"

"High speed?"

"The only way to ride."

Jack adjusted his stance carefully, allowing Kane to support her hips slightly higher. That opened up enough room for Kane to withdraw, the mushroomed head of his cock clinging to her opening. As he pressed in, Jack pulled out, his shaft teasing the nerves deep within and making her sing with delight. One after another they thrust in, slowly increasing their speed, increasing the pressure. The angle brought Kane's groin hard against her clit on each drive and the building orgasm notched up another level.

"So. Damn. Tight." Jack's words snuck out through rigidly controlled gasps.

"I can feel…" Kane broke off and squinted. He swallowed hard and canted his hips again to drive in still harder. "Are you close, Dara?"

"Umm-hum." She ground hard on his abdomen on each pass, "Just a—"

She came apart. Her orgasm rippled along her sheath, clutching Kane's cock. Jack rammed inside her ass, the friction oh so good, and another sudden burst of pleasure exploded. The sensation of her ass pulsing in rhythmical waves caught her by surprise.

"Holy fuck." Jack crushed her hips against him and locked himself deep as her body squeezed and throbbed around both men.

Dara dug her fingernails into Kane's arm as she gasped for control. Sexual satisfaction rolled over her, more and more waves, until she couldn't stay upright and collapsed onto Kane's chest.

He clasped her close. His hips jerked against her, but he kept his grasp careful even as he spoke softly.

"That was the most fucking incredible experience in my life."

Dara laughed and turned her head so she could listen to the rapid pounding under her ear. Her own heart slammed in the same tempo. Jack withdrew from her body, returning with a warm washcloth. He cleaned her gently before crawling beside them, leaning over to kiss the back of her neck. Tender. Soft. His words brushed her ear. "Thank you."

Kane embraced her carefully as he rolled them to the side. His bright blue eyes examined her face, the corner of his mouth cricking up into a smile. "Yes, thank you. For sharing yourself with us. For being an awesome friend."

She kissed his nose before collapsing back, one arm sprawled over each of their torsos. "What? No thank you 'for kicking our butts on the ski hill, oh most wonderful goddess on skis'?"

They all laughed. Kane left her in Jack's arms to hit the bathroom. Jack slid her closer, grabbing the top sheet from the floor and draping it over their naked bodies. "You can kick my butt on the ski slope any day."

Dara scrambled for words. She wanted to say something. Wanted to tell Jack what was bubbling inside her heart. "Jack..."

He tucked her head under his chin and cradled against his long lean body. "Yeah, sweetheart?"

She slid her fingers over his back, along the muscles that shifted as he protected her and held her close. What could she say? She still had no idea which of the guys was the one for her. Misery tried to intrude, but she fought the emotions down. She wouldn't let any regrets mar tonight. She was glad, oh so glad, of the opportunity.

"Dara? What's up?"

She snuggled in tighter. "Umm, can we have burgers for dinner?"

He slipped his hand intimately over her belly and spooned her tight against his body. "For you, anything."

She closed her eyes and prayed he really meant it.

Chapter Nine

Alpine Responsibility Code

Rule #9—Venture "Out of Bounds" at your own risk...

Kane drummed his fingers on the steering wheel. He adjusted the volume on the speakers. Glanced out the window at the rapidly fading daylight and flicked the truck wipers off and on.

"Enough already. Your fidgeting is driving me crazy." Jack adjusted Dara as she snoozed in his arms. They'd skied their hearts out until the final chair stopped running, piled into the truck, and she'd been asleep almost before they left the parking lot.

"I can't help it. I'm trying to figure out what we're going to do."

Jack stared out the front window. Kane gave him time, trying to shove his own chaotic thoughts into order. Was he even sure what he wanted? At the start of the weekend he'd had all these grandiose plans. Dara would fall in love with him, Jack would be fine with it, and they'd kind of carry on like the three friends they'd always been. Stupid really, now that he'd had more time to think about it. And after seeing the way Dara responded to Jack—he wasn't sure he could deny her being with his friend. There were certainly things Jack could provide for Dara that he just wasn't into. For a weekend, it had been fine, but if he never saw a set of restraints again, he'd be happy.

Dara wiggled, settling tighter against Jack's chest. She slipped her legs out and Kane guided her into the most comfortable position. He smoothed her sweat pants over her thighs. She reached out and caught hold of him and damn if his throat didn't tighten.

He didn't want to give her up.

"Jack, man, talk to me."

"You going all girly on me? Want to talk about emotions and shit?"

Kane gave him the finger and Jack laughed softly. Kane tried again. "Jack, I don't want to lose you as a friend."

"You're not going to. Holy crap, what are you thinking about over there? It's not going to be simple, but for now, don't make it more complicated than it needs to be. We're going home after a kick-ass ski trip. We've got the pictures and bruises to prove it."

"And the fact we fucked our best friend silly for three nights doesn't even come into it?"

Jack grunted at him in disgust. "You eat with that mouth? We didn't just fuck her."

Silence fell again. A light sprinkle of snow had begun to fall and the headlamps shone into a hazy distance. It was kinda surreal, holding this conversation in muted tones so they wouldn't disturb Dara as she slept.

Kane couldn't let it rest. "That's what I'm saying. It was more than a sex-fest. She's not just our fuck-buddy, she's our friend. All for one and all that."

"Exactly. So we go home. We give ourselves a bit of time to get settled into a normal routine. Then we worry about the next step. That's the logical thing to do. Simple."

Right. Simple. And impossible. How was he supposed to go home and just let Dara go back to hanging out with them casually when he wanted to have her around 24/7? In his bed, and out of it.

"I don't think that's a great idea."

Jack sighed, his exasperation clear. "Look, you think we should ask her to join us in the sack for the rest of the week? The month? How long you going to drag this out, Kane? She's not a toy for us to play with."

"Don't be a shithead. I know that. That's not what I'm suggesting at all."

"What, you enjoyed being naked around me so much you want to keep that part of it up?"

Kane clutched the steering wheel. "It wasn't so bad. I can handle it."

Jack snorted in derision. "I noticed. I think you more than handled it. In fact, it felt fucking good when we were both inside her. I felt every move you made. Did that turn you on, Kane? Our dicks basically rubbing against each other?"

Kane shot a quick glare at his friend. "Now you're just trying to piss me off."

"Answer the question."

Bloody bastard. "It didn't bug me, okay? That was the hottest thing I've ever done, and it was because it was Dara, and it was you. My two best damn friends in the whole world. If that makes me gay, so be it. There. I was honest. Now, let's hear your confession. You thought the whole weekend rocked, and if there was one thing you'd beg for, it would be for this to be our real life."

"Real life? You're insane. People don't live in trios. People don't set up houses with two guys and girl, not without a lot of shit down the road."

Kane zipped his mouth shut and concentrated on driving for a while. The snow flashed by in sheets, and he had to slow to barely moving to keep on the curvy road. They were obviously at an impasse. For now, getting Jack to admit anything was futile. Stubborn asshole. It was part of the reason they'd always gotten along so well—Kane knew when to shut up and when to push.

This was shut-up time. Jack wasn't ready to listen to reason.

Kane laughed softly at himself. Reason. Really? Somehow in the past thirty minutes he'd come to the conclusion that being with Dara and Jack was a good, scratch that, a fucking fantastic idea.

By the time they arrived home, his eyes were itchy from staring through the increasingly whiteout conditions. Jack woke Dara, her lazy stretch and innocent cuddles as she slowly came awake stirring something inside Kane. He was going to do everything in his power to make sure Dara was happy even if Jack did say no to continuing the relationship.

They carried in their equipment and bags, ending up in Dara's one-bedroom apartment on the final trip. She stepped away from her pile of gear and glanced at them, her hands twisting together.

"So I guess that's it."

Kane cleared his throat. "Awesome trip."

Dara nodded quickly. "We've never had better conditions, have we?" She took a big breath and held it, biting her bottom lip, and Kane wanted to race over and hold her against him. Wanted to pull her lip from between her teeth and kiss the reddened surface.

Her eyes widened as Jack turned to go, panic flashing across her face.

"I have a confession to make," she blurted out.

Jack paused, running a hand through his hair as he turned back. He gave Kane a dirty look. "Seems to be the day for it. What's up, sweetheart?"

"I heard you. Talking about me."

"What?" Good Lord, had she heard them in the truck on the way home?

"A few weeks ago. I overheard both of you saying you were interested in me."

Jack frowned. "You heard us?"

She nodded. "I...I thought that if...maybe. Oh damn it, I thought sex would make it easier."

Kane's stomach fell. "Did you suggest the ménage for our sakes? Jesus, that's fucked up. Why would you sleep with us if you didn't want to in the first place?"

Dara shook her head rapidly. "No, no. That's not what I meant, Kane. I wanted you." She glanced at Jack. "Only I wanted you both, and I thought that if I arranged to get more physical with you I could figure out if I wanted one of you more."

Jack stiffened, his whole body bunched up tight. "And did it work?"

She shook her head. "I thought I could help the situation, but I think I've made a terrible mistake. The past few days have only made it clearer that I don't want to choose between you. I don't want to be with you, Jack, not if Kane's not around. And I can't see loving Kane alone—I'd miss you terribly."

Kane's heart turned over. Holy shit, she was suggesting the same thing he'd been leaning toward. He stepped forward but

Vivian Arend

Jack beat him to her.

Jack took her hands in his, lifting one to his lips and kissing her knuckles gently. He let out a huge sigh. "I'm glad that the ménage was something you really did want, but you're right—in a way it was a mistake. It was a fantasy, and I was more than happy to help you spread your wings, but it isn't something that can continue for the rest of our lives."

"Why not?" Dara's voice quivered, soft in the hushed air.

"Why not? That's an easy question to answer. For how long, Dara? How long do the three of us set up house together? I can see it working for fun, for a short term, but if you overheard us talking did you hear the part about trying for forever?"

"Forever?" Her eyes were huge, moisture filling them. Kane moved closer.

"Yeah, as in marriage, get a dog, have a few kids. How do you think that would work with three partners?"

"I don't know, but I'm willing to try."

Jack dropped her hands. "I'm not."

He spun and grabbed his bag from the floor. Utter misery painted Dara's expression, and Kane wrapped an arm around her as he called after Jack's retreating back. "I never figured you as a quitter."

Jack stopped short of the door. He pivoted and glared at Kane. "I'm not a quitter, I'm a realist. Damn it, am I the only responsible adult in this room?"

Before had been time to shut up, now was time to push. Kane goaded him again. "You want this, Jack. Admit it. You'd like to say screw it to the conventions around us and be with Dara and me because it's the best damn thing you've ever had in your life."

"Fuck it." Jack growled. "Fine, I'll admit it. I want to be with

132

Dara so bad my brain aches. And I'd be lost without my best friend. But just because I want a thing, doesn't mean I can have it. What you're suggesting is impractical."

"If we don't try, we'll never know," Dara whispered.

Jack shook his head and grabbed the doorknob. "I can't lie to myself and wish for the impossible."

He left the room and Dara burst into tears.

Kane twisted her in his arms, letting her hide herself against his chest. Damn Jack for being a stubborn fool. If he wasn't interested, fine. But to admit that he wanted the same thing as they did and still say no...

It had been a long time since he'd actually hit Jack, but he was perilously close to remedying that.

He held Dara while she wept, breathing as slowly and calmly as he could to try and pass on some peace. She wrapped her arms around him, hugging him tight, and the image of being with her, having her in his life, hit him like a load of bricks.

If Jack said no, he could have her to himself.

For one awful moment, he contemplated the idea before realizing that plan was more impossible than any of the future paths stretching before them. It would kill Jack to see him and Dara together, knowing that he could have been a part of a relationship. If she'd actually picked one of them, there would have been bruised egos and frustrations to work through, but now?

They were screwed.

Although, there was still a faint ray of hope. Jack had admitted he wasn't totally against the idea, and as far as Kane was concerned, that meant *maybe*. He and Dara needed to figure out how to convince the jerk to get off his high horse and give them a chance. The sooner the better, as well, because once Jack trenched in it would take a bulldozer to move him.

He kissed the top of Dara's head and she looked up at him. He brushed away a tear from her cheek with his thumb, holding her face in his hands tenderly.

"Do you think we can convince him to change his mind?" Her words came out shaky.

"Perhaps. Come here." He led her to the couch and sat her down, squatting before her to be eye level. "Dara, I want you to think about it and tell me the truth. Why do you want this? I mean, I suppose Jack's a good-enough guy. I know I'm a fairly hot catch as well."

An involuntary burst of laughter escaped her. "And oh so modest."

"Exactly." He winked at her and she gave him an unsteady smile. He kissed her cheek. "That's my girl. We'll get through this, you'll see."

She nodded jerkily. "Okay. I just...I want it so bad. I really did try to figure out another way, but it seems so perfect."

"Why don't you pick one of us and we'll find a way to keep our friendship strong. The changed dynamics will be tough at first, but with a little work—"

"Don't you see? That's what's so screwed up here." She shook her head in frustration, jumping to her feet. Kane took her spot on the couch and watched her pace. "So you two are willing to put the work in to stay friends if you don't have me, or stay friends without gloating if you do. Where's the logic in that? Why not put all that energy into making the three of us a reality? Maybe it is impossible, and down the road we'll have to call it quits, but..."

Kane considered. She was right, and damn if she didn't even have enough logic in there to please Jack.

She growled as she stomped across the room, wiping tears from her eyes. She turned to face him, her hands planted on her hips. "Jack's such an arrogant bastard at times. 'Only adult in the room.' More like the only child. He's not even going to take the toy out of the box to play with it because he might break it."

Kane whistled softly. Man, was she calling it right. "He has a couple of collector's items like that at his folk's place."

Dara's jaw hung open. "You're shitting me."

He shook his head. "You know what? I think you hit the nail on the head. He's afraid. He doesn't want to lose either of us."

"And he won't."

Kane held out a hand to her and she joined him, crawling into his lap. He combed his fingers through her hair. "There're no guarantees here, babe, but you're right. If we don't try, it won't happen."

She stared at him, the remaining tears glistening in the corners of her eyes, and he reached up to wipe them away.

"Are you really good with this?"

He shrugged. "I've got a few concerns. I'd be an idiot if I didn't. But Dara..."

There was a crease forming between her eyes, and he smoothed his thumb over it. He'd spent four years coming to this place, and if he didn't say it now, he'd explode. "I'm in love with you."

Dara stared at him. "What?"

He paused. "You want to interpret that for me? Did you mean 'what' as in 'I didn't hear you'? Or 'what' as in 'I can't believe you said that and I'm going to freak out'?"

She grabbed his face in both hands and kissed him madly

before pulling off. "What, as in I really *really* need to hear you say it again. Oh God, Kane, I love you too. At least I think I do. Only..."

He pressed her head to his shoulder. "You love Jack as well, right?"

She nodded.

"Well then. All we need to do is get Mr. Proper to admit what he feels—because I can tell you he's fucking gone for you as well."

She cuddled in closer and his tensions eased. He leaned back and settled her more comfortably, rocking her gently in his arms. They sat together, breathing each other's air, fingers linked together. Kane kissed her forehead, holding her tight to his body and letting her pulse synchronize with his own. Yeah, the sex had been dynamite, but the skiing each day had been just as spectacular. Spending time with her and Jack outside the bedroom—the memories made him smile. Dara racing fearlessly ahead, teasing Jack about his old-fashioned skis. Smiling and joking and telling stories.

They already had an awesome relationship as a trio. The only thing that had changed this weekend was adding a physical relationship. Hopefully they could beat that fact into Jack's head sooner than later.

Dara twisted to straddle him, bringing her lips against his throat. She opened his collar and touched him with her tongue as she tugged on his shirt. His body was interested, very much so in fact, but he held her wrists and stopped her.

"I think I should go see Jack. Make sure he's okay."

Dara unbuttoned his shirt. "He's being a grump. How will it help to go see him? Maybe we should give him more space to cool off."

Kane was tempted, really tempted, but giving Jack enough

time to rationalize this even more would make their task that much harder. "He doesn't need to calm down, we need to get him really riled up. Make him mad enough to fight for what he really wants because, Dara, he wants you. I know it."

She tilted her head and her expression changed to The Look. The one that made him shake in his boots. The one Jack called her Devil Face.

"You want to make him mad? You up for a little acting? Because I think I know one way to get him to react."

"Oh good Lord, Dara, what are you dreaming up now?"

"It's kind of poetic justice, really. They got us into this trouble and maybe they can get us out."

They? Who the hell is she talking about?

She scrambled off his lap and dug through her backpack. She twirled with a cry of satisfaction, holding up a pair of—

"Walkie-talkies?"

Dara's smirk grew wider. "To the rescue. Let's see what a little eavesdropping does to Jack."

Chapter Ten

Alpine Responsibility Code
Rule #10—Share the responsibility for a safe experience
with others...

Jack sprawled on the couch and sucked on his beer. He stared at the bottle mindlessly for a minute before focusing on the label. The icy cold local brew—called Faceplant—always made Dara giggle when she handed them out, and he gritted his teeth together and turned up the volume on the television. He flicked through channels and wondered if Kane was even going to come home tonight.

Damn it, why'd he leave? He could have been there with them right now, or better yet, they should have hauled Dara into their apartment and his king-sized bed.

He held the bottle to his temple. Right. For tonight. And tomorrow. But what about after that? What about when he couldn't hold back any longer and started taking charge again, not only of Dara, but Kane?

He couldn't do it. He couldn't put aside his need to lead in the bedroom. For the second half of the trip he'd tried that, forcing down his more dominating urges. Trying to change the way he operated had made him lose something fundamental.

Even though he was controlling when it came to sex, he had always connected emotional caring with the physical demands he made. He hadn't even realized that had been missing for the past day until he'd heard Kane as they prepared to take Dara together. Kane had been the one with the soft words, talking about making love. Talking about wanting to be there to support her. Wanting to share the experience so it became much more than just a physical thrill.

Dara and Kane were the ones who deserved to be together, without him coming in and ordering their world. Changing his spots seemed impossible, no matter how much the offer she'd made tempted him.

Maybe I could deal with it if it meant I could have Dara.

Fuck.

No, this was a better way. He'd use the excuse of society, and after a while Dara and Kane would accept it. Somehow he'd find a way to not let them know he was slowly dying as they carried on in front of him.

The door opened with a clatter and he startled upright. Kane entered, his pack on his back. He stared at Jack, looked as if he was about to speak, then turned and headed silently to his room.

Jack stared morosely at the screen. Great. Now all three of them were miserable. He was a fucking genius, he was.

Kane rattled around for a while in the back of the apartment. The shower clicked on and Jack found himself with his hand on the front door before jerking to a stop. His body was ready to return to her without any qualms at all. *No.* He had to give this breathing time. He paced back to the couch.

But there was no reason why he couldn't call her. Just to make sure she was all right.

She answered on the fourth ring.

"Jack?"

"Umm, just wanted to make sure you were okay."

Silence on the line. A soft sniff. "I'm fine."

"You want to come over and watch some TV with me?" Sheesh, pathetic much? Surely he could beg a little harder. Throw in a few grovels for good measure. He'd been away from her for what? Thirty minutes, and he was caving already.

"Kane's coming here." She whispered the words and his heart stopped in mid-beat. "He's just grabbing a shower and some stuff, and said he'd spend the night."

A dagger of pain went through him. His best friend worked damn fast. Still, this was what he wanted, wasn't it? "Okay. Well. Later then—"

"Jack, I love you."

He scrambled for words, but before he could answer, she hung up.

She loved him? He buried his face in his hands. She loved him, but his best friend was going to be the one in her bed tonight.

Because I'm an idiot.

Jack wasn't sure how long he sat there, numb and needy. Wishing he could see a way out of the hellish hole he'd dug for himself. Behind him, Kane cleared his throat, and Jack forced himself to turn and look him in the eye.

"I'm heading over to Dara's. You're welcome to come."

Inside his belly, anger and frustration battled. "I said no."

"You said a lot of things over the past few days, mainly to Dara, but I've been listening as well. You talked about not feeling guilty over what brings you pleasure. About trusting yourself. Not rushing into any decisions."

"So?"

Kane shook his head. "Take your own damn advice. She needs you, and you need her. Hell, I'm the one who should be curled up in a fetal position."

Jack frowned. "Why would you be freaking out?"

Kane laughed mockingly. "Oh, maybe because I found out having you around during sex wasn't nearly the issue I thought it would be?" He held up a finger. "I'm not saying I want to get it on with you, but you were right. It's a bloody big turn-on to be with Dara at the same time as you. Because it's her, and because it's you—my two best friends."

Jack broke eye contact to stare at the wall. "I can't do this tonight."

"She needs you, man. She needs me. Don't throw this away."

Rustling noises followed as Kane hefted his bag and left. Jack sat miserably for a while before grabbing another beer and returning to the television. He cranked it up loud and settled in to watch something mindless.

Over an hour passed before he hauled himself upright. He'd been flipping through the same damn mental pathways over and over again.

He had to change his ways. If he changed he could be with Dara and Kane. But how much more would it hurt down the road to have to call it off if it didn't work, or if he ruined their friendship in the process?

Jack growled at himself in exasperation as he hit his room. He threw his dirty clothes into the laundry and himself into the shower. The steamy water didn't wash away any of his troubles, and when he made the mistake of picturing Kane in Dara's bed, he had to turn the water to icy cold to deal with his instant arousal. He was not going to jerk off to the memories of being with his best friends.

Not when I could be with them.

He snapped off the water and stalked naked into his room to find clean clothes.

And froze at the sound of voices. Muffled, but loud enough to recognize as Dara and Kane.

"Like that?"

"Oh hell, yes, right there. So good, Kane. More, please, more."

The words trailed away but the sounds of their lovemaking continued. Jack searched the room in a frenzy to find where it was coming from. The moaning and grunts of pleasure were driving him mad by the time he found the walkie-talkie. It was tucked into the side of his backpack, the listen button jammed in the "on" position. Fuck it. Somehow the two at the other end must have accidentally triggered theirs as well.

Jack smacked the casing to try to get the button to release. It had been bad enough to be imagining them having sex without him, he didn't need a live play-by-play.

"Kane, would you...spank me?"

Oh my God. The image of her bare butt glowing pink flashed to his mind and his dick went instantly rigid.

"I'm not sure."

"I loved it when you did it the other day. You and Jack, it was so good. Please?"

No. Fucking. Way. Jack couldn't stand it any longer. He cracked open the battery compartment, ready to break the connection when he heard a loud slap and a sharp answering gasp from Dara.

Another slap.

She cried out in pain, not pleasure, and Jack swore.

"Ouch, no. Stop, that hurts."

"Sorry, I didn't mean to...fuck that. I can't. It's not my thing and I think it's for freaks anyway. Jack should have known better than—"

The walkie-talkie fell unminded to the floor, the batteries rolling two different directions as Jack saw red. For freaks, hey? What happened to the little lecture about not feeling guilty about things that brought pleasure? He yanked on a pair of boxers and stormed through the apartment. Just because the bastard had no finesse didn't give him the right to hurt Dara.

He let himself into Dara's apartment with her spare key and shouted a warning.

"Get your hands off her, you bloody idiot. You were all high and mighty a little while ago, feeding me back my words—"

He thrust open the door to her room, fully expecting to see them naked and tangling the sheets. Or Dara rubbing a sore butt cheek, eyes filled with tears. Instead the bed was covered with a Monopoly board, and Dara and Kane, fully clothed, fists full of popcorn, reclined on either side of the game.

"Hey, just because she asks me to sell Park Place doesn't mean I've got to." Kane snickered as he glanced Jack up and down. "Nice choice of attire, man. You wander the halls of the apartment like that and Santa's going to put you on the naughty list for sure."

"Jack? You okay?" Dara slipped off the bed, concern filling her eyes. "You look upset."

What the hell was going on? Jack glared at them. "How did you do that?"

"Do what?" She frowned before slipping a few popcorn kernels into her mouth.

Was he going insane? He could have sworn he'd heard them. He scrambled to recall the actual words, but there was no way he could have misinterpreted the sexual sounds for people playing a board game. Kane turned his face away, but not before Jack caught a glimpse of a smile.

Kane...smiling? Even though Jack stood ready to pound the shit out of him for hurting Dara? What the hell was going on? Understanding broke over him, and for a second he wasn't sure if he should leave, slug Kane like he'd planned in the first place, or burst out laughing.

"It wasn't real. What I heard wasn't real. How the fuck did you... Damn it, you set me up."

Dara approached cautiously, as if concerned he was going to growl at her again. "Kinda?"

"Hey, no 'kinda' about it," Kane gloated from the bed. He leaned back, hands crossed behind his head, wiggling his brows at Jack. "That was a damn good ruse. He fell for it—hook, line and sinker."

She turned slightly and put her finger to her lips. "Shh, he doesn't need to hear that yet. We can taunt him later."

"It's more fun when it's immediate." Kane reached beside him and pulled away a pillow to expose a walkie-talkie and his laptop computer. The open screen revealed a shot of Jack's bedroom from a high angle.

Jack jerked in disbelief. "You set up a camera in my closet? If you wanted to see me naked, you could have just sat on the bloody bed."

"It's my cell phone, and yeah, well, you tell me this didn't get your attention right where it hurt the most."

Jack glanced back and forth between the two of them. On his right, his best friend grinned openly. On his left, stood the woman he cared about the most in the entire world. Only these two would have the gall to pull him out of a funk before he could wallow in it, because they were the only two that knew him, inside and out.

144

To hell with caution, it was time to take a chance. But they needed to know what cards he was laying on the table. If they'd take him, the *real* him, he was willing to try.

He held his arms out and Dara's face lit up in the split second he had to see it before she threw herself at him. She burrowed in like a nesting animal, tucking tight to his side. "Please, Jack..."

"Spank you?"

From across the room Kane shouted in dismay. "Hey, none of that."

Jack offered a smirk. "I wasn't offering to spank *you*."

"Thank God."

Dara wiggled in his arms with her laughter, and he arranged them so he could look her in the eye. "Please what, Dara?"

She took a quick breath and held it for a second before blurting the words out. "Give us a chance. It might not work, but it might. It's worth a shot."

Jack waited, watching the emotions roll over her face. He imagined she saw the same kind of things in his. Some fear, tons of need. Rising hope.

Falling in love?

"Sweetheart, it's not as easy as that. All weekend I've been thinking about how right it felt to be with you. When I wasn't feeling jealous, I even loved watching you with my best friend, even though he does have a serious issue with exhibitionism."

"Hey!"

Jack flipped Kane the bird, never taking his eyes off Dara's face. Kane laughed out loud and she smiled as she lifted her hand to his face. Her touch was infinitively soft against the stubble on his jaw.

"But, Dara, I've got to tell you the truth. I like to be in charge in the bedroom."

"I noticed." She flushed hard. "I liked it."

He paused. "What if I get even more bossy? Could you still enjoy it? I toned it down a lot the last couple of days, and if we do this thing, I'm not going to do that again." Jack glanced at Kane who was sitting at attention, listening to his every word. "And you. What if I start ordering you around as well? Especially when it's the three of us together?"

Kane grinned. "I'd say hallelujah and pass the plate for more."

Fuck.

"Seriously?" Jack asked. Could the whole issue be solved this easily?

Kane nodded. "When it's the three of us together, having you call the shots was pretty incredible. I didn't mind at all. Of course, if you interrupt Dara and I when we're alone, or try to touch me yourself, I will break your face."

Dara laughed softy. "Jack, we've got a lot of things to figure out while we work through this, but I loved how you had such power over me. The restraints, the spanking you made Kane give me, even making me wait for release... I've never felt more loved and cared for than when I let you take charge."

She turned and pointed to Kane. "And it all balances out nicely with Mr. Showoff here, who made me smile by cutting it up in the ski line, or chasing me down the hill like a sex maniac. I love the unique things you both bring to me, and it's always been that way as friends. Why should I expect you to be anything but yourself when it comes to sex?"

Jack stared into her pretty green eyes. It was true. They'd never asked him to do the changing; it had been his idea in the first place. To find out it hadn't been necessary—the relief hit him hard, although if he could kick himself in the ass right now he would. He'd wasted part of the time they'd had together.

He cleared his throat. "Damn it, you two. I'm supposed to be the logical one of our trio."

Kane laughed out loud. "Right. Like we'll fall for that load of bull."

Dara rested her head on his chest and hugged him tightly, squeezing the final bits of fear from his system.

He lifted her chin until he could see into her face.

"I hoped I'd get a chance to do this privately somewhere down the road, but I suppose what we're entering into means 'private' has new definitions. Dara, you want to move in with Kane and me? I really care about you. I think I love you, and I'd like to see where we can take this."

A mischievous expression flashed over her face. "Hang on..."

She slipped from his arms and out of the room. Jack watched her go, uncertainty seizing him.

"Good one, Jack, you scared her off already."

Jack pivoted slowly, giving Kane a glare. "Freaks?"

"Exhibitionist?"

They both laughed and Kane rose to give him a huge bear hug. They pounded each other on the back in typical guy fashion before Kane grabbed him by the arms. "This only works because it's you. We've been there for each other forever. This is just one more adventure."

Jack nodded. "We're going to have to get a bigger apartment."

"Bigger beds."

"Another ski-getaway in February."

Kane laughed. "Definitely."

Dara strolled back, her hands tucked behind her back. Jack eyed her carefully. Tricky woman. Between her and Kane, he was never going to get to relax again. "You didn't answer my question."

"I thought this would be the best way." She pulled out three chocolate bars and passed them around. "They're from the freezer, so don't break your teeth."

Kane scooped her up and spun her in a circle. "You're a goof."

"Takes one to know one."

It seemed more than appropriate. Jack held up his 3 Musketeers bar with ceremony. "Ahem. I hereby proclaim we're all for one..."

Kane lowered Dara carefully, keeping her tucked under his arm. She held out her free hand and took Jack's in it, linking their fingers together before raising her chocolate bar to meet the other two.

"...and I'm the one for all," she declared.

The three of them burst out laughing. Jack cupped the back of her neck and drew her in for a long, slow kiss, letting the taste of her wash over him and clear away the remaining concerns. For now, this was all they needed to be together.

Loving, freestyle.

Rising, Freestyle

Dedication

Darling daughter—you're still too young to read this book, but I appreciate you so much. You encourage me to reach for new heights both on and off the wall. I can't believe we managed to sweet-talk the pizza delivery guy into doing the "Drop of Doom".

Chapter One

Beta: Climbing slang that means to gather information about a route.

"Go on, you can do it."

Melanie remained immobile, gaze glued to where her fingers wrapped around the holds on the climbing wall. The dark Adonis holding her safety rope had been nothing but positive and upbeat with her since she'd signed up for the private climbing lessons. Even without looking she could picture him, his wide smile bright against his tanned skin. Dark hair slightly messed, chocolate-brown eyes that made her think all kinds of naughty things.

"The next hold in the route is that blue one, off to the right. Match your feet, transfer your weight and you'll be there in no time."

As she moved to follow his instructions, she wondered for the millionth time if he was staring at her butt simply to help her find the best route, or if he was staring at her butt for more nefarious reasons.

She could only dream it was the second.

Derrick James was everything she'd dreamed of in a guy. Tall, dark and good with ropes. Now if she could get up the nerve to make a move on him other than when they were checking each other's harnesses for secure straps.

Concentrate. She needed to focus on the wall, not the dry spell in her sex life. Even if dry was the wrong word to depict something comparable to the Sahara during a drought.

A few adjustments later she'd made it to the hold he'd described.

"Awesome job. You want to go higher?" he asked.

Oh man. There were many things she wanted. She wanted to drag her fingers through his long hair and pull his head to hers for a kiss that would make her toes curl. If he happened to use his strong fingers on her back for a massage that somehow turned into a more erotic playtime, that would be fine as well. Maybe letting her crawl over him as they writhed together in wild, passionate lovemaking that would leave her gasping for breath and sexually sated. All of those were on the instant "hell, yeah" list.

Going past the fifteen-foot mark on the vertical climbing wall? That one wasn't nearly as easy a decision.

Melanie stared upward. The holds were simple on this section of the wall, the route easy to follow. Old training patterns kicked in and she automatically shifted her weight as she saw the correct sequence to reach for next. She could do this.

Until she turned and looked down. The floor wavered beneath her, fading farther and nearer like some freaky optical illusion. She clung to her handholds as her tongue stuck to the dry roof of her mouth. Fear laced through her, a shot of adrenaline making her limbs shake and all the blood rush from her head.

"I got you." The harness around her hips snugged upward as Derrick took in the slack of the rope and secured her in place. "That's as high as you're going right now, Melanie. Just take a deep breath. You're okay."

The bulging muscles of his arms as he held the belay ropes blurred into the background as she stared into his eyes. Her heart pounded, there was a ringing in her ears and she needed to pee. It took too much effort to squeeze out the words, and she sounded like a two-year-old. "Don't drop me."

"I've got you," he repeated. His expression was no longer the sexy one that got her blood pumping. There was deep concern, and suddenly the corner of his mouth was the most important thing for her to concentrate on. Because if she looked at his mouth, and thought about kissing that spot, then she didn't need to think about the fact she hung in the air above a hard floor. Didn't have to think about how much it would hurt if she fell again. "I need you to look at the wall, Melanie. Just turn and look at the wall so I can lower you. You understand? I'm not going to drop you. You're safe, but I need you in position to get you down."

"Scared." Throat tight. Breathing tough.

"I know, but I promise you're safe. I'm not going to drop you, and you know it. Want me to lift you a tiny bit? Prove that you're secure?"

She nodded rapidly. He leaned back and pulled easily, no more than a couple of inches. It was enough to make her body rise and take the weight off her shaking legs. Mel snapped her head back to face the wall. It took conscious effort to loosen her death grip and press her hips away from the wall. Letting go of the handholds made her heart leap to her throat, but she didn't change elevation. Derrick held her in one spot, rock solid and firm. Quickly, she wrapped one hand around the rope at her chest level, the other thrust toward the wall for protection. She moistened her lips so she could speak.

"Lower." The climbing command stuck in her throat, but she got it out.

"Lowering. Good girl." His deep voice enveloped her and she let the warmth act as a protective barrier.

Her descent was so smooth and slow she had time to walk her way down the wall like a little child inching down a sidewalk following a snail. She hung in a modified sitting position as she relied on him to control her motion. He did an amazing job—even the stop at the bottom came smoothly, no sudden jerk to startle her already overwrought nerves.

Why in the world had she thought facing her fears and learning to climb again was a good idea?

Her butt landed on the crash mat with a delicately soft touch, and she breathed a sigh of relief, laid back and closed her eyes. Only fifteen feet and she'd had a freaking acrophobia attack. After three weeks of hard work, that was all she'd accomplished? How was she supposed to get back to living a full and exciting life when she couldn't even get past the baby marker?

Beside her shoulder, the mat dipped, and she wearily popped one eye open to spot Derrick seated on her left. "I know you probably don't think so, but you did great."

Bullshit. "Define great." That sexy smile of his was back, and at least now she could blame the way her heart beat out of control on something other than her annoying new fear of heights.

"You didn't expect to be able to hit the ceiling so soon, did you? Go back to free climbing and lead climbing as if nothing happened? You had a major fall and it's going to take time to get over—"

"Shut up." Mel snapped to a sitting position to glare at him across a more even playing field. Damn, that was inexcusably rude, but she didn't care. The intensity of anger that hit came as a surprise, yet it was a welcome relief to counteract the paralyzing fear that controlled her life. She tilted her chin and met his gaze again. "Don't tell me it's going to take time. It's been three years, and I'm still so chicken I'm afraid to walk across the street without looking both ways twelve times."

Confusion flashed over his face. "What does that have to do with climbing? Or your accident? The ropes failed. It was a freak situation and never should have happened, but you've recovered and—"

Melanie slammed a hand onto the mat next to her. "Recovering. I'm not nearly as strong as I was. Before the accident, I was always traveling and exploring the wilderness. Set new routes for others at outdoor sites in the summer. I used to climb all day and dance all night. And it's all gone, okay? The exploring, the friends. The dancing and enjoying being with other people. I've been living like a hermit. Shit, I haven't had sex in three fucking years. So when the hell am I going to get over being afraid?"

Oh my God. She hadn't said that. She scrambled to her feet and turned her back on him, fumbling to undo the figure-eight knot holding the rope twined through her safety harness.

Strong arms surrounded her, his hands blocking her attempts at the knot and holding them still. He was a wall of muscle behind her, hot and firm, making all her earlier thoughts return. Sweaty, needy, entangled bodies and...she wasn't going to be distracted from the fact she was pissed off. She struggled and his grip tightened as he backed up a pace, moving away from the wall.

"Melanie, it's okay." He didn't release her, but his clasp changed, one hand locking her immobile, the other caressing her gently. Prying her hands from the rope until he could slip his fingers over hers, his fingertips teasing the webbing between each digit. The motion was intimate and soothing even as it sent a tingle up her arm.

She closed her eyes, the heat in her face slipping to her chest and farther inside—a rush of warmth that tightened her throat and made it tough to breathe.

He nuzzled at her nape, the warm air of his breathing a caress down her neck. "Melanie?"

Right there in front of her was the wall that had defeated her again. She tilted her head to stare at it, fear making her legs quiver the higher her gaze rose. Only this time Derrick was solid at her back, his warmth a cocoon of safety.

Longing to move forward hit like a thunderclap. Longing for the touch of a man—this man—intertwined with her desires. She'd been afraid for so long.

Melanie twisted in his arms to stare into his eyes—dark midnight pools that were filled with something more than concern. Derrick brushed a knuckle against her temple, smoothing back a loose hair. All the time his gaze fixed on hers.

Then he leaned closer, slowly. Giving time for escape, for retreat, before his lips made contact.

Whisper soft. Not hesitant, but careful.

Too careful. Melanie leaned in harder, accepting his offering. Derrick responded, becoming more forceful and direct. Heat built between them as he ravished her mouth and her mood flipped again. All her stored-up frustrations burst out into glorious lust and she opened her lips willingly. Somehow she found her fingers tangled in his hair like she'd dreamed of earlier. He showed his approval by clutching her hips to him, his arousal evident even through the mass of webbing in the harnesses lashed around their hips. The safety rope wove between their bodies; the hard surface another contrast against the delicate brush of his fingers as he trailed them up her arms.

He kissed her, his tongue teasing along her teeth, tickling her lips, plunging deep. Their breaths mingled as they separated for a second to gasp for air then dove back for more. The tight knot of fear in her belly slipped into an aching need a handspan lower, centered between her legs.

Maybe she should have freaked out sooner. Maybe coming to the climbing wall and forcing herself to get back into a harness was the best thing she could have done.

Maybe she should just concentrate on the man she wanted to climb up and swing from the rafters with. Her swelling desire shoved the lingering stench of her anxiety into the corner as she let the thrill of arousal take her away.

Derrick figured he'd be kicking his own ass once this was over, but for now he reveled in the woman melting in his arms. For the past three weeks he'd been as patient and gentle as a saint. He'd ignored the urge to make a move, sensing her nervousness, thinking it was about her getting back into the swing of climbing again. He'd forced himself to stay aloof and make the situation as peaceful and serene as possible, all the while longing to find out what Melanie Dixon tasted like.

Even the fact she was related to a good friend wasn't enough to stop him from expressing interest in the dark-haired beauty. Kane's little sister was grown up enough to know her own mind, and what she'd said she needed was to regain her courage in the climbing arena.

If she had given him even an inkling of what she'd just shared, he would have been all over her weeks ago. Now he was finally getting the chance.

Screw the consequences. She needed this—maybe even more than he did. And he needed it bad.

God, she could kiss. She held his head in traction between her palms, lips tight to his. Every breath he dragged in tasted like her, with that damn tongue exploring and rampaging through his mouth. He cupped her butt and dragged her higher to line them up better, thrusting his own tongue along hers, pulsing it like he wanted to pulse into her body. Her moan of approval rippled along his spine, and he went from hard to utterly rigid. The confining straps of the harness holding his khakis in place pressed on him violently enough to cut off circulation.

Derrick took another step back. There was a sudden jerk as the rope between them snagged and he tripped. Melanie let out a little scream. He rolled instantly to his back to catch her, swearing at his own stupidity in giving her any reason to not trust him. *Great, asshole. Drop the woman who's afraid of falling.*

Nothing happened. He lay flat on his back, but instead of the sudden contact of her body slamming against his, he heard a peal of laughter echo off the high walls of the climbing gym.

"Damn it, Derrick, get me out of this mess."

Her voice came from directly above him, and he looked up to see her face hovering over his. It took a second to follow the lines and figure out what had happened. The loose end of the rope was tangled around his torso, pinned in place by his body weight. The middle of the length rose to the ceiling, looped through the support hooks as it should and returned down to where Melanie's harness was secured into the other end.

She hung suspended a foot over him, facedown, with the rope caught over one shoulder. Her feet were planted on the wall, holding her in place. She looked as if she were laying flat on her tummy on an invisible diving board.

He stared into her face, checking for any signs of fear, but all he saw was amusement. "Are you okay?"

She snickered. "I'm fine, but a little stuck. Could you please get me down?"

The situation was too tempting to resist. He gripped the rope to keep her in place, then swung himself into a direct line. When he released the rope, letting it slide through his hand an inch at a time, it lowered her all right.

Directly on top of his waiting body.

It felt so damn good, the increasing weight of her settling on him. The warmth of her thighs met his legs, her breasts crushed against his chest. Her gaze bore into him, and he wondered if he'd overstepped his boundaries for the second time.

"Did you plan this all along?" she asked.

He shook his head, trying to ignore the violent urge to rub their groins together to satisfy the hunger burning inside. He couldn't do that, not unless she showed some indication she was agreeable.

Tying up a woman to get into her pants—it wouldn't be the first time, but he only did that with willing partners.

"Couldn't have planned it in a million years," he confessed.

Her eyes darkened as her gaze darted over his face, landing on his lips with a hungry stare. "Damn, I'd hoped it was on purpose."

Hallelujah. He let go of the rope and rolled her, diving back into the kiss. Only this time the feel of her under him made him crazy. She opened her legs and his hips settled in tighter, except for the layers of harnesses between them. Like some kind of modern chastity belt, the wide webbing snagged together as he rocked his hips, stopping him from rubbing his erection against her mound. He growled out his frustration.

She grabbed one of his hands and tugged it to her breast.

Okay, he could be pacified for a moment or two.

They slowed the frantic kisses as his need to taste her skin grew beyond restraint. While he licked and nipped his way along her jawline, her fingers skipped over his back, tugging his shirt upward until she reached bare skin. Her short nails weren't enough to scratch, but her strong fingertips dug in and pulled a groan from him.

He wanted to be naked with her. He wanted to strip off the long-sleeved shirt and sports bra she always wore, and suck on her firm nipples until she screamed. Then he'd—

A buzzer went off and they both tensed. They glanced toward the clock on the wall and Melanie let out a huge sigh. "Opening time."

The after-school crowd was waiting for him to open the door to the climbing gym. *Screw it.* They could all wait for a few minutes.

It took an extraordinary amount of time to untangle themselves and find their feet. Derrick held her close for longer than he needed to, pretending it was to make sure she had her balance. He just didn't want to let her go.

The damn buzzer went off again, this time accompanied by banging fists on the doorframe.

"Your students are eager to get started." Melanie stared away from him, all her concentration centered on untangling the knot tethering her to the rope.

He wasn't going to leave it this way. A wild tumble on the climbing mats and nothing more? "Would you like to go for dinner with me?"

Her head snapped up, a small smile appearing. "Tonight?"

Derrick nodded as he headed for the door. "I can get away

around six thirty. Seven if you're okay waiting that long."

Melanie paused and he held his breath. "I'd like that. You want me to come here?"

Excitement raced through him to rival any teenage boy planning a first date. "That would be great."

"Okay."

They were grinning at each other like fools, he was sure of it, but he really didn't give a shit. Not about the continued protesting at the door behind him, or the faces peering in. Not about his lack of finesse. She turned and headed for the change room, and he watched her ass with a growing conviction that fate had intervened today and that tonight was going to be the start of a fine relationship.

Melanie wanted to relearn how to live? He could help her with a lesson or two, and if somewhere along the way they happened to get involved in some heart-pounding, body-aching sex?

He was good with that as well.

Chapter Two

Rope Gun: Slang title for the climber who does all the leading.

Melanie pivoted in front of the mirror, frowning in dissatisfaction. She smoothed her hands down the second T-shirt she'd layered on. Unless a person knew exactly where to look, no signs of her accident showed. Of course, that equaled no skin visible anywhere, which meant she wasn't very sexy, and therein lay her dilemma.

There had to be some kind of rulebook she'd neglected to read that could guide her through this situation, but the feverish heat pulsing through her veins and the ache between her legs continued to distract her. A girly-girl she wasn't, but surely even she could manage to pull together one outfit that was a little less "here I am, I'm covered" and a little more "here I am, want to uncover me?"

She changed clothing five times before she forced herself to stop.

In a few short minutes, Derrick James had turned her on and left her revving on high. Although she was embarrassed at her emotional outburst, it hadn't seemed to bother him. On the contrary, he must have had getting close to her on his mind before that moment. Guys got turned on fast—she knew that from too many years of close contact in confining quarters when her co-ed team had traveled to competitions. But Derrick? He had struck her as far more mature than the trigger-happy youths on her climbing team.

And the way he'd kissed her? Okay, the idea of being in someone's bed hadn't been on her agenda for a long time for a lot of reasons. After her last horrifying experience, she was not only afraid of his reaction, but her own. She didn't want it to all be a bunch of motion with no grand finale. The fear she wouldn't be able to relax enough to enjoy sex haunted her, and she wasn't the type to fake an orgasm for anyone, especially herself.

After the lust-inspiring grope they'd shared, she wasn't that concerned Derrick wouldn't be able to get a response out of her.

But would he be able to handle what her body looked like under her clothing? And was she really ready to let anyone see the scars? The lingering pulse of interest said she might be willing to find out.

She walked back to the climbing center, the air warm enough she didn't need a jacket with the long-sleeved shirt she wore like protective armor. Hiding from the stares of other people on the street had become second nature to her by now— and took far less energy.

Five minutes later the pounding pulse of a rock beat shook her before she even laid a hand on the door. She slipped inside and leaned on the wall, taking a slow look around to see who was climbing on Thursday night.

Families, youths and couples all filled the place with noise and laughter. Derrick had done a great job making the center somewhere for more than the elite to gather. She smiled as a dad belayed his son up the closest wall, the little guy maybe five years old and clinging like a gecko as he chatted excitedly.

Except when the kid breezed past the marker line where

she'd frozen, Melanie turned away in disgust. Yeah, whatever. Next time she'd force herself to go higher. There had to be an end to fear at some point, right?

She spotted Derrick roped into a harness, lead belaying one of the stronger climbers. The biceps in his arms showed nicely as he fed out the rope a portion at a time, watching his partner closely. Adam swarmed up the wall, smooth and rhythmic in his motions. She was far enough to the side Derrick must have seen her, at least in his peripheral vision, but he did no more than wave a finger, his gaze fixed on the climber.

Adam reached to clip his rope into the hook of the next carabiner on the overhanging wall and missed. Melanie's stomach tightened in a rush as the young man fell. A split second later she fought for breath—the rope Derrick held that attached to Adam's harness had jerked him to a safe stop well above the ground. Good-natured laughter rang through the room as Adam was lowered the remaining distance, shaking his head sheepishly.

Derrick clapped hands with him and pointed at the holds, probably suggesting something different to try the next time. Adam nodded and the two unroped and separated. Derrick headed directly for her.

"You okay?" The concern on his face was touching and annoying at the same time. God, even watching another person fall made her stomach roll.

"Just a little shaky. Think I need some food."

He undid the straps securing his waist belt. She tried not to stare in fascination at his hands working directly over his groin. Part of her wanted to reach out and volunteer to help him, any way she could. When she dragged her gaze higher, he tossed her one of his spine-melting smiles, his own interest shining in his eyes as he looked her over.

"I need to wash the chalk off my hands and put my belt away, then we can head out."

It wasn't that much later they were on the sidewalk, forced into close side-by-side proximity as newcomers brushed past them to enter the facility.

"You sure you can get away?" Melanie asked. "It looks busy tonight."

"I'm fine. There's enough staff on, and I usually take off Thursdays and work the late shift Friday and Saturday."

"That must interfere with your social life." *Oh, that was smooth, Mel.* Not. Way to sound as if she was digging for information. Which she totally was, but still. She didn't think he had a regular girlfriend, not with the way he'd kissed her. He had asked her out, but before she dove into anything, she'd like to know a little more about the big picture. Their private lives were not a subject they'd discussed over the past weeks.

"I get plenty of time for friends. The gym is closed at nine those days, and five on Sundays, so it's not like I'm there until two a.m. or anything." They dodged a group of skateboarders hanging out in a circle on the corner of the street. Derrick pulled her closer to his side as a few of the gang turned and eyed her.

The touch of his fingers as he kept hold of her trickled tiny rays of heat up her arm and into her body, and she suddenly wished she'd been brave enough to simply wear a tank top so he'd be touching her skin.

Hmm, skin on skin. Another item to add to the collection of things she'd like to try again. Soon.

They were in the restaurant in two minutes flat—one of the joys of small-town living. Derrick pulled out a chair for her on the deck built along the main street. In the winter, Main Street was an eclectic shopping vista, with cozy coffee shops to hide from the weather. In the spring and summer, the town turned the downtown lane into the center of attention, with multiple outdoor sitting areas and the ever-present buskers providing street music for tossed coins.

"How are you enjoying living here?" Derrick leaned back in his chair. He was seated beside her, his right arm close to hers as he placed the menu back on the table. The hair on his arm brushed the back of her hand and her nipples tightened.

She was a sexual time bomb waiting to be triggered. She blew out a breath, ruffling her bangs, then smiled at him. "It's been great. My brother told me this was a fun town to visit, but a little crazy to live in. He's right."

"You see a lot of Kane?"

She shook her head. "I had dinner with him and his roommates when I first moved, but he's been gone pretty much ever since. He's got a full schedule of wilderness trips booked until the end of summer."

They chatted for a little longer until their order was taken. Light conversation about what she'd done in school, about him and the house he was renovating even farther up the steep slope of the mountain than where she lived. All the while she admired him—his dark hair with the slightest bit of unruly curl at the ends hung loose, brushing his shoulders. He had the darkest irises, somewhere between brown and black, and a jaw that made her want to turn down dinner and just nibble on him for a while.

A climber's body—lean muscle, not bulky—every movement he made coordinated and smooth. He wore a T-shirt that clung to his biceps, fit snug to his chest. Heck, it was tight enough when he shifted position she swore she could make out the ridges of his six-pack. She knew he had one—she'd rounded the corner the second week at the gym when he'd stripped off his shirt and pumped out a set of chin-ups to the rising cheers of his climbing mates. She'd had to wipe away her drool.

Their food arrived and they both reached for the salt at the same time, bumping hands. He laughed and gestured for her to take it first, his strong fingers with neatly trimmed nails catching her eye as he picked up his burger and bit into it heartily.

Melanie attacked her own multilayered wrap, juice from the spicy barbeque sauce escaping to trickle down her chin as the flavours burst over her tongue. He caught a drip from the corner of her mouth and that electric pulse returned. Harder. Hotter. Their conversation faded away to nothing as the sexual tension at the table rose tenfold. Every bite, every swallow. Flames licked her skin, and there wasn't enough of a breeze in the air to cool her off. She grabbed her water glass and purposely looked in the opposite direction, needing a second to regain control.

"What would you like to do after dinner?" Derrick rubbed the back of his knuckles against the thin fabric of her shirtsleeve provoking an instant rush of desire. "There's a movie we could catch, or we could go for a walk along the lakeside."

There were a whole lot of unspoken questions in his tone.

What *was* her agenda for the night? Going to a movie was safe, in a way. At the most they'd be able to do a little necking like teenagers, but they wouldn't get to talk. And while more kissing with Derrick was on her list, if they were going to take the interlude they'd started any further, they definitely needed to talk. "I'd like to walk, if you don't mind."

Thirty minutes later they slowly strolled the boardwalk curving the perimeter of the park. On their left, the lake spread out, lazy ripples undulating on the surface as the occasional kayaker floated past. Melanie reached for his hand and snuck her fingers into his, and he smiled, squeezing lightly and letting her set the pace.

Enough of keeping secrets. If she was going to do anything more than kiss him, she had to tell him. Part of facing the future, right?

"You know my brother pretty well?"

He nodded, his thumb brushing the back of her knuckles with a light, teasing touch. "We've worked together over the years. When Kane's arranged wilderness excursions with rock-climbing components, I've come along and coordinated. I do occasionally hang out with him, Jack and Dara for kicks. Great guy, lots of fun."

"Did he ever tell you about my accident?"

Derrick pointed off the main path to a bench facing the water. "He'd said you were a top-ranked climber, but you'd had a fall. Never mentioned much more. That was also about all you told me when you came in and asked for private lessons."

Melanie shifted uneasily, ignoring the open spot next to him on the bench. She'd prefer to be on her feet for this one. "I guess I don't want a lot of sympathy, but..."

She sighed. Damn fall. Of all the stupid things to be worried about right now.

"What's wrong, Melanie? How can I help?" He reached forward and grabbed her hands and tugged her toward him. His knees were spread wide and she stepped into the protective circle of his body. The warmth from his torso and the sincerity in his eyes helped a lot. "I'm interested in you. Not just as a client."

He slipped his hands around her hips and suddenly fingers touched bare skin where her shirt had ridden up in the back.

"Wait..." She pulled back and his face fell.

"Sorry. I thought you—"

"No, it's not that. It's just..." Damn. She dragged her hand through her hair. *Pull in your courage. It shouldn't be this tough.*

He tugged on her arm again. She plopped onto his knee and clutched his shoulders for balance. Slowly, as if expecting her to run away again, he leaned his head toward her and their mouths connected.

Melanie dove in wholeheartedly, letting the arousal that had simmered all afternoon come to a full boil. Yeah, she still needed to tell him about her scars, but just in case she scared him off, she was going to store away one last session for future fantasy material.

As her willing lips meshed with his, the strumming in his body kicked up a notch. Thank God, it wasn't that she didn't want him. Derrick adjusted her on his lap so he could lean back and let her full weight rest against his aching groin. She had to be the most emotionally volatile woman he'd met in a long time. Frightening thought in some ways, but he liked his woman to have both the fire to stand up to him, and the mental strength to submit. It was never the cool and in-control ones he enjoyed the most. Whatever psychological turmoil had Melanie in its grip, he was more than content to see where this thing between them led.

She wiggled, her lips leaving his to dip into the scoop of his neck as she squeezed tight against him. Her small breasts rubbed his chest, her tight nipples visible as he glanced down at her dark, long-sleeved T-shirt. He ran his hands up her back, careful to stay over top of the fabric, and swore lightly when he realized she wasn't wearing a bra.

The heat in his body kicked even higher. Three weeks of watching and wanting to touch her. Yeah, he was ready for this to go a whole lot further than simply kissing.

They had enough privacy here to get into a moderate public display without getting arrested. There were only the joggers at his back who could spot them, and they always seemed intent on the end of the trail. He clasped her hips and lifted her across him. She helped by raising her knee, coming down to straddle his thighs. Off in the distance, a cheer rose from the parents watching their children at the soccer fields.

She scraped her fingernails down his shoulders as her tongue continued to dip into his mouth. He captured her taste, the warmth of her wet lips, and another pulse of desire raced through him. This much contact wasn't nearly enough. He lowered his hands back to her hips to grind her over him, connecting the ridge of his bulging erection with her crotch. She moaned in approval.

Derrick tore his mouth from hers and dropped his head to her shoulder, stilling their frantic gyrations and dragging in a breath to control himself. "I want you. Let me take you home."

She stiffened, but her fingers continued their teasing touch at the base of his skull. "I want that too, but..."

He cupped the back of her head and held her tight. Maybe it would be easier if she didn't meet his eyes. Maybe it was the wrong time of the month, as if that wasn't the most awkward question ever. "But what? Not a good time right now?"

Melanie out-and-out laughed, leaning back to display a smirk. "Oh God, sorry for making you ask. No, it's nothing like that, but I am...embarrassed." Her words tumbled out in a rush as if she had to say it quickly, or not at all. "I've got scars from the accident. I wasn't sure what you'd think of them."

All the tension that had built in him as he'd considered the dire reasons she could have for putting him off slipped away in a smooth eddy of relief. "I've got a few scars of my own. Thirty years of rock climbing and outdoor adventures invites wear and tear on the body. I don't think there will be a problem."

"Yeah, well...that's what someone else told me too. Only it was a problem."

Shit. As soon as she uttered the words she'd gone as rigid in his arms as a tightly coiled spring. Suddenly he understood. "Is that why it's been so long since you've had sex? You think guys don't appreciate what you look like? Or did some ass insult you and you never tried again?"

She hung her head. "Walked out on me in disgust."

Rage flashed inside, along with a deep need to take apart the guy one piece at a time.

"He was an idiot." He cupped her chin and waited until she looked him fully in the eye. "I swear there's nothing about your body that can make me not want you. You've been driving me crazy since the minute you walked through the door of my club."

She raised a brow. "Even though I've worn nothing but long pants and full sleeves since day one?"

Derrick smoothed a hand down her cheek, reveling in the heat she exuded. "It's not just about the way you look. Your stubborn determination to learn to climb again is more of a turn-on to me than seeing you in a skimpy pair of underwear with flawless skin. The way you move makes me hard. I smell your skin, and I'm ready to beg you to touch me."

"God, you're good."

He trailed his fingertips down the front of her shirt, scraping a nail over her nipple and smiling as it popped up to poke the fabric. "It's the truth. You tell me—any of your injuries affect what we can and can't do when we get naked?"

Her nipple fascinated him, and he continued to play with it,

171

teasing lightly in circles, pressing the tight nub with his fingers. It took a minute for him to register she hadn't responded. He glanced up to see her pull her mouth shut and a red flush staining her cheeks.

"When we get naked, there is nothing we can't do."

He let his satisfaction show. "Then there's nothing to worry about. Will you come home with me? So we can do the naked thing?"

Melanie straightened her back, but her smile was nothing but naughty. "Oh, yeah. If you're sure, I'd like that very much."

It normally took him fifteen minutes to walk home from the park. With all their pauses to kiss each other, they didn't make it to the gate of his backyard for thirty. Once he yanked the stubborn thing open, she was back in his arms and he had her pressed against the solid wood, their mouths together again as he gave in to the need to massage her breasts through her shirt.

The compact mounds just filled his hands, her nipples spearing into his palms. A growl escaped, tearing from his lips as his desire broke free. He bent over and nipped at the hard peak through the thin material and she moaned. Moisture from his mouth soaked her shirt, and he sucked right through the fabric, making her squirm. It wasn't enough, not nearly. It took all his will power to draw away, staring at the wet circle left behind. "I want to taste you, everywhere."

His voice had dropped a level, dark and lust-filled. Behind his jeans, his cock pressed the fabric to its limits, his balls tight to his body as she writhed against him.

"Not outside. Please?"

Of course not. Not considering she was concerned about showing herself in the first place. The thought of seeing her totally nude in the sunlight did crazy things to his groin though, and there was no way he could walk right now. He propped his hands on either side of her head and gave her one last needy kiss before pulling back.

"Inside."

He unburied his keys from his pocket and dangled them in front of her. Melanie grinned mischievously, snatched them from his fingers and ducked under his arm. She ran down the back path and halfway up the stairs to the deck before he could follow. He chased her with an exaggerated roar. She fumbled at the lock before popping it open and slipping inside with him right on her heels.

The back door opened onto the kitchen, but she darted through into the next room, dodged around the couch and coffee table and scrambled for the stairs. He slowed, letting her remain ahead of him.

She paused at the top of the landing and leaned over the railing to beam at him. "Shall I make myself at home?"

His cheeks ached from grinning so much. "Please do. Anywhere you want to go is fine with me."

Melanie disappeared around the corner, and he stomped his way after her, deliberately loud as he took each step, loving how her responding laugh echoed off the walls. He slowed as he reached the door of his bedroom. Every nerve in his body wanted to grab her and bury himself deep, but his brain was getting the biggest kick out of the whole chase scene.

He hadn't had a lover he could play with in a long time.

She waited on the far side of his mattress, the curtain half-drawn behind her. Backlit, her hair tumbled around her, a halo of shimmering highlights. "Am I being too forward?"

"You ended up right where I wanted you." Time to start the naked business. If she was uncomfortable, he'd do what he could to help her. He reached for the bottom of his shirt and stripped it from his body. Admiration painted her face as her

173

gaze dropped over him, lingering on his abdomen and the front of his jeans. Staring at her as he continued, he popped open the top button. She bit her lower lip, her hips wiggling from side to side, her arms wrapped tight around her.

The width of the bed separated them. He unzipped his jeans, pushed them from his hips and stepped free. He knew his cock strained against the front of his boxer briefs. Hell, he'd probably already left a wet spot on the fabric after all their fooling around. Melanie once again seemed to square her shoulders. She grabbed the bottom of her shirt and shimmied it upward, slowly exposing her smooth belly with a flash of a jewel at her navel. The outline of a rib, then those perfect little breasts were bare to him, and his mouth watered. He wanted to cover the dark circles with his lips and suck them until she moaned in ecstasy.

"God, you're beautiful."

The words burst free—unplanned, unrehearsed—and she choked out a cry. It was somewhere between laughter and pain, and as he searched her face for the reason, she pivoted, twisting to expose the left side of her torso.

Ribbons of stark white showed against her skin, plastering her arm and shoulder, her breast. Her rib cage was covered, and the scars marked her all the way down to disappear under the edge of her soft cotton pants. The lower they dropped, the more extensive the damage, the single lines meshing into crosshatches and batches of uneven dips and valleys where the skin and muscle had been torn away prior to healing.

"Shit—that must have hurt." He sat on the bed, patting the place beside him then reaching a hand to her. She joined him hesitantly, crawling over to bury her face in his neck, her body shaking against his.

"Sorry, I thought I could do this. I thought I was strong

enough, but I'm still freaking out." Her voice was a whisper, and he carefully wrapped his arms around her and held her close.

"Shh, it's okay. Tell me what happened."

"I slid. Thirty feet free fall down the wall, most of it jagged granite. The rocks were sharp enough they cut my clothing away, and shredded my harness. By the time I landed, I had broken four ribs and my left leg, dislocated my shoulder and had lacerations from wrist to ankle. A concussion that put me out for a couple of days. The rescue crew was amazed I hadn't broken my neck. They figured my flexibility and muscle strength saved me."

"You survived because you're strong."

Melanie shrugged, her ear resting on his chest. "My life changed."

He smoothed her back with tiny circles, caught in an erotic torture as her bare breasts rubbed his chest. Damned if he'd move ahead until she was ready, but shit, he hadn't lied. Just the smell of her skin made him hard, and now holding her half-naked body in his arms? Screw the scars, he wanted her badly.

So tell her.

"I understand why you're afraid, but..." Maybe actions would speak louder than words. He caught her hand and pulled it between their bodies, pressing her palm against his cock where it rose between them. "Does it seem as if I'm turned off at the thought of being with you?"

Melanie laughed again, this time a short gasp. She'd been on the verge of tears, and that was not where he wanted this to go. He would wait as patiently as possible. Of course, while he waited, he could make it clear he had no objections to her body whatsoever. He lay back on the bed and took her with him, draping her over his chest and continuing to stroke her warm skin. She squirmed and her gorgeous tits pressed tight to him again. His cock jerked against his briefs. Her temple was within reach, so he kissed it. Then with a little roll they were side by side and her lips were once again accessible.

Kissing her breathless seemed the best way to get her mind off what wasn't an issue. Not tonight. Not with him. And kissing his way down her body to her breasts was the next natural progression. He held her gently, thumb and forefingers creating a half cup to press the mound of her breast upward. A slow lick over one tip, the hard point wonderful against his tongue. When she moaned, he tore his gaze upward to make sure she was still on board. Melanie struggled up on her elbows, shaking her head slightly.

"What?" He moved his other hand to play with her nipple.

"It really doesn't bother you?"

"Kissing you?"

She rolled her eyes. "Now you're being deliberately obtuse. My scars."

"They don't bother me." All he wanted was to touch her. To get back to what they were doing. He wasn't ignoring her pain, or the damage the accident had done to her mind and soul, but wanted to show her the fears about her body at least were groundless. He leaned in and took her nipple into his mouth again, the one on the side where the scarring was. Working slowly, he skimmed his fingertips along the sides of her torso, touching and teasing her skin. Slipping his fingers under the waistband of her pants, he pulled them away.

He slid down the mattress to dip his tongue into her belly button and play with the tiny purple jewel nestled there. All his senses were heightened as he tasted her. The sweet scent of her soap clung to her skin and turned his exploration into an olfactory delight. He planted kisses along the top of her panty line, stroking the side of her body in long sweeps, cupping her ass. She rolled one hip upward, and he snagged the edge of her underwear and dragged it down, exposing her sex to his sight. Oh yes, this was what he'd been waiting for.

Nudging her legs apart with his shoulders, he settled between her thighs, swirling a fingertip between her curls to open her.

"Please." Melanie lifted her hips higher, and he rewarded her with a slow swipe of his tongue.

He shuddered as her cream hit his system. Too good to stay slow, he covered her with his mouth and ate greedily. Tongue dipping in, then rising to torment the hard nub of her clitoris. Driving in hard until Melanie grabbed his head and called out her pleasure. It happened far too quickly, so he carried on feasting. He brought up one hand, slipping a finger into her core to enjoy the pulses of her orgasm that rocked on and on. Languid pumps followed as he continued to lap and suck her sensitive clit.

She dug in her heels and ground against him, and he willingly gave more. Two fingers now, stroking the front of her passage until she shook. Derrick pulled away and leaned on the bed, his fingers moving constantly as he looked into her face. Two bright red spots flushed her cheeks and her eyes were half-lidded. Pleasure streaked her face when he brought the heel of his hand in contact with the top of her mound. He moved to kiss her again.

Her fingers twisted in his hair, her tongue tangling with his. The taste of her pleasure passed between them, and she arched, rubbing against him like a cat.

She broke the seal between their lips. "I want you inside me."

Oh, yeah. Derrick kissed her one last time then reached over her into his side table. Her warm hands were busy at the elastic of his briefs, stripping off the fabric and enveloping his cock with her tight grip. He rolled to his back and let her play, watching with delight as she explored his length, stroking and caressing with her fingertips.

"You okay?" he asked.

She shuffled closer, kneeling half over him as she turned her bright eyes in his direction. "I'm wonderful. I want more."

"So do I." Every firm stroke brought him that much closer to finishing, and he wasn't ready yet. He grabbed her wrists in his hand and stilled her caress. "You're driving me mad."

Melanie smiled and leaned over to nab the condom. He took the opportunity to swipe at her breast as it came within reach, and she paused, moaning as he suckled. "That feels so good."

He smiled around his mouthful, nipping the tight tip. She gasped and pulled away, her bottom lip caught between her teeth.

"I like your body, Melanie. All of you. You are one nice package."

She raised a brow and sat back, the condom wrapper tossed to the floor as she held his cock in her hand again. Ball-breakingly slow, she rolled the latex down his shaft. "Speaking of nice packages."

They laughed together before he tipped her chin up. "You want to be on top? It's been a while."

She answered by dropping to the mattress and tugging his shoulders. "You do all the work this time."

He had no objections with that at all. He covered her with his body, the warmth of her skin teasing him. The expression in her eyes enticing him on. Then the tip of his cock slipped through her folds, and the raging heat of her body surrounded him. He squeezed his eyes closed, fighting to restrain his eagerness. One slight rock after another, he forced his way into her tight passage. Melanie drew her knees wider to the side, opening space for his hips as they meshed together. It felt so fucking good as pleasure slid down his spine and pulsed in his balls.

He hovered over her, allowing their bodies room to rub as he thrust in, slowly at first. Unhurried and deep, his cock slid into her passage as her cream spread over him. His ability to resist melted and he sped up, switching to hard and fast thrusts. Each plunge better than the last, each drive slamming their groins together. His balls slapped her body, her peaked nipples grazed his chest. When she dragged her fingers down his back, he swore and pounded in wildly. There was an inferno blazing between them, and he wasn't going to stop until they went out together in a burst of pleasure.

Derrick leaned on one arm and slipped a hand between their torsos to find her clit, pinching in time with his thrusts, and Melanie screamed. Her fingers dug into his shoulders, her heels digging into his butt. She hauled him into her core, and as her orgasm squeezed him, he released all control and exploded into the condom. His balls pulled up, his cock jerking again and again until she'd drained him completely. The room spun, and there was a loud roar in his ears that blocked out all other sounds. Her panting breath hit his cheek, and he took in the scent of sex filling the room.

He could handle more of this. A lot more.

Derrick collapsed to the side, his arms quivering with reaction to the intensity of his release. "Holy shit, that was..." Words escaped him. His brain was mush. She cuddled in closer, his cock still buried in her body, and let out a contented sigh.

"Oh yeah, it was."

They stared at each other, satisfied and sated. "Round one?"

Melanie raised her brows. "I'm game for more, once I can move."

Exactly. He kissed her forehead and just lay there. More in a minute. Right now he needed to get some blood back into another part of his body before his limbs would operate. He lazily ran a hand over her naked torso, both the smooth and the scarred. She tensed, but only for a second, before leaning into him and relaxing.

Derrick smiled against her hair. Yup. There were some things said more clearly with actions than could ever be said with words.

Chapter Three

*Sketched Out: Feeling insecure, a lack of
confidence in the current situation.*

She hadn't changed much. Not in the nearly ten years since he'd last seen her. Her petite body was still powerful, lean and made his body ache as she clung to the wall and traversed her way across, staying only a few feet off the ground.

Nathan King rested his chin on his hands, leaning forward in his seat in the balcony area as he watched Melanie bouldering. She wore full-length yoga pants and a long-sleeved shirt—no evidence of her accident was visible, but he knew it was there. He'd seen the news-file photos taken immediately after Mel's fall.

He'd gone off in another direction long before her mishap, and until his most recent assignment had crossed his desk, he'd put all thoughts of her out of his mind. She'd been underage the first time they'd hung around each other, him always careful to stay on the outskirts of her crowd.

Nathan stared across the room, his fascination rising. She wasn't too young anymore.

He clicked a couple of candid shots from the upstairs seating area before packing away his camera equipment and descending the stairs to greet her.

He hung back along the wall and waited for her to spot him. She spoke animatedly with another climber, the woman laughing at something Mel said. Nathan admired how her eyes lit up, a smile brightening her face just like he remembered. Except the slope of her cheek was all woman now, no baby fat or maturing left to do, simply a dark beauty that shone through her healthy glow.

Taking this assignment was looking more positive all the time.

Melanie lifted her head and glanced in his direction. A crease appeared between her brows, a cloud of confusion in her eyes. The moment she figured out who he was, everything changed.

"Nathan? Oh my God, it's you!"

She raced across the floor and threw herself into his arms. The warmth of her torso hit like a thunderbolt, streaking through him and electrifying his entire system. He grabbed on to stop her from falling, bracing his legs to keep them both vertical. Her arms squeezed him tight and he was suddenly aware of the intimate contact between their bodies. Her breasts were compressed against him, his cock against her belly. She squirmed and he let her go, her cheeks flushed as she stared.

"Hey, monkey."

He easily blocked her instant punch to his torso, grinning as he realized that even after all these years her response to his tease hadn't changed.

"What are you doing here? I haven't seen you in forever." She motioned him to the side of the room to a safer place to talk out of the way of climbers and curious onlookers.

"I came to see you."

Her eyes widened, panic-stricken. "Katy. She's okay, isn't she? You didn't come to tell me—"

"Whoa, hang on. There's nothing wrong with my sister. She sent her love when I told her I was heading west to meet with you." Nathan looked her up and down slowly, letting his admiration show. This might be partly a job, but that didn't mean that was all it had to be. He was single, and she was all grown up. This could be a lot of fun for the short while he would be in town.

He was rather looking forward to it.

Her tension dissipated only to be replaced by a frown. "I'm glad she's all right, but I don't understand. Why are you looking for me?"

"Does that surprise you so much? That I'm interested in seeing you?" He couldn't resist. With the back of one finger he stroked her cheek, enjoying how her body jerked in response to his touch, her face heating even more.

"Nate, I'm..." She backed up, flustered just like when she'd been a kid and he'd paid attention to her. Although he'd done his best back then to keep his attraction hidden.

"Can I buy you a coffee? So we can talk?" He knew he was staring, but he couldn't seem to stop. Under her tight T-shirt, her nipples had hardened and now poked against the fabric. The facility had the air-conditioning on high enough it wasn't sweltering hot in the place, but it wasn't cold enough to make her body react.

She fumbled for words. "I'm not done with my workout."

"I can wait." Somehow his hand was on her arm, a gentle caress.

She crossed her arms, casually slipping away from him, and it was his turn to feel embarrassed. He hadn't meant to make a move in public. Not after so many years apart. No matter that the chemistry between them seemed to be heating up in a hurry.

"Melanie. Is there a problem?"

The dark-haired man he'd seen behind the check-in counter stood beside her, glaring at Nathan with suspicion.

Mel blinked hard right before she leaned on the other man's chest, slipping her arm behind his back and settling intimately against him. "Derrick, this is Nathan. He's my best friend's big brother."

Ah, shit. Flirting without asking questions could be detrimental to his health.

Nathan held his hand out to Derrick, fully expecting the guy to crush his fingers in a display of macho strength.

Instead, Derrick gave a friendly grin. "Glad to meet you."

Nathan noticed he didn't do anything to move Melanie any farther from his side. Point made. She was taken.

Shit again.

"I was just asking Mel if she'd join me for a coffee. You're welcome to come along."

Derrick glanced at the clock. "I'm good to go anytime. Melanie? You done or did you want to climb for a little longer?"

She leaned up and kissed his cheek quickly before stepping away. "If I finish my workout now I don't have to come back later." She turned to Nathan. "Are you okay waiting for a bit? Tell me your timeline. If you've only got a few hours in town I can totally change my plans."

"You can finish. I'm staying around for a while. Got a room at the hotel on the lake, so no rush."

Melanie nodded, glancing between them before retreating to the wall she'd been traversing. Nathan watched in fascination as she shook out her hands then stepped onto a tiny foothold, her body close to the wall, arms extended overhead.

"Family friend? You know Melanie well?" Derrick moved

closer and Nathan hid his smile. The third degree started now. That was fine. He had a few questions of his own, and this was as good a way as any to get information.

"I moved away for college and have only seen Mel a couple of times since then. I'm on the road a lot. What about you? You work here at the climbing center?"

"Own it. What do you do for a living that keeps you traveling so much?"

Nathan pulled his camera bag forward. "Photographer. I don't do war zones, but just about anything else—still life or action—I've shot it."

"You taking pictures around the area for a travel magazine or something? I can make a few suggestions of easy places to access."

"Thanks. I do need some nature shots, but this assignment is human interest."

Nathan's gaze was drawn again to Melanie. She was leaning at a nearly ninety-degree angle, long legs stretched to the side and spread wide, the edge of her shirt separating a bare inch from her pants as she lowered herself down the wall doing a modified chin-up. The amount of strength in her upper body was incredible, and he could just picture the kind of shot he could take, getting in close to angle from—

There was a nudge to his arm and Nathan snapped back to attention.

"Human interest? You want to take pictures of Melanie?" Derrick's disapproval rang through loud and clear.

"I think I should talk to her about it first, if you don't mind."

The pleasant expression on Derrick's face had vanished. Nathan didn't even bother to try and hide his smirk. The boyfriend was going to be protective, was he? Well, Nathan didn't remember Mel ever needing much protection.

"Of course." They stepped aside to allow a couple to access the wall behind them. Someone called Derrick's name. He waved at the couple before motioning to Nathan. "Wait in the viewing gallery until Melanie's done, then we can grab that coffee."

He didn't offer it as a suggestion. Nathan nodded briskly before taking the stairs two at a time. Well shit, the fact that Melanie was attached sucked. He'd been looking forward to getting to know her better over the next weeks. He leaned on the railing, peering down into the climbing area. She fluttered glances upward a few times, her cheeks bright, gaze darting away whenever they happened to make eye contact.

Then again, maybe the boyfriend thing wasn't going to be an issue. Nathan grinned. In fact, there was nothing he liked better than a challenge.

Melanie squirmed in her chair, her body far too hot and needy to deal with this situation. Nathan King. Of all the people to show up now, why him? She leaned against Derrick's side. Yeah, she was hiding. The kind of physical thrill that had hit her when she'd caught sight of Nathan was completely inappropriate considering she'd been sleeping with Derrick for the past three months. Except sleeping was such a weak, pathetic word to describe what they'd been doing. Romping, sweating and screaming out in pleasure. The man didn't do anything by half measures. Not her climbing lessons, not their dating, and certainly not the sex. After she'd gone on birth control and they'd both gotten clean bills of health, their lovemaking had become even more spontaneous. There were a few days she'd truly understood the concept of not being able to walk afterward.

So why did Nathan make something in her core quiver like a needy bird?

"You guys grew up together?" There was a low timbre of stress audible in Derrick's voice. He might be attempting to keep the situation laid-back, but there was no getting around it. Somehow she must have let her unwelcome attraction to Nathan show. Guilt hit. Her growing relationship with Derrick was about more than simply sex—she didn't want to hurt him.

Nathan popped open his wallet and passed a picture to Derrick. "My little sister Katy and Mel were best friends growing up. I think since day one. Our gap in ages meant I wasn't around that much, though."

Enough for her to have had a mad teenage crush on him. Melanie scrambled for safe topics. "Katy said you were working for *Rave* magazine. How's that going?"

Nathan flashed his bright smile and she fought against the spark it lit inside her core. "It's been the best move of my career. With bimonthly releases, I get a ton of work from them. I'm on assignment, and while they occasionally call with last-minute shots they want for the files, most of the time I'm out for a couple weeks at a time doing human-interest stories. Like right now."

Human interest? In this neck of the woods? "Who's so interesting around here? One of the environmentalist programs? Bear handling?" Melanie teased, sipping her coffee.

"You."

She choked on her mouthful, spitting back into her cup. "Me? What are you talking about? I just moved here. I have nothing to do with the area."

He laughed. "It's not the location, monkey, it's you. We've got a series of 'where are they now' articles in the works, and you're—"

"No way." She leaned back in her chair, the ache in her hip a clear reminder of what he was talking about. "You want to talk about the accident? *Jesus*, Nate, I thought the bloodsuckers got all the mileage out of that disaster back when it happened."

"It's not like that, Mel, just hear me out."

"I don't want to show the old pictures—"

"We won't."

Derrick slipped an arm around her. "You don't have to do anything you don't want to."

"It's not about the past, it's about where you are now. What you've been doing and how you've headed into the future." Nathan's piercing blue eyes locked with hers and refused to let her go. "When they mentioned your name I thought it was a brilliant suggestion. Do you know how many people you could encourage? How many victims of car accidents or burns could see you living life to the fullest and become motivated to do the same?"

Her stomach fell, all the simmering sexual interest vaporizing and drifting away on the breeze. How could she be an inspiration to others when she had barely peeked her head out of her own personal hellhole? She'd made some headway since moving, and getting involved with Derrick had done wonders for a bunch of her psychoses, but as a role model for others?

Bullshit.

"Nathan, I...I can't do it." Her mouth was completely dry, her tongue stuck to the roof of her mouth. "I mean, I'm employed at the post office. It's not as if I'm a brain surgeon or a schoolteacher or anyone who makes a difference in other people's lives."

188

"But you could make a difference. Mel, I saw you in the gym. You were working that wall, pumping it out when I know damn well you didn't walk for months after the accident. It took a lot of determination for you to get back to being physically strong, and I think you've underestimated how remarkable that is."

It was too much. She turned to Derrick and buried her face in his shirt. He held her close, rubbing her back. He remained silent, not taking over and she was so grateful. It took a minute to regain enough control that she could twist her head to stare at Nathan while remaining in the safe shelter of Derrick's arms.

Nathan's princely good looks had matured, or maybe it was the fact she was no longer looking through love-struck teenage eyes. He'd cut his dark hair into a close, professional style, and she imagined all the women at his magazine vied for his attention when he was in the office. No doubt tossing themselves at his feet and willingly crawling between his sheets on a nightly basis.

But right now, with the firm beat of Derrick's heart under her ear, and his arms supporting her, there was nothing in Nathan's eyes saying sexual intent. There was compassion, and a streak of stubbornness that she'd expect from him.

Could she do this? Talk about a forced move into the light. Letting Derrick see her naked and touch her scarred body—that was one thing. They'd shared enough time over the past couple months to make being with him seem normal. It was private, and usually she was so sexually turned on by the time she stripped that passion smoothed away any remaining nervousness that arose.

She still hadn't managed to show her damaged skin in public. Not even a regular T-shirt. The thought of anyone other than Derrick seeing her made bile rise to the back of her throat.

189

Imagining the potential taunts and questioning glances threatened her breathing. She had no guarantees people would be cruel, but it was no use.

She might be trapped in a cage of her own making, but she was trapped, nevertheless.

Anger rippled through her. She wanted to live. Fully. Wasn't that her goal? And while she wouldn't give up what she had with Derrick for the world, she still had a long way to go.

Melanie squeezed Derrick's arm, thanking him for his silent support before facing Nathan straight on. "What are you thinking about?"

His eyes lit up. "Two parts. The first is for the magazine. They need a couple dozen pictures for the article, indoor and out. I'd take a mix of pictures—some at work, some at your home and some at the climbing wall. I'll do a short interview, but the pictures are my main contribution. The second thing is a project I've got an idea for on the side—it's a graphic presentation. Images telling the story. We can take pictures wherever and however you feel comfortable, but I can show you some samples of what I've got in mind. We can discuss that in more detail later."

He wanted to take pictures of her showing her scars to the world. To show her living in spite of the accident that never should have happened. Oh Lord, this was going to kill her. "Do I get to see the pictures?"

Nathan responded immediately. "I'll give you total control over what pictures I hand over to my magazine."

The hair at the back of her neck stood upright. Derrick squeezed her fingers. "You don't have to do this," he repeated.

It was too much to decide in an instant. She examined Nathan's face. Years ago she'd wanted nothing more than to have his undivided attention. Now she dreaded it. Life was unfair in how it granted wishes.

His smile stroked her. In spite of its warmth, there was a nagging ache inside warning her this experience could be hell for more reasons than baring her scars.

"I need time to decide."

Nathan's hopeful expression faded, but he nodded. "I can understand that. I deliberately didn't phone ahead of time—I thought this discussion would be better in person. But if you could let me know in the next couple of days, I'd appreciate it. I'm not trying to rush you, but I have deadlines to meet."

He returned the conversation to Katy and what was happening with her and the rest of the family back in their hometown. Light, newsy information meant to put her at ease.

The coffee burned a hole in her stomach with every sip.

When they'd finally finished their drinks, Nathan plopped a light kiss on her cheek, then disappeared down the street, his camera bag slung over his shoulder.

She and Derrick walked in silence back to his apartment. His fingers twined with hers, strong, supportive. Her mind raced with images and discussions from the past, distant days as well as the more recent time she'd spent in Derrick's presence.

At what point would she be able to let go of her burdens?

Derrick led her to the couch where he proceeded to cuddle her in his lap and rub the tension from her shoulders until she was able to let out a long slow breath. She twisted to face him. His forehead was creased with worry and she smoothed a finger between his brows.

"Hey, it's not that a big a deal."

"It is to you. Mel—I know you're trying to be strong and move forward with your life, but that doesn't mean you have to say yes to this offer."

He was right. There was no one holding a gun to her head. There was no life-and-death decision that needed to be made this instant, like grabbing a safety rope as a hold gave out. But there was a time that waiting became the wrong response, and she was never going to reach her goal if she didn't keep moving.

"I know I don't have to, but what if I should? What if this is like Nate said? Something not only for my sake, but to help others." She closed her eyes, trying to ignore how her stomach squirmed as she imagined baring herself. "I'm not the only one with scars, and I got mine in a fairly innocent way."

"What the hell are you talking about?"

Melanie shrugged. "It was an accident, and there was no one to blame. You said it—a freak rope failure. I was climbing, which has intrinsic dangers. What about the people hurt in car accidents or house fires? They had no hand in their situations, but they're still scarred and have to deal with it."

He reached out to cup her face in his hands, his thumb tracing the thin line of the single scar on her cheek—the only visible cut on her face. "Sounds as if you've given this a lot of thought. You can't have come up with all this since we left the coffee shop."

"I did tons of therapy with a sports psychologist after the accident, but frankly? It's a hell of a lot easier to say it than think about doing anything with it. Being told my injuries were somehow better since I didn't get them from a vicious rape or a drunk driver slamming my vehicle—"

"That's absurd." Disgust rang in his voice. "I can't believe anyone would ever say anything like that to you."

She sighed and leaned her cheek harder into his hand. "You'd be surprised what things people feel are their right to tell you. To be sure you know how lucky you really are."

Derrick shook his head, then brushed his lips over hers. "Again, just because Nathan offered this shot doesn't mean you have to do it now. If you are interested in the idea, you can arrange to do it at your own pace, with anyone."

"Maybe. But *Rave* magazine? That's a hell of a platform." Melanie snuggled in tight to his chest. "No, Derrick, I think this might be the right time, and the right place. I trust Nathan as a photographer. But..." She dropped her volume, forcing the words out. "I need to ask a huge favour."

Because if she was going to show off to the world, she needed his help. She didn't want to have a crutch in her life. Not a thing, not a person, but giving up Derrick's comforting touch and presence right now was impossible. "I can only do it with you there. Is that possible? I know it's a huge imposition, but if you're present it will help. So much."

He pulled back to stare into her eyes, his gaze thoughtful as he examined her face. The caring lover she'd grown to appreciate over the past months—he was probably considering what was the best for her. Derrick nodded slowly. "How about this. If you and Nathan can work around the hours the climbing gym is closed, you can use the place to do your shots. There will be no distractions and no audience."

Extreme relief shot through her. Oh God, she hadn't even thought about that part. She hugged him close, burying her face in the vee of his neck, loving the way he created a wall of protection to hide behind.

"Thank you." And the rest? She sat back quickly, catching his gaze again. "And you'll be there?"

"As long as you want me."

Wasn't that a loaded question? She shifted, straddling him to be able to reach his lips easier. "I want you. I want you now."

She wanted to be held and caressed. Distracted from the

heavy burden in her brain. He kissed her with just the right touch of compassion and rising lust, and her body softened. Warmed in all the right spots. He ran his fingers down her back, and she arched against him, breasts growing heavy with anticipation.

He kissed her jaw, held her firmly, yet tenderly. A wave of need swept past, followed by guilt. She'd been turned on back at the climbing wall as well, and that had nothing to do with Derrick.

She pulled away. "Oh damn."

A low rumble of discontent escaped his throat as he paused. "What?"

"Oh *damn*, I need to tell you..." Sure, how was she supposed to say this? Mortification hit hard, and the heat flushing her face was more from shame than the expectation of Derrick's lovemaking.

She didn't realize she'd dipped her head until his fingers under her chin brought her gaze back to meet his. "Mel? What? Is this something to do with me watching the shoot? Is that going to embarrass you—?"

"Oh hell, no. I'm just trying to tell you..." She'd sworn to be honest in her relationships, and she wasn't the type to let a situation start that could cause them trouble down the road. "I need to tell you about Nathan and me."

One brow snuck upward, his expression highly amused. "You mean the fact he wants to get in your pants, or the fact he turns you on?"

Her jaw must have hung open for a full minute before she found her voice. "You're kidding. You figured that out how?"

Derrick grinned. "Sweetheart, I'm not stupid. I know a guy putting on the moves when I see it. And your response? You have this little habit of flushing right here—" He dragged a

194

finger down her throat and over her chest. "When you get excited, it shows."

She was so embarrassed. "I had a crush on Nathan from the time I was about thirteen. I followed him around Katy's and his house one entire summer. He must have been so freaked at having a teenager dogging his heels."

Derrick stroked her back, smooth and even. Tantalizing circles that pulled her a tiny bit closer to him on each rotation. "And did you do anything about that attraction?"

"I was fifteen, he was like twenty. Of course not."

"So, you've got the object of your teenage crush hanging around." Derrick linked his fingers with hers. "Mel, I've been enjoying our time together, a lot. I don't think the fact the guy turns you on is bad, it proves you're human. Call me crazy, but the fact he's attracted to you is okay with me as well. Maybe that's a guy thing—I've got you, he doesn't. You know, caveman attitude."

Melanie laughed softly. Sexy, kind and understanding. She'd have to have her head examined to give this up. "You are who I want to be with. Not him."

His grin lit the room. "Then I don't mind if he gets your motor running, as long as I'm the one in your bed."

He cupped her face in his hands and kissed her.

Chapter Four

Dyno: A dynamic movement where momentum is required to propel the body to a new position.

Melanie grabbed him by the shirt and clung to him as their lips meshed. A gentle caress of mouths, with no teeth, no frantic moving to the next stage. Almost as if they were exploring each other for the first time.

It was an offering, a sacrifice. Something to affirm that while having Nathan show up created a new situation between them, the foundation they had built was solid and worthwhile.

Derrick rolled her under him on the couch, working his way down her body. Removing her clothes, kissing all the tender spots he'd discovered over the past months. His fascination with her breasts made her smile.

"I still can't believe you like them that much."

Derrick hummed happily. His palms forced her nipples upward so he could more easily suckle one, then the other. "More than a mouthful is too much."

She laughed. "Barely a mouthful. Oh, that's good." She held on to his head, keeping him close. His lips surrounded one tip, his fingers pinching and drawing the other nipple tight and ready for his hot mouth to lick. Circles followed by long, slow licks. A shiver raced along her spine and she pressed harder to his lips, looking for a little more.

The soft fabric cradled her torso as he tugged her toward the end of the couch. She laughed as he pulled her yoga pants from her in one smooth practiced move. Somehow he caught her panties at the same time, and she lay sprawled totally naked before him.

He stared at her, his gaze intent, hunger on his face. "I know why Nathan wants you."

She hesitated. Why was he bringing up Nate?

Derrick rose to his feet, looming tall and muscular over her. He still wore all his clothes, and she realized with a start she wasn't embarrassed in the least to be completely naked before him.

"You have no idea how beautiful you are." He rasped out the words—lusty and low.

"Right."

He squatted beside her, shaking his head slightly as he drew a finger down her body. "Your body is powerful. Slim in the right spots, curved perfectly in others."

His palm cupped her hip for a second before slipping back to cradle her ass.

The expression on his face, even more than his words, stroked her. "I'm glad you like how I look."

He grinned wickedly. "And the way you smell."

"Oh my God." He had picked up her legs and draped them over his shoulders, and her sex clenched. Wanting something to grasp, to fill her. She didn't have long to wait. Maintaining eye contact, he lowered his head and breathed in deeply.

"The way you taste."

She would have protested, but the words smeared into a

197

moan as his mouth made contact. His tongue, gentle but thorough on the outer edges of her sex. Teasing, offering a glimmer of satisfaction then stealing it away. He avoided her clit, instead lapping everywhere until she was squirming to find what she needed. His hands tightened on her ass then his tongue thrust in deep and she squealed.

He fucked her with his tongue. The peaceful, slow attack sped up along with her heart rate, along with the sizzling in her core building to explosive levels. "Oh, Derrick. Yes, *yes, yes.*"

She couldn't stay still. The velvety caress of the couch under her back contrasted with the firmness of his hands. Soft noises carried in the windows, the birds adding a nature soundtrack to the sounds of his mouth moving eagerly over her. When he finally pulled back far enough to make contact with her clit that was all she needed to begin riding a wave of pleasure. Melanie closed her eyes, concentrated on how good it felt to have him carry on touching and lapping until the tremors died away and let her draw a normal breath of air once again.

Her ears were still ringing, and she missed the moment he rose to his feet. The next thing she knew she'd been flipped, her legs draped over the armrest, leaving her ass high in the air as the cool air of the room drifted past her wet core.

Then the hot hard tip of his cock touched her and with one slow, deliberate press, slid in deep. The stiff fabric of his jeans brushed the backs of her legs on every thrust. In contrast, the smooth heat of his shaft filled her. She felt so alive as the forceful motions of his hips rocked her on the couch. The slight abrasion against her nipples kept the heat building from her earlier orgasm. She twisted her head to the side, resting her cheek on the seat cushion to look back at him.

Derrick smoothed his hands over her ass cheeks in circles before holding on tight and bracing her for his forward stabs.

His gaze danced over her, watching where they joined together as if fascinated.

"Even here, you're beautiful. Wet, tight. Oh God, so good." He closed his eyes for a second, face tight in a grimace. Melanie squeezed her internal muscles as hard as she could, loving the way he sucked in air, his eyes popping open. "You're dangerous."

She snickered and repeated the move.

"Fuck. Do it again."

Melanie obliged, the increased pressure drawing her nearer to completion as well. He wiggled his hips, nudging her knees farther apart and let his cock slip even deeper on the next thrust. All her breath pushed from her lungs, and when he reached between her legs and stroked her clit, she lost it. The wave of contractions spread like happy ripples through her sex, dragging a shout from Derrick's lips and he came, hot seed spilling into her.

He collapsed over her back, the pressure of his clothed body over her skin perfect, enticing. He tenderly kissed between her shoulder blades, caring in his touch.

"Like I said, beautiful."

The word described him and his heart completely. How could a man be so trusting to understand that she was attracted to another man, and still give to her so fully?

She wasn't going to question why. When she managed to find enough energy to drag him out of the living room and to the bathroom to clean up, she tried to return the favour and show a bit of what she was feeling.

That she was maybe even starting to fall in love?

"Slowly turn your head upward. There. Perfect. Okay, go ahead."

Nathan snapped off another series of shots as Melanie twisted her way across the lower half of the wall. At his request, she'd worn only a sports bra instead of her usual long-sleeved shirt.

It had taken her a long time to remove her shirt and step onto the climbing floor.

Her left arm and side showed the scars, but the main focus was the muscles flexing and moving smoothly as she grasped the wall.

Derrick stared from his position across the room, wondering if he wasn't the sickest bastard in creation. They'd turned up the air-conditioning in the gym, but with the extra lights Nathan had arranged all over the place, the heat level had risen, causing a slight sweat to break out on all of them. Melanie, even with the minor amount of effort she was currently putting out, had a shining slick to her skin that made him want to drag her off the wall, drop her to a mat and fuck her senseless.

Right there in front of Nathan.

Of course, that was the other part of the heat filling the room. Melanie had been upfront about the attraction she'd felt for the guy. It was impossible to miss, and seemed unstoppable.

The disturbing part was Derrick had no desire to rip Nathan's head from his shoulders. In fact, as Melanie's pulse picked up, Derrick's fascination increased. Every time Nathan helped position her on the wall, his hands firm and confident on her body, Derrick's dick got harder.

Melanie's breathing accelerated, that telltale flush covering her chest. Derrick took another long swig of his water bottle and wondered if the two of them would notice if he pulled out his cock and jacked off right here and now.

Fucked in the head, that's what he was. Watching his girlfriend get as good as fondled in front of him, seeing her get turned on, and all he could think was how happy he was for her and how much he needed to ease his balls.

Nathan lowered his hand, the camera dangling from his fingers. "Take a break. I want to try another angle and need a second to set up."

Melanie dropped to the mat, landing as soft as a cat on her feet. She shook out her arms, wiggling her fingers to get the blood moving again. Derrick peeled himself off the wall he'd been holding up and strolled over as casually as he could with his cock a solid brick against the front of his pants.

He stepped around Nathan to reach Melanie, rubbing his hands up and down her arms to help relax the muscles.

She stared at him, her flush spreading farther as she pressed in for a kiss and the ridge of his cock met her belly. There was no way she could avoid feeling it. Her tongue darted out to moisten her lips, and if it was possible, he got harder. Derrick leaned over to whisper in her ear.

"How you doing?"

She swallowed.

His lips brushed her earlobe. "Other than needing to be fucked?"

Her eyes widened. "Oh hell, I'm sorry, but..."

Derrick brushed back a strand of hair that had escaped her braid. "It's hot in here, isn't it?"

She nodded. "It's the lights."

A burst of laughter escaped. He stroked her arm, brushing the side of her breast. "Nice try."

Melanie leaned in and squeezed him tight as she whispered

in his ear. "Are you sure this isn't pissing you off?"

"Positive."

"I feel so guilty. I don't understand my reaction—I mean, I might have been interested in him years ago, but I'm happy in my relationship with you. Why am I reacting like a dog in heat?"

Because Nathan was treating her like a desirable woman?
"I'm not mad. Although—fair warning? When you're done with this shoot, I'm going to drag you into my office, lay you on my desk and fuck you until you're a boneless heap."

Her eyes widened to saucer-size. "How the hell am I supposed to keep climbing after you say something like that?"

"Guys? I've got an idea." Nathan's announcement broke in and cleared Derrick's brain for all of two seconds. "Derrick, can I get you to do some assists?"

"You want me in the pictures?" That idea kind of sucked. He hadn't seen that suggestion coming at all.

"Only parts of you. I'll show you." Nathan motioned to the wall. "Melanie, climb up. I want you to lean back and have Derrick reach across your body."

She willingly stood on two small footholds, grasping the larger jugs he'd had her use earlier, but she frowned. "I'm not sure what you mean."

"Just get set up and I'll show you." Nathan gestured, and Derrick moved in to help. They had no ropes this time, even though both of them still wore their harnesses. Melanie was only a foot off the ground, bringing her head level with his.

"Okay, like this now." Nathan abandoned his camera and moved in closer, hands landing on her hips to align her the way he wanted. He slid one hand up her side, so concentrated on what he was doing he seemed oblivious to the fact his palm slipped over the bare skin on her right side before pausing on her torso directly in line with her breasts. "Lean against me a little. That's it. Now, Derrick, check this out. I'm going to hang on to the wall, but lean out of the way. Got that?"

Derrick nodded, trying to ignore the surge of blood headed south as Melanie licked her lips and closed her eyes. The more excited she got, the more he ached to do something about it.

Nathan stepped back and reached for his camera. "Now take my place. I'm looking for the contrast of a more masculine limb next to Melanie's feminine figure."

Melanie's gaze followed Nathan's retreat for a second before she turned to face Derrick. She mouthed the words *Oh my God* and he snorted.

Yeah, she was turned on big time.

He took his place and deliberately copied everything Nathan had done, including rubbing his way up her body to get into position.

"Bastard," she muttered.

Derrick stepped to the side, making sure the only thing in the shot was his arm. That meant his hips were pressed tight to her ass, letting her know exactly how hard his dick was. "I'm so looking forward to helping you get into position in the shower later."

"Awesome, guys." Nathan stepped around the open area, clicking madly. "Derrick, if you can reach the wall with your other arm—yeah, there. Perfect."

A trickle of sweat rolled down the side of Melanie's neck, and Derrick instinctively brushed his face against her. She arched, just the tiniest bit, but it was enough to press her tighter to his groin, and he groaned out his approval. The tips of her nipples were hard, stabbing the thin fabric of her bra. Her breathing sped up as he stared over her shoulder and planned exactly what he was going to do to her when this session was over.

Nathan strolled from side to side, clicking away merrily. Melanie wiggled for a second, her ass rubbing his dick in an innocent coincidence—or was it?

"You need something, sweetheart?" He whispered the words, letting the tip of his tongue brush the dangling lobe of her ear.

"Stop it."

"You mean that?" He forced the side of his arm to her torso and adjusted his grip. The movement made him rub her nipple and she moaned.

"God, I'm going to explode."

The secretive conversation was made even raunchier knowing Nathan watched them through the lens of the camera. They weren't alone. Every nuance, every touch, Nathan was there, a silent observer.

Maybe it was a touch of possessiveness that made Derrick rock his hips, the minute motion mimicking what he wanted as soon as humanly possible.

"Change of position," Nathan called.

Derrick scooped up Mel and hugged her close as he stepped away from the wall. He lowered her, letting their torsos rub together until her feet touched the floor.

Her bright eyes stared into his, a tiny smile quirking the corner of her mouth. "I will get my revenge," she promised.

"Bring it on."

They grinned at each other before turning to face Nathan.

Nathan strategically arranged himself behind a chair to

hide his erection. The generic shots were turning out fine—not as spectacular as he hoped to see for his special project, but more than sufficient for the *Rave* articles. And after getting a glimpse of how Melanie reacted to Derrick... Well, even though Nathan longed to be the one making her respond, with a little direction the boyfriend could assist in capturing some potential award winners.

Over the years Nathan had learned how to pull a response from his models. It wasn't the lighting or the framing of a shot that made it unique and mesmerizing. It was the emotion portrayed in the eyes, the faces. The tension of muscles under skin. The merest whisper of a frown or a bead of sweat—that's what made people remember a photo days or even months later.

Sometimes he'd arrange to shoot the pictures at a location that pushed the project to that incredible next level. Returning a family to the site of their lost home, the burnt remains a backdrop for them facing the future, or a child walking past the hospital where they'd spent the past Christmas—Nathan sensed how to get what he wanted, but he only ever did it with the full consent of his models. It wasn't about taking advantage of them, but working with them to prove they were capable of the next step.

Like Melanie—although he had to admit his emotions were more conflicted when it came to her. She oozed sensuality from every inch of her skin, scarred or not. When he'd planned this trip, all kinds of mental images of what they could do together had bombarded him. He'd wanted to be the one making that sheen of desire rise to her skin, wanted it to be him taking her home at the end of this session and playing sexual games until they were both sated.

But in the end, as long as the shot worked, he would settle for Derrick's participation. At least for now. It was all about timing—the lights, the energy levels.

And like taking baby steps, it was time to move to the next stage. Nathan put down his camera and strode over to turn off the extra lights he'd brought into the gym. "I want to try something else, but you have to tell me if you're comfortable with it."

He sat in one of the folding chairs and dug a couple of water bottles from the cooler. Melanie and her sidekick accepted them, and Nathan waited. He wondered if Derrick was really as calm and peaceful a guy as he portrayed. If Nathan had made a miscall, this next move would get his ass wiped all over the dusty floor mats.

Only one way to know for sure. He pulled out a file folder.

"So far what I've been doing are basic shots for the feature article. I've just about finished them."

"That quick?" Melanie wiped water from her mouth, and Nathan forced himself to stop staring at the perfect swell of her lower lip. The fact he was also imagining what those lips would look like wrapped around his cock had nothing to do with why he was here.

"I will need a few shots outdoors—and I hope you'll be able to help us out there, Derrick."

The dark-haired man nodded slowly. "There are a couple places I can lead you to that are less popular, yet good solid climbing walls. But, Nathan, you're aware Melanie isn't up to climbing anything technical yet, right?"

She stiffened in her chair. "I'm capable of doing what needs to be done."

Derrick dropped a hand on her knee. "I agree. You are capable of anything you put your mind to, but I'm not belaying you up a technical route when he should be able to get the pictures he needs without pushing your boundaries. You've come a long way. That's the goal, a little at a time."

Hmm. Melanie sat back quietly and Nathan examined Derrick closer. Seems the guy wasn't just brawn and no brains. Time to see how he'd react to this push.

"I agree. I can work with whatever you feel is appropriate. I don't need a shot of Melanie dangling in midair against a huge backdrop. What I want is at the base, outdoors, creating another step in the big picture. I won't push beyond what you feel comfortable with, okay, Mel?"

She nodded and he smiled at her.

"We're got barely an hour left before you said the wall officially opens. The natural lighting is awesome right now with the sun coming in through the skylights. I'd love to take a few shots for that other project I mentioned."

"The coffee-table book?"

Nathan pulled proofs from the file. Here's where the shit was going to hit the fan—or not. "Again, only what you're comfortable with, but here're some sample shots I took last winter. It's all about playing with the shadows and light. The human body is a work of art, and that's what I'm trying to show."

He passed over the pictures and held his breath.

Chapter Five

Sandbag: To underestimate a route's difficulties.

Melanie's eyes grew wide, but it was Derrick's expression as he peeked over her shoulder that made Nathan the most hopeful. The boyfriend's gaze shot up to meet Nathan's, and there wasn't anger in his eyes, but intense concentration.

"Holy cow, Nathan, you taking pictures for *Penthouse* or something?" The light joking in Melanie's voice didn't disguise her touch of interest. "Because I have to tell you upfront, there's no way I've got the body for this."

She had no idea, did she? "Mel, that's bullshit, but that's not the point. No, it's not *Penthouse*, and I swear the intention is not to give teenage boys wet dreams. Think Greek statues, Renaissance painters—this is a celebration of the human body. But I want to show more. I also want to celebrate the human spirit, and that is where you are such a fantastic example."

She rotated the eight-by-ten she held toward him. It was a shot he'd taken last winter of a female skier, lounging on an emergency blanket in the middle of a snowfield. The black and white proof made the contrasting textures even more stark.

Long smooth lines of skin, the grainy surface of the snow in high relief, the woman's naked torso reflected like a mirror image on the silvery blanket. Her skis, boots and poles scattered in a heap beside her like a sacrificial-offering pyre. He was proud of the shot, and his model had been even more thrilled.

"This woman is totally naked, Nathan. I'm not posing for you in the buff."

He held up his hands in surrender. "Didn't ask you to. But—would you be willing for me to use some artistic license and make it *look* as if you're wearing a lot less than you've actually got on?"

She narrowed her eyes. "Using computer editing?"

"Nah, good old-fashioned methods of shooting from the correct angle." Nathan glanced at Derrick. "With a little help from you. Want to try a couple shots then tell me what you think?"

"These aren't going to *Rave*. Right?"

"Of course not, and remember, I promised you'll get to pick the ones I do offer them in the first place. I don't know which five or six they'll actually use. I have no control over that, but you'll know upfront which shots will be possibilities."

Derrick leaned closer and whispered in Melanie's ear. Nathan waited as patiently as he could, hoping this wasn't the moment that the whole idea collapsed around him.

The expression on Melanie's face wasn't giving anything away either. Except for her uneven breathing, which he'd noticed happened a lot during the photo shoot. Hell, his own breathing wasn't much smoother. The chemistry in the room had been enough to make them all hot and horny.

Nathan hadn't had a steady girlfriend for years. Love them—thoroughly—then leave them happy had become his motto. With his travel schedule there was no other way, and really, it wasn't that bad a life, being responsible for no one but himself.

Melanie sat up and cleared her throat. "If you take a few shots today, can you develop them and show me what you mean? That way I can decide better what I'm agreeing to."

Shit, yeah!

"Oh course." He stood and examined the walls closer. The perfect place to begin? "Stand in the corner and let me grab what I need."

He deliberately turned away to let Derrick and Melanie have a moment without his attention. He forced himself to breathe and keep his body loose and relaxed. Sporting an erection right now wasn't the way to keep Mel relaxed.

Oh hell, the images racing through his brain were going to kill him. Just because it seemed he wasn't going to get any action this trip didn't mean his body was happy about the fact.

He called over his shoulder as he gathered his gear. "If you can roll the top of your pants down a little, but leave the harness on, that would be great. I want it to look as if there's nothing on you but the climbing belt. If I shoot from the right angle, all we need is one small twist to your climbing top and a little assistance from Derrick."

Nathan strolled back to where Melanie waited in the corner where there was a beginner's climbing route. Back in the day, he'd seen her climb something like this freestyle, no ropes, laughing as she flew past the caution line and made her way to the top unprotected.

He wasn't going to demand anything that wild.

She stood strategically again, the side of her body with the scars tucked to the wall. Derrick remained close, a fierce guardian. Fine—Nathan had no objection to using the guy to get what he needed. Nathan put the camera away for a moment, then stripped off his shirt.

Melanie's bright laugh burst out. "Oh my God, Nathan, why

are you wearing a bra?"

He grinned at her, thrilled to see the girl he'd been attracted to peeking from her shell. "Demonstrating what I want you do is easier with visuals. I need you to adjust your shoulder straps so that your shoulders are left bare. Like this—"

Nathan twisted and squirmed until all the fabric in the sport bra lay across his chest in a narrow band. He'd picked up the thing at the thrift shop the previous day, and now stood in a ridiculous pose. Her giggle of a response delighted him.

Melanie smiled hard. "You goofball."

"This must be big-city fashion or something," Derrick teased, a low rumble of amusement in his tone.

Nathan grinned back. "You're just jealous that you too don't have a fine article of clothing such as this to wear."

"Oh hell, yeah. I'm so envious I'm going to go get my feather boa out of storage."

Nathan good-naturedly flipped him the finger. The easy banter between them smoothed the tension, and the next thing he knew Melanie had popped out from where she'd hidden behind Derrick, her bra now twisted in imitation of the one he wore.

"Like this?" She cleared her throat. "I don't..." She blew out a slow breath. "This is tough, Nate. I never knew how tough it would be."

He stepped forward. "If it's too much, we can stop."

She shook her head, but tucked in against Derrick's side. "I'm okay, just, can I close my eyes or something?"

"Of course."

Derrick kissed her temple. "Give me a second. I've got an idea."

He snuck away, heading behind the front desk. As soon as

he left, Melanie wrapped her arms around herself.

Nathan's heart was breaking. He hadn't expected her to be so fragile after all this time. He lowered his voice. "I mean it, monkey, if you want to stop, I have no objections. I'm not going to be pissed off or report you to Katy for banana stealing or anything."

The pain in her shining eyes contrasted with the stiff determination of her mouth. "I said I'm fine. I want to try. I want to see what the pictures might look like, because I can't honestly tell you yes or no otherwise."

He nodded before turning away, removing the sports bra and replacing his T-shirt, trying to make the situation easier. He didn't look at her until Derrick returned and held out a scarf to Mel.

She took it gingerly. "You're going to blindfold me?"

Derrick glanced at Nathan. "It shouldn't matter for these shots if there's extra fabric in the way, right? They're just samples for Mel to check out?"

It was brilliant. "I can work around that."

Mel handed the scarf back to Derrick. "You better stick close, that's all I'm saying."

"Like glue, girl, like glue."

Derrick wrapped the bright blue fabric around her eyes twice before tying it off, the short tails falling down the back of Mel's head to land on her bare shoulders.

Now that he wasn't worried about her catching him staring, Nathan allowed himself to finally look his fill. The skimpy line of fabric covering her breasts was no barrier to his appreciation of the firm swells. Her muscular arms and trim waist made him long to be able to smooth his hands over her body and enjoy her more intimately.

A soft cough brought him back to the sudden realization Derrick was probably at that moment planning his demise for openly lusting after Melanie. Only the expression on Derrick's face was unreadable—his own interest in the woman standing at his side crystal clear in the ridge bulging the front of his pants.

Derrick was just as turned on as Nathan, and Nathan hadn't a clue what to do.

So he did the only thing he could think of. Picked up his camera and directed Melanie and Derrick into the positions he wanted. He started slowly. After getting Derrick to place Melanie back in the corner, leaning on the wall, Nathan took the simple shots first.

"That's right. Relax your neck, let your shoulders fall. I'm taking a picture from the neck up, arranging the shot frame with the top edge of your sports bra."

"I still don't understand how you think this will produce anything someone will buy for a coffee table. I'm rather ordinary to look at, Nathan, really I am."

"Bull." Derrick beat Nathan to the punch this time. "Don't put yourself down or I'll make sure you know exactly how attractive you are."

Nathan's fingers skittered on the shutter button as he compelled himself to hold the camera steady. Derrick had placed a single finger on Melanie's throat, hovering over where her heart beat visibly. He dragged his hand downward, stroking softly. Nathan kept clicking, catching her shiver, the resulting line of goose bumps that rose over her arm.

"You don't have to fit some textbook-model stats to be gorgeous, Melanie. You've got grit. You've got the most incredible smile. But your body? Hell of a package." Derrick leaned in and dropped a kiss over her heart and Melanie instinctively arched her back, breasts reaching forward.

Nathan was going to fucking die. He had barely enough brainpower to somehow keep snapping shots.

Melanie cleared her throat. "Derrick—Nate's watching."

The words whispered out, chased by her tongue as she licked her lips. The blindfold remained in place. Nathan kept silent, waiting to see what Derrick's response would be.

"Of course he is, but he doesn't matter, babe. I'm the one who's telling you how beautiful you are. Don't you believe me?"

"I do, but...he's watching."

"Doesn't matter. Pretend he's not. Pretend there's no one here but us."

Derrick stretched his arm across her body and took her lips like a starving man. Melanie snuck one hand up, fingers tangled in Derrick's hair. Her other hand splayed against the wall as she got caught up in the kiss.

Maybe he was a bastard, but Nathan never stopped taking shots. He dipped to his knees, twisting to achieve the camera angles he needed. While Derrick and Melanie's lips meshed, their panting breathes echoing off the two-story ceiling, Nathan focused less on big-picture shots and more on revealing a mosaic of flesh and need. The arch of Melanie's shoulder, the smooth curve of the upper swell of her breast. Derrick's hand hit the wall next to her torso, the line of his biceps perfectly covering the swatch of fabric over her breasts. The muscular arm appeared as the only thing keeping her upper torso from full exposure to the camera's lens.

Gorgeous.

In his peripheral vision, Nathan spotted a beam of light inching closer as it fell through the skylight to hit the mat at their feet. Inspiration hit, and Nathan didn't hesitate.

"Derrick, help Melanie to the floor. Place her in the sun."

The other man dragged himself away, blinking hard as he fought his way back from the lust-filled creature Nathan had been capturing. Derrick nodded agreement, slipping his hands up Melanie's torso until he could lift her, taking her to the off-kilter square of brightness marking the center of the gym.

"Nate?"

God, the lost-little-girl sound trembling on her voice was going to kill him. "Don't worry, monkey, nothing scary is happening. It's as if you're back in drama class and you have to pretend to be a tiny little seed. I want you to curl up into as tight a ball as you can."

She nodded slowly, her fingers still linked with Derrick's as he stood to her side. "Do you..." She cleared her throat. "Do you want me to take off my top?"

Oh shit. That was so like the Melanie he remembered, attempting to push her own limits far sooner than she needed to. Nathan's gaze shot to meet Derrick's. The warning shake of Derrick's head wasn't needed. Nathan nodded silently, acknowledging his understanding. She wasn't ready for more, not today. "Nahh, these are test shots, right? Just plop your butt down and let me take advantage of the light."

The visible relaxing of her body showed they'd made the right decision. With incredible grace, Melanie sat, pulled her thighs to her chest and wrapped her arms around her shins.

"Do you need me to do anything?" Derrick asked.

Nathan stepped in circles around his subject, working as he spoke. "Not this time. Since it's just the test shots. Wait—yes, in a second I'll use your shadow. Okay, Mel, remember that drama-class thing? You're a seed, and it's springtime. Let's see you grow."

Melanie lifted her head from where she'd buried her face

215

against her knees. Her eyes were still covered, but her smile shone out clear and bright. "Oh, come on, you're not going to tell me what kind of flower I am? What's my motivation? Am I a good seed? Or a bad one? I can't possibly do this kind of improv without more direction."

Nathan and Derrick both laughed.

"You're nuts, that's what you are," Derrick teased.

"Ahhh, a peanut plant. See, that's what I mean, Nate. Give me instructions, and I can do anything."

As if by magic, the high sexual tension and lingering fear that had fogged the space around them for the past couple of hours faded away, and for the next thirty minutes there was nothing but easy camaraderie between them all.

Friends. Nathan finished his work even as he struggled through what was a massive mental change in game plan. It was becoming crystal clear that Derrick and Melanie were more than something casual, and although a part of him still wished he had been the one kissing Melanie senseless earlier, he wasn't planning on sticking around after this assignment. Fucking up someone else's life wasn't something he wanted to take the credit for.

As hard as it was to accept, being friends with Mel was all he was going to get.

Derrick stirred his coffee slowly, the thoughts racing through his brain enough to madden him. The whole photo session had made him harder than a pipe, and there was no way he could simply let it lie. He wasn't usually the type to get demonstrative in public, yet the rush he'd gotten taking charge of Melanie in front of Nathan had been undeniable.

And that was only the start of the issue.

His normal go-to guy in terms of talking about women and relationships was out of the question. He could just see it now, asking Kane for suggestions about dealing with his sister in regards to sex. Not happening.

So instead, he was going with the back-up help. He made his way over to where Jack sat, his fingers flying over the surface of an iPad.

"Okay, geek boy, put the toys away."

Jack grinned at him and clicked off a few final buttons. "Ass. Just because you hate technology doesn't mean the rest of us need to ignore it."

"Don't hate it, but I can live without it most of the time. I do love my GPS."

The sunny outdoor patio was filled with locals and tourists taking advantage of the gorgeous August day. "Jack, got a tough one, and I need some suggestions."

Jack raised a brow. "Me? You're talking about a woman situation here? Because you always go to Kane for that kind of thing. I thought I freaked you out."

"Yeah, but since this involves Melanie, I can't ask Kane."

"Right, you two are going out. I hope it's nothing bad, because while I'm not her brother, I'll still beat your ass if you've done something to hurt her."

Derrick shook his head. "Things are great, the woman is a goddess, and I have no intention of hurting her. It's this old friend of the family, Nathan King. Did you hear about him being around?"

"Taking pictures of her for some news article. Kane wasn't a hundred percent happy about it."

Oh boy, this was not easy. "Look, I need your honest

opinion. You're involved in a relationship with a woman who is also involved with another guy. How does it work?"

Jack hesitated. "You're not asking about the physical dynamics are you?"

Now there was a discussion he didn't want to have with Jack. "Hell, no. I know you and Kane are both doing Dara, and I don't care if it's together, from the rafters or painted with whipped cream. It's the emotional side I'm trying to figure out. I'm not stupid, it's clear this is more than a fling for you three. It's not as if you've been hiding it in public, especially not over the last few months."

Resignation and amusement both flashed over Jack's face. "I must have 'let's talk about our deepest feelings' written on my forehead. Yes, Derrick, spill all your emo questions on me. I'm used to it now, after all this time with Kane."

Kane? "Really?"

Jack laughed. "Just tell me what's up."

Derrick nodded, still slightly disturbed by the image of Kane and Jack having long, deep meaningful conversations, and yet—why was that strange? They would have to talk through some major shit if they were going to survive having three people involved in a relationship.

He pulled himself back to the present. "Here's the deal— Melanie and I are solid as far as I can tell, but she's still got issues in terms of body image because of her scars. And yet, up pops this dude from her past, and she's not only interested, he is as well. And I'm fucking freaking out because instead of wanting to kill him, I'm thinking this is exactly what Melanie needs—to be admired by someone else, and not just me."

Jack stared out the window at the street for a moment, a heavy sigh escaping his lips. "You do this crap even better than Kane. That's a tough one. I'm no shrink, but when someone's been through an incident like Melanie, it makes sense that it's a long road to full recovery. It's probably a positive sign that she's showing an interest in someone. I mean, not that it's great for you or anything."

Derrick waved a hand. "I mean it—things are good between us. She confessed to me she had a crush on him way back when. He obviously has an interest in her. He was taking pictures earlier, and the room just screamed with this *fuck me* tension. Only, I'm wigging out because I'm not..."

He trailed off, not sure how to explain it right.

"Feeling possessive?"

Derrick swore. "I'm fucked in the head, aren't I?"

Jack laughed. "Well, that makes us even, because I get the same damn reaction every time I catch Kane and Dara getting naked together. I wait for the flare of anger to hit, and when it doesn't arrive I wonder if my balls are going to shrivel up and fall off in punishment for denying my manhood."

The picture of totally-in-charge Jack taking a backseat didn't sit right, but the confession made Derrick's hope rise. "Really? I'd always thought you meekly sharing a woman seemed crazy."

"Trust me, there's nothing meek about it. It pissed me off for the first couple months at times, but now that we've been together in a committed relationship for eight months, I'm not sure how we managed before." Jack held up a hand. "Don't get me wrong, we still have fights, but considering there are two of us to deal with Dara when she's hormonal? Much easier than having to figure out a woman all by yourself."

"I'm not talking about forever, Jack. It just struck me maybe Nathan would be good for Mel short term."

"Help her know that someone else feels she's attractive?"

"That kind of thing, yeah." Derrick laughed at himself. "Insane, right?"

Jack leaned back in his chair and crossed his arms. "Actually, no. I mean, it depends on the way you go about this. You're not talking about taking off for a few weeks and letting the guy bonk her, are you?"

No freaking way. "Screw that. If she's doing anything, it's going to be with me there, making sure she's okay all the time."

"See, there's where your situation and ours is different—although I guess our crazy situation began for a similar reason. You're talking about something that helps you get to the end result that's best for Melanie. Confidence in herself."

"Right."

Jack nodded. "I hear you. The only reason we started our three-way relationship was because it was the best thing for Dara at the time. And then it turned out to be the best thing for us all. Kane officially told his parents last month we've got this insane setup going. We're..." Jack rolled his eyes. "Oh God, it's fucking contagious. Now I'm the one acting like a girl. The three of us are buying a house together. Dara's expecting."

"Holy crap." Derrick paused, considering. "Congrats."

Jack's instant brilliant smile wiped away the question if this was a good announcement—the pregnancy—or not. "Thanks. Keep it under your hat for a bit, though. We just got it confirmed, and Kane wants to be the one to let the rest of his family know. And before you ask, because it's written all over your face, no, we don't know who the dad is. Chances are we'll figure it out when the kid arrives, since Kane and I have such different colouring, but we pretty much don't care."

A million questions rolled through Derrick's brain, none of them related to his real dilemma. "You guys have a lot of guts. It's not going to be easy, raising a kid in your unique household."

"It's going to work, because we're committed to make it work. Like any long-term relationship." Jack tilted his head at Derrick. "What about you? If this is serious, you and Melanie, you willing to do what it takes? Your situation isn't exactly like ours, but it's still the same question at the root of it."

No, this wasn't Jack and Kane's situation with Dara at all. Derrick was sneakily suspicious he was falling in love with Melanie, and yet having Nathan join in and help show Mel that she was an attractive, vibrant woman in spite of the scars, seemed like the right thing to do for her sake.

The only reason she was doing the photo shoot was to help others. Screw that. She had needs as well, and he was willing to push past his comfort zone and make sure she got whatever it took for her to get that "full life" she longed for. Even if his solution wasn't typical, adding another guy in the picture might be just the cure needed.

"You're shitting me."

Derrick ignored his comment, instead handing over a list. "You can get most of these things at Kane's shop. I'll loan you what I can, but you should make sure you have these items that fit properly."

Nathan swore his mouth flapped like a fish while Derrick went on and on, continuing to list the places in town to find the camping supplies needed for their overnight trip.

Hell, no. That wasn't where the first part of this conversation was going to stop. Nathan held up a hand, fingers spread in an attempt to arrest Derrick's rapid info dump.

"Back up, man. What the fuck did you just tell me? Before

the camping shit." Because he really had to be going deaf.

Derrick sighed as he turned back to his desk. "Damn it, don't make me say it more than once."

"I think you need to repeat it until it sinks into my brain. Did you just suggest that while we're out on this trip, I should try to seduce Melanie?"

"Not...seduce. I want her to be able to call all the shots." Derrick leaned one hip on his desk, tension hovering around him. As if every muscle waited on the edge of exploding. "Level with me—do you find her attractive?"

Nathan reeled back. *Just the type of question I want to answer to a seemingly jealous boyfriend with enough muscles to beat me silly.* Fine, Derrick was going to ask the tough ones? Nathan went for broke. Maybe he was about to get a fist to the face, but screw it. "Hell yeah. I've been thinking about her ever since I got the bloody assignment."

"That's what I thought. And if I hadn't been in the picture, you would have done what?"

This wasn't happening. "You're a strange bastard, Derrick. I would have asked her out while I was here. But she's not alone. You two are seeing each other. I don't mess with other guys' women, not when they're in a happy relationship."

"She wants you."

The instant silence in the room rang in his ears. Then anger joined his confusion. Maybe Derrick was going to be the one nursing some bruises soon. "What kind of boyfriend are you? Are you trying to pimp her out or what?"

Derrick rose to his full height, which let him peer down at Nathan with a rather intimidating presence. "Shut. Up. That's the farthest thing from what I'm suggesting. God damn it, I'm just—" He turned to slam a fist on the surface of his desk. "*Fuck.*"

He shook his head and dragged a chair over, collapsing onto it as he leaned his elbows on the desk. Nathan waited, ready to bolt, still wondering how the hell this turn of events had happened. He hadn't dreamed it though—Derrick had suggested he let Melanie know he was attracted to her.

Derrick made eye contact before speaking quietly. "She's been self-conscious of her body since the accident. You saw some of that in the gym the other day, but it's not just a cosmetic issue. The questions she used to get from the public are annoying, but it's deeper than that. Some asshole insulted her the first time she attempted sex, and until I came along, she'd been letting her sensuality get buried by fear."

"Shit." The urge to go and rearrange the idiot's face flashed white-hot. "Who was he?"

"Doesn't matter." Derrick pointed a finger in his direction. "What is important is the fact that you turn her on. She's had this major crush on you since she was a teen, and if you had shown disgust in her body and scars, the impact would have been devastating."

Nathan frowned. He'd known about the crush. Kind of been counting on getting to take advantage of that attraction now that they were both grown-ups. "What's wrong with her body?"

Derrick grinned, and the anxiety level in the room dropped. Maybe this wasn't going to end in physical violence. "Exactly— there's nothing wrong, but you're probably the only other guy she knows who sees *her* and not some mass of scarring." He gestured to the chair next to him and Nathan sat. The conversation was unbelievable, and yet made perfect sense.

"That's a screwed-up thing to do to a woman. Melanie went through hell and back physically recovering from the accident. I'd like to find out who the jerk was and make sure he knows better than to hurt someone like that ever again."

"I agree, but at the same time, it's more important to be there for Mel, as satisfying as administering justice would be."

They stared at each other, the gentle sounds of the small town making their way in through the open window. The conversation turned in a new direction, as if there was a connection between them. No longer were they were on either side trying to get Melanie's attention, but on the same side, buoying her up. Nathan took a deep breath. "Now that I'm over my shock, can you try that again? What exactly do you want me from me?"

"I'm not suggesting you do anything you don't want. I'm not telling you Melanie will even agree. The only thing I'm saying is that as her friend, and more, I'm fine with you letting her know how attractive she is. Even if that includes things of a mildly sexual nature. I'm going to be there one hundred percent of the time, but this could be something that helps get her past a tough part of her recovery."

Nathan shook his head. "The whole idea is bizarre. I mean, it makes sense, but it's not anything I've ever heard of before."

"I know, but I think this relationship between Mel and me has the potential to be long term. I'd far prefer to have her face this side issue of her body image with you, someone she trusts, and now, than have her carrying the hurt for longer and have to deal with this shit somewhere down the road."

"You're still a fucked-up bastard, you know that. Right?"

Derrick laughed, slapping his hand on Nathan's knee. "Trust me, I was the first one to realize that."

Unbelievable. Nathan paused, realizing this was one of those moments where he could head down two different paths and his world would be totally different because of his choice.

Only this time, the decision wouldn't only affect him.

Derrick rose to his feet. "We'll be two days in the bush.

Just—act natural." He grinned at Nathan. "Sweet-talk her like you've been doing."

Bastard. "Are you going to tell her what you told me?" Nathan couldn't imagine how to even start that conversation. This one had been freaky enough.

Derrick raised a brow. "When it's needed, yes, but for now, I'd like to just play it by ear. What do you say?"

There was no way he was turning down this opportunity. Nathan let his grin loose. "I'd say Melanie is going to damn well know that she's an attractive woman by the time we get through with her."

Chapter Six

Gumby: A novice climber.

Melanie rolled her head, stretching the tight muscles in her shoulders in an attempt to loosen them. After the drive to the trailhead, the hike, and setting up in their remote campsite, she'd thought they'd take it easy for a few hours, but no... Immediately after lunch Nathan hauled out his camera equipment and started gushing about the light being perfect.

Three hours later, she was praying for clouds.

"Freaking slave driver."

Derrick laughed and dropped his hands on her arms, rubbing in more sunscreen while at the same time pressing so perfectly on her muscles he dragged a groan from her lips. "Nathan's not a bad guy. Not when it comes down to it."

She gave him the evil eye. "You're not the one doing one-hand hangs for half of eternity here, dude."

"Yeah, yeah, life sucks, doesn't it, sweetheart."

She swung at him, and he ducked, grabbing her around the waist and twirling her in a circle until she shrieked with laughter. "Put me down, oh my, Derrick, stop it."

Nathan peeked from behind his tripod, broad grin firmly in place. "Okay, recess is over, children. Time to get back to work."

Melanie gave him her middle finger, then stuck out her tongue. He retaliated by snapping a picture, and she rolled her eyes. "You did not take a picture of that."

"Got one of you flipping me the bird as well. I think I'll blow it up to portrait size and give it to your parents for Christmas."

She stuck her fists on her hips. "Hey..."

He clicked off another shot and she gave up.

"Jackass."

"Monkey."

Melanie spun on the spot and returned to the rock where they were bouldering, her chin held high, letting her hips wiggle as she walked.

She couldn't believe it. Aching muscles or not, she was having the best time ever. It was like a flashback to her climbing days. Joking around and just hanging out with her buds. Nothing serious to accomplish and lots of new routes to try.

While he'd made her pose and not simply lounge around camp, Nathan had been pretty low-key about the whole picture-taking thing, compared to how closely he'd directed them back in the climbing gym. She'd even forgotten he was there as she and Derrick worked one section of the new route—arranging where they had to touch in order to go along the same path. Following a route had always been her favourite climbing activity.

This afternoon, she and Derrick were bouldering. No ropes, nothing farther off the ground than six or seven feet—low enough to stop her anxiety levels from flaring. Just a wonderful, tough physical challenge.

They'd started at the bottom edge of the huge rock, where a section of the base had caved away years ago. The first hand

and footholds they chose placed them face up toward the overhang, butt and back only twelve inches off the crash mat they'd brought with them for safety.

If she fell making the first moves, she wouldn't fall far. And she had lost her grip, a couple times, until she'd figured out how to use the proper leverage to get around the corner and cling with her fingertips to a protrusion that had barely enough space for two fingers. That allowed her to use her stomach muscles, haul up one leg to a hold, cantilever herself to the side and finally make it to the vertical wall to work the next section.

Nathan cut in. "Hurry up, guys. I've got all the pictures I need of you on that hunk of rock. How about getting to the new territory?"

Melanie wrinkled her nose at him. "It's not as easy as it looks, Nathan."

He shrugged. "Whatever."

Oh really? His smirk lit a spark inside—one that wanted to challenge his cocky grin. She had aches in all the right spots, her muscles nice and warm. Melanie paused as she realized she hadn't thought about her scars once in the last couple hours, not even when she'd heated up enough she'd stripped down to her sports bra. The rush of excitement that washed over her made the dare burst out. "I bet you can't do it."

He lowered the extra camera he'd been playing with while waiting for them to carry on. "You've made all of three moves, monkey. Not like it's a huge challenge yet or anything."

"Oh, brother, are you in for it now..." Derrick muttered.

Melanie set her fists on her hips and smiled sweetly. "Put your money where your mouth is. I bet you can't do this route, not even if we show you an easier way."

Nathan sneered. "I'll offer chocolate if I can't."

Oh God, he was so going down.

"Right this way."

Derrick stepped aside and Melanie gestured Nathan forward. He crawled under the overhang willingly and grabbed the handholds.

"Your feet go to the right... Yup, that one. And the other over here."

"Here?"

She giggled. Nathan was tall enough once he did touch the holds he was going to have a hell of a time getting his ass off the mat. "Perfect. Now, lift your hips."

He flexed his muscles and managed to get into the first position.

"Impressive. Now go for it."

Nathan tried, and while he had the strength, he didn't have the technical experience to make the moves. He slipped off the rocks and smacked into the mat, flat on his back.

"Well done. *Not.* Where's my chocolate?"

Nathan blew a raspberry at her. "Patience, monkey. That was only my first attempt."

She shrugged. "First, tenth. Same result."

He set up again, and again. The fifth time his ass hit the mat, she snorted. This was getting more and more entertaining.

"Damn it." Nathan growled.

"He's got the wrong foot pressure." Derrick pointed out.

Melanie checked Nathan's position. "Oh, you're right. Nate, this time, push off with your right foot completely, but keep the left foot on the wall. It will give you the extra reach you need to make the catch."

He leaned his head back and flashed that deadly grin, and

something else warmed inside, not quite so competitive in nature. Damn, the man was a walking advertisement for testosterone and how to use it well. "You're going to have to give me a little help, darling. I was watching through a camera lens before. Where am I reaching?"

She touched his outreached fingers with her own. "You're here. You need to slip your fingers this direction—" She connected with the hold, keeping her elbow in contact with his hand. "See, it's only a few more inches. Course, you should just let me know where the chocolate is now, so I can enjoy it while I watch you fall on your ass another dozen times."

"Ha, ha. I can do this."

"Suit yourself." She stepped back, slipping next to Derrick where he leaned on the neighbouring rock face. He snuck his hands around her waist and tugged her closer, fingers caressing the bare skin at her side with delicate strokes, and her heart rate accelerated.

Nathan fell twice more, but her attention was drawn away by the increasingly intimate caress Derrick applied, sneaking his hands casually higher to brush the sides of her breasts.

"Stop that. You're getting me all tingly," she whispered.

"That's the idea." He chuckled and tugged her directly in front of him, aligning her so the length of his erection pressed between them. "You've been driving me mad. Your ass looks marvelous in those climbing pants."

So much for worrying about needing sexy, skin-revealing outfits to turn him on. "Animal."

"*Snaaarl.*" Derrick nibbled on her neck and Melanie sighed with happiness.

"Damn it, Mel, how the hell did you get around this corner?"

The pitiful question from Nathan interrupted the direction her thoughts were heading—which was fine, since there wasn't going to be much opportunity to get naked with Derrick for a while anyway. Not with them all camping for the night in a single four-man tent.

"Hang on, Nathan, Mel will show you how."

Melanie glanced at Derrick, pulling a mock pout. "I will? Why would I do that?"

"Sportsmanship?"

She narrowed her eyes.

"Come on, give Nathan another chance. He's not as experienced as you are. Go under and demo again." Derrick patted her on the ass.

Melanie planted a quick kiss on his cheek before slipping onto the mat and grinning at a frowning Nathan. "You really think you can do this?"

"I'm close, but I'm missing something."

Five years of practice? "Try again and I'll watch from here."

Lying beside him allowed her to see exactly what he was doing wrong as he extended his torso and attempted to catch the next hold. It also let her see every muscle in his body flex— and while he wasn't as cut as Derrick, it was still a fine view.

He'd been working hard, both earlier in the sun and now, and a fine layer of sweat made his skin shine. She breathed in deeply, the musky scent less dirty and far more arousing than she hoped. Melanie tilted her head back to see Derrick squatting outside the cave area, watching, and she shivered. Why did it feel as if he wasn't keeping an eye on her to make sure nothing happened, but almost as if he hoped something would?

She cleared her throat. "You still aren't using the muscles

in your left leg right."

"I pushed off," Nathan complained.

"You did. But it's not a push you need, it's an extension, and you have to employ your full toe and calf muscle."

Nathan dropped to the mat and groaned. "Show me again."

Mel nodded. "I will, but first, try once more in slow motion, and I'll point out the muscles you need to use."

Nathan set up as she wiggled toward the base of the wall, planting her hand on his thigh before she thought it through.

Oh my God, he was solid. Unyielding muscles flexed under her fingers, and she forced herself to concentrate. "This is where you need to push off, then you can…"

She traced down his calf muscle, caught hold of his ankle and tugged slightly. "Up on your toe. There. That will give you an additional three inches, and that's all you need to reach your goal."

"Additional three inches, hey? Never been told I needed it."

She flushed instantly. What was she supposed to say to in response to that? "Move over and I'll show you one last time."

Nathan dropped then slipped to the side to let her access the first holds.

Melanie dragged her gaze off Nathan, wondering if she'd caught some kind of a flu that made her insanely hot and feverish. There was no excuse for this. She'd told Derrick she found Nathan attractive, but that didn't give her the right to fantasize about the guy right there in front of him.

She lifted her hips and got into position.

"Nate, you'll never see what she's doing from over there. Come over to this side," Derrick ordered.

Melanie's hands nearly slipped off completely when instead of crawling out to come around to her left, Nathan wiggled under her. There wasn't enough room for him to pass by without brushing their bodies together, no matter how close to the rock face she clung.

And it seemed she wasn't the only one feeling the heat. He was most definitely hard more places than his arm and leg muscles. Melanie held her breath as he passed, glancing at Derrick to see just what the hell was going on.

He winked.

Winked?

"Okay, Mel, do a slow-motion reach. Nathan, put your hand on her left thigh and feel how the extension starts—it's not only the thigh, it's the calf as well and the toe as a final move."

Nathan wrapped his warm fingers around her leg. His palm cradled the back of her thigh as he stroked downward.

She tried to concentrate on the climbing move, but her focus was gone. A burning sensation skittered along her nerves in direct opposition to the path of his hand, heat flaring into her core. Melanie slid off the rock and lay still for a moment, heart pounding. This was insane. Impossible. Nathan stared into her eyes, his gaze fixed on her as he flipped his grasp to cover the top of her shin. Inch by inch he smoothed his palm upward. The new grip meant his fingertips tickled the inside of her thigh, edging closer to her sex. Fiery shots raced ahead of his touch, and she bit her lip to stop her panting breaths from escaping and revealing exactly how turned on she was.

Maybe she should ignore him. He was going to stop any second—this was a totally innocent move on his part, and she shouldn't make it dirty simply because she was horny enough to want to strip and crawl all over him—

Sudden energy flashed to her muscles, and she scrambled out from under the rock, crawling crablike away from Nathan. Escaping, retreating. She stood, teetering briefly before a broad body made contact with her.

She spun, squeezed her face tight to Derrick's chest, wrapping her arms around his torso like a tangling vine. If she didn't look at either of them, she could pretend she hadn't just considered letting Nathan King touch her intimately. Fake that the issue was her scars, when this time her damaged body had been the last thing on her mind as she'd lain in the arms of her teenage fantasy.

Derrick stroked her head, his solid body tight in all the right places. Including—*oh my.* He was hard? That in itself wasn't unusual, but now? The timing seemed improbable. He reached under her hips and lifted her, allowing her to cling tighter to his neck, their faces now level.

"Derrick, I—" How to explain? Make an excuse or tell the truth?

He kissed her. So, so tenderly. The moist heat of his mouth as he nuzzled her cheek, her temple, made tears spring to her eyes. One brush passed over her lips. One landed on the tip of her nose before he tilted his head to recapture her gaze. "I think you're a very beautiful woman."

She flushed. He thought she'd freaked over her scars. For a moment she debated taking the easy way out, letting him continue to blame this on her past fears, then guilt hit. If she truly cared about Derrick, and that was the way her heart seemed to be heading, she would not lie about something this important. "I'm sorry."

"For what?"

He'd turned them so her back was to Nathan. What was he doing? Had he followed them? "This whole picture-taking thing is getting to me. I've never felt like this before."

Derrick's dark eyes crinkled at the corners. "Because you feel attracted to Nathan? As well as me?"

"I don't want to hurt you." The confession was barely audible. She might have shared about her past interest in Nathan, but it *was* the past. She didn't want to do anything to screw up her future with Derrick.

He shifted position, adjusting until he found a comfortable rock to sit on. She was in his lap now, resting on his strong thighs. His broad shoulders under her hands were strong and yet relaxed.

"I'm not upset with you." He wrinkled his nose. "I am at a loss for words though, so excuse me if this sounds stupid."

Melanie wiggled upright. "What?"

Derrick's smile had a guilty twist to it. "Mel, you know I find you attractive, but I'm not the only one. Nate thinks you're pretty incredible as well."

Air stuck in her throat. "You... How do you know that?"

The guilty expression spread, becoming more obvious. "We talked about it."

Holy shit. The guys she'd hung around with on the climbing team had talked about girls all the time, but it was locker-room talk. Conquests and game plans. Surely Derrick and Nathan were above that kind of thing. And why was Derrick looking so sheepish?

"You talked about me? What specifically did you discuss?"

A hand brushed her neckline, and she startled, nearly falling off Derrick's lap. Two sets of hands caught her, Derrick's familiar touch on her hips.

Nathan's firm grasp on her shoulders.

"We talked about the fact I can't keep my eyes off of you." Nathan stood close behind her body, heat from his torso making her insides squirm. He loosened his clasp and slid his fingers down her arms, the light stroke causing a reaction in her core similar to putting flame to kindling.

Derrick pulled her hips in tighter until her sex rested against the very apparent ridge of his arousal. "I told him how important you are to me, and he shared how much you've meant to him. As a friend, and someone he greatly admires."

Melanie wasn't sure if she was holding her breath, or if her body was incapable of performing the simple tasks necessary to survival. When Derrick dipped his head, brushing his lips against hers, his kiss gave her something to cling to. She accepted the worship of his mouth even as her mind spun.

The vulnerable sensation rippling through her body had nothing to do with her past injuries. It had everything to do with the rising lust she seemed helpless to resist, the yearning to be caressed by the two men who mattered the most.

A warm hand slipped across her belly, palm in full contact, and she froze. Nathan was touching her. He delicately circled her bare belly button—she had taken out the ring for climbing—before pulling his fingers back to wrap them around her waist. Settling directly on top of her scarred skin.

Oh my God.

Instant fear surfaced, even though she had buried it under layers and layers of barriers. Bile rose to her mouth, in anticipation of the coming agony. Any second now Nathan was going to recoil in disgust, and his response would rip her soul in two. A blur passed in front of her eyes as she waited for the dagger to stab into her heart.

"Breathe, Mel. Come on, I'm here, holding you. There's nothing to be afraid of."

Derrick's voice dragged her back from the wall of anxiety that had rushed up, blocking all possible escape routes but sheer panic. She took a deliberate breath of air through her nose before lifting her gaze to his.

He remained waiting like a rock, something solid to cling to. Still, the mixture of terror and desire clouding her brain made concentration difficult. "He's t-t-touching me."

Derrick nodded. "If you like it, he'll continue to touch you. But only if you want."

"You're a very desirable woman, Melanie." Nathan swept his hand over her abdomen again, ranging higher this time. The tips of his fingers brushed the underside of her breasts and sent jolts of excitement to her nipples, her core.

In spite of the ache in her body, she needed to know. Her heart was fragile—even more fragile than her body had been three years ago as she lay crumpled at the bottom of the hill. Melanie spoke her fears. "I don't understand. Derrick—what's happening? Are we not a couple anymore?"

"Oh, Mel." Derrick cupped her face in his hands. "No, that's not it at all. I need you, I want you, and have no intention of letting you go. But I also care enough about you to give you what you need."

"What I need?" Another gentle pass of Nathan's hand over her sensitive skin caused a shiver that consumed her entire body. "You think I need...Nathan?"

Derrick soothed her, hands and lips petting her softly. "You tell me."

Sunlight wavered around them, the tall trees swaying in the breeze making the shadows dance around the clearing. It was the most peaceful of settings, and she closed her eyes and soaked in the serenity around her to force out the fears rocking her world.

Sexually aroused, emotionally anxious—and stunned by what she grew more certain was love shining in Derrick's eyes.

Melanie twisted until she sat sideways in his lap, both legs dangling to the side. She glanced behind them where Nathan squatted. There was no mistaking the heated interest in his expression as his gaze roamed over her body.

Derrick thought she needed Nathan. Did she? Her first response to him touching her scars had been worlds apart from her reaction earlier in the gym, and on the bouldering wall. Instead of a rush of desire, she'd felt dread.

Why? Why the change?

Because he'd made actual contact. That's when she'd been rejected before.

She touched Derrick's face. "You want me to let him touch my scars. To prove that they don't mean anything."

"To prove your attractiveness is far more than skin-deep."

Even as fast as her heart fluttered, there was a twist of irony in the setup. "This seems a radical form of therapy."

Derrick bumped his nose against her cheek, breathing from the vee of her neck. The warm puff of his breath slid down her skin like a delicious secret. He spoke for her ears alone. "Doing is much better proof than discussing for hours. I'll be right here, and you can say stop whenever you want. Kiss him if you want, touch him, allow him to touch you." He pulled back, staring possessively at her lips. His tone dropped, thick with lust. "And when you've had enough, I'm making love to you until you lose all doubts about how desirable you are."

She squeezed her legs together at the instant response his promise created in her body.

"Do you understand?"

Melanie nodded slowly. It was preposterous. Fantastic. Slightly mad.

Derrick paused. "If this is what you want, it's up to you to take it."

Brilliant. There would be no chance down the road she

could claim this was something she'd felt pressured into. If she wanted, she could act. Make it her decision to step forward to prove herself attractive to more than just one man.

A rush of self-reproach hit. Why *wasn't* being attractive to Derrick enough? He'd been so consistent and caring, and she still hadn't been able to move beyond her limitations. Melanie lifted her lips to his and accepted his kiss. Hard for a moment, both of them affirming their connection, needing proof of it. Derrick eased back, a questioning expression on his face as he waited for her decision.

Having Derrick in her life was the start of healing, but she still felt caged. And it was past time to fix this problem.

This offer—to try and break the final chains that wrapped her in bondage—it was as if a lifeline was being stretched to her. Even though her limbs trembled, she turned to face Nathan, because she damn well needed this for her soul.

"Monkey?" Nathan's knuckles were white where he'd dug his fingers into his thighs as he waited a few feet away. The grass lay crumpled under his knees, a smear of dirt along the edge of his shorts. Patient, and oh-so masculine. No longer the young man she'd lusted after before she even knew what lust was.

She shook her head, casting aside all her childish connections. "I'm not a monkey anymore. I grew up." And the grown-up woman had needs the teenage fantasy couldn't answer.

But the man before her could.

Nathan's response was a skin-tingling, body-melting smile. "I noticed."

She shuffled forward on Derrick's lap, the firm base of his thighs giving her a chair-like base to rest upon that allowed her feet to touch the ground. With one hand she reached for

Nathan, and he moved to accept it.

His fingers were less callused than Derrick's. Not soft, but not the hands of a climber. With her wrist captured, Nathan rotated his hand, delicately holding her palm upward in the circle of his fingers.

"Derrick is right. You can say stop at anytime. I find you very attractive, Melanie Dixon, and I can't wait to prove it. In detail."

She couldn't tear her gaze away. He seemed fascinated with the tendons in her wrist, tracing them with the fingertips of his other hand, inching his way up the sensitive skin of her arm until he made contact with the inside of her elbow. Traveling in conjunction with his touch was a freaky sensation somewhere between being tickled and being held at the edge of a rocking orgasm.

Was it possible to climax without a single sexual touch?

"I want to kiss you, Mel."

He waited for her response, his long dark lashes that she'd envied as a teen lazily fluttering as he stared at her mouth.

A kiss would be good. If she remembered how to talk, she would tell him that. Instead, she managed a nod, and his smile arrived right on cue. He released her wrist, slipping one hand all the way up until he cradled her neck. His other hand dropped to rest feather-light on her thigh.

Nathan leaned in until his mouth made contact with hers, tracing his tongue over her bottom lip tentatively. Even as she pressed closer for more, Derrick's firm grasp reassured her, his thumbs stroking slowly back and forth over the curve of her hipbones, adding to the desire rocking her core.

The situation was bewildering, but the actual increase in her pulse had everything to do with arousal instead of fear and she could have cried because it felt so wonderful.

240

She crushed her lips against Nathan's, not allowing him to remain delicate. His response was immediate—passionate and demanding. He held her head in place and took her mouth by storm. Thrusting with his tongue, biting her lips, rocking the pleasure in her to a higher level in a split second. It was unlike any childish fantasy she'd clung to and, *oh God*, it was good.

The heat behind her confirmed Derrick was still there. That when she'd had enough of Nathan's caresses, her lover was going to make her body sing like he had proven over and over he could—

The line between panic and pleasure blurred further. It might have been fear that started her heart racing in the first place, but it was the sensation of Nathan's hand moving on her thigh that pushed a needy cry from her throat.

Chapter Seven

Crux: The hardest move on a route.

The breathless sound echoed in his ears, and Derrick felt the same damn shiver of lust that occurred when he was the one making Melanie respond. He was a fucked-up bastard—Nathan and Mel's lips were locked together, the man's hands were moving on her body and not one single iota of jealousy registered. If anything, Derrick had gotten harder in the last minute than he'd been before.

He stroked her skin under his fingers, smooth on one side, pocked and marred on the other—there was nothing about her body she had to be ashamed or worried about. If having Nathan touch her could convince Mel of that forever, this was the cure to use.

She gasped again and Derrick tightened his grip on her hips. Centering her, being there for her. Listening for any indicators she wanted to retreat, but even while she leaned away from Nathan's kiss, Melanie reached up to catch hold of his head.

"That was way better than when I was sixteen."

Nathan grimaced. "You weren't supposed to know it was me who gave you that kiss."

She wriggled in Derrick's lap as she laughed. "Oh my God, are you serious? Even blindfolded I knew it was you."

Blindfolded?

Then there was no chance to ask any questions as the train moved forward in a rush.

"Take off your top." Nathan flicked a glance over Mel's shoulder at him then returned his full attention to her. Under Derrick's hands, she'd gone tight. Rigid as a rock wall, and Derrick wondered if Nathan had pushed too hard.

She leaned against his chest and took a deep breath. Nathan waited, silent yet demanding. Derrick was on the verge of speaking—of suggesting this wasn't needed. That he'd made a mistake, when Melanie surprised him.

"Close your eyes," she ordered back, and Nathan complied, snapping them shut. His hands remained resting on her thighs, hunger on his face.

Mel twisted her head. "Derrick, you still with me?"

"All the way, whatever you want." Whatever it took to make her happy. Derrick was more convinced every minute he was in for the long haul.

She nodded, then maneuvered the sports bra from her body, dropping it to the grass beside them. Derrick peeked over her shoulder to admire the tight points of her nipples poking from the rounds of her breasts.

"Hmm, can I touch as well?" he asked, and Melanie reached back and caught his head, tugging until their lips met. Passion rocked through him, a thunderous noise in his ears as they kissed—so right and familiar now, yet new and unique each time. Derrick wrapped his hands around her torso to cup her beautiful breasts. He played with her nipples between forefingers and thumbs, lightly teasing the tips, rolling and tugging and pinching until she moaned.

Moisture touched his fingers, and Derrick swallowed the exclamation she made before pulling back to observe Nathan come in for a second slow swipe over the exposed peak of one breast. Nathan had kept his hands locked on Melanie's thighs, only his mouth touching, tongue darting out to flick the tip again and again.

Derrick adjusted his hold to bare more of her breast, and Nathan took immediate advantage, wrapping his lips around the entire nipple and sucking.

Melanie writhed on Derrick's lap, her ass rubbing his erection as she arched and pressed closer to Nathan's eager mouth. "So good. Yes, like that..."

As Nathan moved his hands up to cradle and caress, Derrick slipped his out of the way, simply enjoying the heat of her in his lap, the brush of her skin against his torso as she continued to lean in his direction. He watched. Assessing, judging, ready to act if her enthusiastic response changed, but there was no need. She caught Nathan by the hand and directed his touch, their fingers linked as she allowed her old friend to brush the damaged skin on her torso, the side of her breast.

More kisses followed, hot and needy, as Nathan took Melanie's lips again. When he leaned away Melanie sucked in air as Nathan's gaze flashed over her body.

"Every inch of you makes me want you. No scars can change how attractive you are. Nothing can."

A hesitant smile crossed her face a split second before he recaptured her lips. Then he kissed his way down her throat and across her collarbone to once more worship her breasts.

A purr of contentment escaped her. Derrick rejoiced. That was what he wanted to hear, to witness. Every inch of her craving sexual release, no thought of her scars or the trauma she'd gone through.

And sexual release she would get. Derrick snuck his hand over Melanie's hip and under the elastic of both her climbing pants and panties. Over the soft curls covering her sex, wetting his fingers in her cream and drawing it higher to rub her clit.

Together he and Nathan took her to the edge of pleasure. They whispered words of admiration, stroked her skin, kissed her bare torso. Nathan bit one nipple then suckled hard, and Derrick took that moment to thrust two fingers into her core.

"Oh *God.*" She squirmed, not in retreat, but to allow them both to reach her better. "More. Please, more."

More? They gave it to her until she gasped for air. Derrick ground the heel of his palm against her clit as Nathan pinched her nipples, kissing her hungrily.

The flush of arousal over her chest heightened in colour, the sounds she made shifting from words to guttural mutterings then moans. Tiny cries and gasps until she went silent, the calm before the storm.

Melanie shook as she came, her sheath pulsing tight around his fingers, a long low keen of satisfaction rising on the air. Nathan dropped his head against her chest, his dark hair covering her skin, his breath escaping in rapid gasps. Derrick clung to his own sanity for a moment. He needed her like crazy.

More than that, he needed to finish this as a couple, not a trio. He wasn't about to toss Nathan in the dirt, not after he'd given so willingly to Melanie, but the next step was going to be him and her, alone. Urgent desires and violent passion swirled inside, and Derrick caged them both as he waited for the right moment. This was for her.

She relaxed, boneless in his lap, one arm rising to cling to his neck, the other reaching out so she could brush her knuckles over Nathan's cheek.

"Wow."

Nathan grinned. "You liked that?"

She laughed, sitting up to deliver a quick kiss over Nathan's lips. "I liked it a lot. But I need—"

She glanced over her shoulder and Nathan hummed. "You need time with Derrick. No worries." He rocked away, slowing his breathing.

Melanie twisted to curl up in Derrick's lap, as if a bird seeking shelter. She tucked her face into his neck, and he hoped she wasn't retreating. Then he realized this time she hadn't hid the scarred side of her torso from Nathan's gaze.

The two men locked eyes. It wasn't a complete cure, but it was a step in the right direction. Derrick dipped his chin and Nathan nodded acknowledgment.

Melanie burrowed her hands under Derrick's shirt and scratched his back, and the rush of need that assaulted him nearly tossed him to the ground. It tore open his barely contained ardour. Foreplay was over and there was only one place this was going. He lifted Melanie into the air as he stood, leaving Nathan behind with their gear.

Melanie sighed, resting her head against Derrick's chest, the heavy thumping of his heart rhythmic in her ear. Every step he took rocked her body against him. "That was simply—"

"Don't talk." The words were ground out so low and guttural she peeled herself away to see what was wrong. He shook his head, his nostrils flaring as he carried her back to the wilderness campsite they'd set up. She forced her lips together to keep from blurting out her questions.

He dropped her on the solid wood of the picnic table, and she bounced as her butt landed on the flannel cloth she'd spread earlier.

"Take off your pants," he ordered.

Derrick ripped off his shirt, the rigid planes in his abdomen flexing as he reached for the snap on his pants.

It wasn't anger driving him. Relief shot through her, and she remembered his promise from earlier. As stupid as it was, shyness hit and she glanced toward the trees where Nathan remained. "But—"

"Now."

She'd never seen this side of Derrick before. Need and desire pulsed from him like a tangible thing. His hands were on her pants before she could protest again, stripping the fabric away. He tugged her to the edge of the table then buried his face between her legs.

Crazy emotions jumbled together with her instant physical response to his touch. His tongue drove her mad as he took possession of her hips and forced her into a position he liked better.

Melanie let her worries and concern wash away as Derrick brought her back up to the verge of another release so rapidly she thought she'd have trouble ever taking a full breath again. Every time she attempted to fill her lungs, he thrust into her core and made her gasp with pleasure. When he exchanged his fingers for his tongue, her sheath wrapped tight around him and her desires whipped into a frenzy. The cloudless sky overhead spun in a circle as an orgasm washed her from toes to brows, and her mind went numb.

Then he stood, dropped his pants and slammed his cock into her with one thrust.

"Derrick!"

He supported her knees in the air, her thighs lifted to

vertical as he pounded his groin against her body. Every thrust powerful and deep, stretching, filling her to capacity. Making her weep with want.

"So. Fucking. Beautiful. Every bit of you."

He stopped, cock buried in her core. His eyes flashed, dark obsidian globes backlit with the fire of passion. He ran his hands up and down her thighs, tiny rocks of his hips keeping the intimate connection going, but dragging the sensory overload farther into her extremities. When he pushed her knees toward her chest and leaned over her, his cock pressed even deeper.

A whimper escaped.

Derrick stopped instantly. "Mel?"

"Oh, *God*, do that again." More. He'd have her begging if he didn't move.

Slow, tortuously slow. His deliberate control as he withdrew caused the wide head of his shaft to stroke all the sensitive places inside her.

"I couldn't stand it anymore. I needed you," he confessed.

Another plunge forced a gasp from her lips. "Need you too. Oh please, Derrick."

The teasing edged her back up like a sizzling fuse. Her climax hovered just out of reach. Melanie grabbed her knees, folding herself in a virtual pretzel. Giving him everything. Begging without words for him to continue.

He grinned, the flash of his teeth bright against his tanned skin.

"You like this?"

She couldn't speak. Forced herself to nod.

He sped up slightly, strokes still long and powerful. "Even better?"

She opened her mouth as he snuck his fingers between their bodies and found her clit. He pressed the aching nub between his fingers and buried his cock deep.

Melanie closed her eyes to concentrate on just how damn good it felt. "Oh, yes. Do that."

It wasn't an easy position for either of them, but she'd lost her fear of where they were and could only sense what she needed. What they both needed.

Each other.

The boards were solid under her back, the sun heated their naked skin. The summer-turning-to-fall scent floated past on the light breeze. All her senses seemed to be turned on high, even the taste of the air more robust than usual. She should have been cold with all her exposed flesh, but there wasn't an inch of skin that wasn't steaming hot.

She opened her eyes to meet Derrick's, and this time, it was the tenderness she saw that made her dissolve. The physical connection between them was good, but it was that something extra that made sex magical. Tipped her over the edge, made her fall in headfirst, her body's response pulling him along, her heart succumbing as well.

Nathan remained motionless, indecision locking his limbs. Hard physical need urged him to follow—to demand more from Melanie. He'd barely gotten a taste of her, and what he'd experienced wasn't nearly enough.

But when she twined herself around Derrick and the man carried her away, Nathan hesitated. This wasn't about him, never had been. The whole insane scenario had been for Melanie's sake.

He collapsed back onto the grass, arms flung to the side, willing the blood that had pooled in his erection to vanish.

249

Pleading for the images in his brain to fade enough he could get to his feet without the violent desire to interrupt the lovers and throw himself into the action again.

A slow roll allowed him to crawl to his knees, then fight his body to vertical. There was a distinct lack of blood in his brain as he found himself picking his way through the woods toward where they'd made camp. Responsibility motivated him—he needed to make sure Melanie was okay. He hadn't believed the idea was a great one in the first place. Letting her know he was attracted to her? That was easy. But Derrick should have known Melanie wasn't the type to want to fool around. This could have been a huge mistake, no matter how much he'd enjoyed touching her. No matter how much more he wanted to experience.

He pushed aside a branch and froze. He'd been a fair distance behind, intending to give them space, let them settle and talk things through. Only the sight that greeted him wasn't the two in deep conversation, or Melanie in tears. Instead her naked body was arched in ecstasy as Derrick lapped at her pussy like a starving man.

Nathan had forgotten that part of the discussion.

Her moans of delight did what Nathan thought was impossible—made his dick hard again. She'd teased him unintentionally all day, but seeing her spread out and in physical rapture?

He stepped back into the shadows and rubbed his palm over the fly of his pants, attempting to soothe his aching hard-on.

The erotic tableau before him evolved again. Derrick thrust into Melanie's sweet body, and by instinct Nathan's hips jerked.

Fuck it. He lowered his zipper and pulled out his cock, finally able to see straight as the pressure eased. There was nothing to distract him as he stared, mesmerized, letting the semen escaping from his cock ease his hand on his shaft. There was nothing light and delicate about his touch. He bucked into his fist matching the tempo of Derrick's hips, and with everything in him, Nathan wished he could feel Melanie surround him. Experience her wet heat, the tight pressure squeezing on his cock. Touch her body and let her muscles drag him over the edge.

It was dirty and gritty, being a voyeur, and yet he couldn't tear his eyes away. So much for apologizing for his earlier behaviour—he was ready to explode just imagining being intimate with her. Thrusting like a madman into the woman who had taunted his dreams.

Derrick rearranged Melanie's limbs, and the view got even better. Nathan had a clear visual line on every plunge, every snap of Derrick's hips against her ass. The sounds she made were enthusiastic and vigorous, carrying on the air to where he stood.

It wasn't enough. He wanted to be the one making her moan. Sucking on her breasts, licking in endless circles over her skin until she screamed in pleasure. He closed his eyes and thrust harder, his balls dragging higher to his body until the spark of fire flashing up his spine exploded out his cock.

Holy. Crap. Nathan pumped into his fist, strands of semen spurting out to coat his fingers, splay over the plants at his feet. His legs grew shaky, and he barely managed to catch hold of the nearest tree to keep upright.

Of course that was the moment Melanie shouted, Derrick's cry overlapping hers only a second behind. Nathan automatically thrust again, even with nothing left to spill. Feverish heat raced over him, all sweaty and sticky and void of all mental ability.

251

What the hell had just happened?

Nathan staggered a pace or two, propping his back against a tree. His breathing was ragged. His softening cock hung in the air while his pants flapped around his knees. There was a sweet twittering as birds floated past. Branches wiggled—probably from a squirrel or some other kind of small animal. He was surrounded by the freaking animal kingdom, and he'd just shot his brains out the end of his dick.

"I am so fucked."

Nathan forced himself upright. Scrambled to put everything in place. Finding his footing wasn't as easy, then he remembered the equipment still left at the boulder. He should go back. Retreat and gather their gear. Give Melanie and Derrick time to clean up and get themselves together.

That's what he should do, but the temptation to witness the conclusion of the story was too great. He twisted and stared at the picnic table. Derrick had pulled Melanie to a sitting position, and they were kissing tenderly, bodies still joined. The portrait was incredible—sexual, explicit and affectionate all at the same time.

An unfamiliar emotion stabbed deep. Even as Nathan admired how well the lovers suited each other, while he appreciated the esthetic beauty of the contrast of feminine and masculine bodies, the ache inside had nothing to do with missing a great photo op.

Nathan whirled. He staggered unsteadily for a second before catching his balance and making his way back to the boulder to gather their abandoned equipment. Maybe if he kept himself busy he'd be able to ignore the truth. Wanting to have more physical contact with Melanie was explainable, both from the perspective of their past history and general male admiration for a beautiful woman. But it was the unmistakable signs that the other two were falling in love that made him insanely jealous.

He was honest enough to admit that while he didn't want her forever, the connection Derrick and Melanie shared was looking more desirable than he'd ever imagined.

Chapter Eight

Epic: A really big adventure.

Derrick sent Melanie into the tent to find clean clothes while he wrapped a towel around his hips. He got a big pot of water boiling and laid out supper supplies. Cleaning up from their escapade would be a little tougher in the outdoor setting than it would have been at home with hot showers, but the whole experience had been too spectacular to complain about the extra work.

A soft cough brought his attention to the edge of the clearing where Nathan stood, hands full of gear. "Is it safe?"

A mix of guilt and gratitude washed over Derrick. "Nate. Come on. I've got things started for our meal."

He gestured toward the table and Nathan deposited the collection of belongings they'd left behind.

Derrick smiled with approval as he picked out Melanie's top. "I didn't expect her to go for it that quick," he confessed.

"So, everything's okay?"

The unusual tone in Nathan's voice drew Derrick's attention upward. The other man's bright smile was absent, and Derrick hurried to reassure him. "Everything's aces. Mel's great, and I have no issues. You?"

Nathan glanced toward the tent before sitting on the bench and speaking quietly. "She's an incredible woman, Derrick, and I can see why she means so much to you. That indomitable spirit I always admired—she's still got it."

Pride and possessiveness swelled in Derrick. "Her fears are being taken down one by one. You did a good thing earlier. Thank you."

Nathan snorted. "Trust me, it wasn't a hardship." He paused, although Derrick could see he longed to say more.

"What?"

"Is that it? I mean, how do you expect me to act for the rest of the trip?"

Oh hell. "Like do I assume you're not to touch her anymore?"

Nathan nodded.

It only took a moment to consider. "You know what? I don't think I'm the one you need to ask." God, this was tough. Derrick wanted nothing better than to say hands-off, but the reasons he had suggested this scenario in the first place still applied. Once was not a cure. And he had to admit, it had been pretty hot seeing Melanie that turned on. "Keep playing it by ear. I'm not going to kill you in your sleep, and if Mel wants this trip to continue with both you and I paying attention to her—I'm willing to give her what she wants. You?"

The playboy's grin was back, even though the smile didn't seem to reach Nathan's eyes. "As long as she's willing. I find I'm a glutton for punishment."

The zipper on the tent opened and both of them swung to look. Melanie's hair stuck up in a tousled mess as she poked her head out the front flap. Her gaze snapped to Nathan, her cheeks flushed bright.

Derrick waited. It felt like he'd been doing a lot of that lately.

"Can I have a washcloth, please?"

Nathan rose and stepped to Derrick's side. "I'll take over supper prep. Give her a hand. Can I use a little of that water as well?"

Derrick nodded, pouring a container half-full and adjusting the temperature with cold water from another jug on the ground. "There's another bowl in the rubber tote by the table. Help yourself. Just give us a few minutes."

He left the tent unzipped to let in more light and allow the fresh breeze to play over them. Melanie waited with her arms curled around her legs, the vivid red spots on her cheeks making her look healthy and full of life.

Derrick stroked her cheek, loving how heat radiated off her. "Lay back, sweetheart, and let me help you."

The washcloth remained warm even after he wrung out the moisture, and as he slid it over her, she relaxed on the sleeping bag, a contented expression playing over her face. One long, satisfied sigh escaped her lips. "That feels marvelous."

"How you doing? Did I wear you out?"

"Not completely. I'm still up for more climbing this evening."

He rinsed the cloth a few times, enjoying the chance to wash every inch of her so intimately—her total trust in him clear as she watched him intently.

"I told Nathan the rest of the trip—what happens is up to you."

"I heard."

Derrick put aside the cloth and lay next to her, his head supported on an elbow as he stared admiringly into her face. "Is that okay?"

She nodded, then pulled him down for a slow kiss that reassured him the fires between them weren't going to stay banked for long.

They dressed, crawled out of the tent, joined Nathan at the table—all normal activities and far more comfortable than it could have been. Melanie laid a hand on Nathan's shoulder for a moment before seeming to change her mind and wrapping him in a huge bear hug. The man's pleased smile lifted Derrick's heart.

Whatever happened, they were all in it together.

After a bite to eat, they went back to climbing. Nathan snapped photos. He stopped at times to join in and attempt a few moves. They talked non-stop—about Nathan's previous assignments, his travels. Derrick shared climbing stories. Melanie's laughter flowed easily. The whole situation was easy and comfortable, like three good friend sharing time together. Nothing more than casual hugs and easy caresses occurred between them, but more importantly in Derrick's mind, Melanie allowed pictures to be taken regardless of whether her scars were in the picture or not.

She was slowly accepting. Hesitantly opening up more.

They called it quits for the day when the sun started to fade around eight, and made their way back to the campsite to grab a snack.

The discussion ebbed and flowed. Derrick rearranged one of the logs in the fire. Bright sparks flashed upward, and Melanie *oohed* in delight. Derrick took his seat on the blanket they'd draped over the ground, and she crawled into his arms. Quiet peace settled as he stroked her hair and the back of her neck. Streaks of brilliant sunset filled the western sky, and the red glow of the fire added a layer of intimate relaxation to the setting.

He squeezed the arm he'd wrapped around Melanie's shoulders then turned to face the other man. "Spill the beans, Nate. You never did explain how you ended up in the middle of a game of spin-the-bottle with Melanie."

Nathan shook his head, firelight reflecting in his eyes. "Stupidest move ever. I was back from college for the holidays and wandered downstairs to discover Katy's Christmas party had devolved to the point of darkened lights and giggles in the corners of the room. I slipped out of sight as fast as I could, but I didn't know they were doing some weird variation on the kissing game. They had planted girls in each of the downstairs rooms and blindfolded them."

Melanie held up a hand in protest. "We were trying to make it less embarrassing for the people who didn't get picked to be kissed. It was your sister's idea."

Derrick laughed. "Let me guess. You walked into a room and found Mel."

Nathan swirled a finger around his head, as if wrapping it with something. "And they'd covered her eyes completely, so she had no idea it was me and not one of her teenage boyfriends."

"That's what you thought," Melanie muttered.

"It's true. You finally squeaked out like a mouse and asked why I wasn't kissing you."

"Not a mouse. Just trying not to give away I knew it was you. Because there was a slight chance you might kiss me if you *thought* I didn't know it was you."

"Bullshit."

Melanie slapped Nathan on the knee. "Dude, none of my

'boyfriends' were old enough to have five o'clock shadow. Plus there was that scent—probably only deodorant, but I knew the type you wore. I smelled it the instant you opened the door."

Nathan groaned as he rubbed his temples. "Shit."

She smirked. "Anyway, he finally stopped being a chicken and kissed me. Never slipped me any tongue, much to my dismay, but he held the back of my neck, and I think I nearly came from that alone. It was as if I'd stuck my finger in a light socket and gotten an electric zap that went all the way down to my toes."

Derrick laughed as Nathan pretended to be electrocuted, shaking his limbs and torso rapidly. Melanie smiled happily at Derrick, her body warm and intimate with his. She reached for his hand, linking their fingers together.

Derrick basked in the obvious connection she was making with him.

"I'm sorry I ruined all your teenage fantasies." Nathan winked, then poked the fire thoughtfully.

Her tongue slipped out to moisten her lips a second before she spoke. "Well, we all have to grow up sometime."

She turned and brought her lips next to Derrick's. The warmth of her breath washed his cheek, and she brushed her lips against him before whispering in his ear, "I want to make love to you by the fire."

Oh hell. His dick flashed to rock hard, the images of flickering light dancing over her bare skin driving up his lust. "And Nathan?"

She drew back far enough to look Derrick in the eye. "I want him to take pictures. For his book."

Was it hypocritical his mind protested the idea of being on display like that while he longed to see *her* naked in the firelight? "Of us making love? That sounds rather kinky."

Melanie rolled her eyes. "Well, I don't want to make a porn flick, but if he can take pictures and make them—presentable—I'm game. If he's interested."

A sharp gasp escaped Nathan. "Are you serious?"

Melanie nodded. "Serious. Nate—" She paused, then the rest of her words rushed out. "I've thought about it all evening. I like you, and you turn me on, but it's Derrick I want to be with."

Derrick's heart swelled. Her confession made everything that much brighter.

Nathan touched his fingers to her cheek. "And I have no trouble with that. Honest. I like you too, and I understand."

She broke free and stood, stepping to the edge of the firelight and grinning at them both even as her chest continued to heave. "Tell me what to do."

"Monkey, you've just made my year. Let me grab my camera bag." Nathan leapt up and scrambled toward his gear. Derrick glanced at Melanie thoughtfully.

"You sure about this?"

She nodded. "I've been trying to force another panic attack, and it's not happening. Being with you two has been perfect. Since this photo shoot means a lot to Nathan, I thought this might be a good time. I loved those shots he showed us earlier. I really, really want to try this."

Derrick leaned back on the cushioned log, letting his admiration for her show. "Then I really, really want to see you naked."

She looked out from under hooded lashes. "Even if it means you might be in some of the shots?"

Nathan had said all the pictures would be theirs to veto. "I get to make love with you. How could there possibly be a downside to this scenario?"

He stripped off his T-shirt before rising to his feet and reaching out a hand. She slipped into his arms so perfectly, the soft flannel of her shirt teasing his naked chest as he held her tight to his torso. One hand he spread wide over the curve of her lower back, with the other he reached up and caught her neck. Nibbling along her jaw, sneaking up on her lips to make her his. It was going to be his touch that took her all the way to paradise.

Beside them, Nathan drifted like a helpful specter, rearranging the heavy blanket closer to the fire, smoothing it out. Then he moved in one last time and kissed Melanie's shoulder, stroking his fingers down her back. "Have fun, kids."

He faded out of the light. Became only a darkened figure in the background, another of the flickering shadows dancing in their peripheral vision. Derrick forgot he was there. Forgot everything except the woman before him and the fact she wanted him.

One button at a time he opened her shirt, the smooth glow of her skin between the swathes of fabric appearing golden in the firelight. She hadn't pulled on a bra. Derrick's mouth watered as he stepped back to admire her.

Melanie's gaze caught his, trapped him. Held him like an animal mesmerized in a bright light. Only the light came from within her as she shrugged off her shirt and let it fall to the ground. His gaze dipped to her naked breasts, peaked nipples revealing her own arousal.

"Take it off," he ordered. Derrick palmed his erection, rubbing forcefully to give a moment's respite from the aching need he had to fill her completely. "Take it all off and show me how incredible you are."

The hesitation she'd shown a few days previous had vanished. She snuck her fingers into the waistline of her pants and slid them down, stepping out from the puddle of fabric. Her skin glowed in the firelight, and even the smooth flawless right half of her torso was dappled with patchy colour from the flickering flames. The tiny pair of panties she wore covered only the smallest part of her mound, silky ribbons all that held the sides over her hips.

Derrick panted with urgency as she turned, displaying her ass, a single strip of fabric disappearing between her cheeks. Some women could wear a thong well—and *hot damn*, Melanie was one of them. He longed to cup her ass cheeks in his hands. To rub the muscular swells and cradle them in his palms. To nip and bite his way along the crease between her leg and ass. To lick everywhere until she screamed in pleasure.

"You like what you see?" Melanie played with the ribbons on the sides of her panties. Teasing him, making him so mind-fogged he was ready to forget everything except being inside her now. One side at a time she tugged the knots loose. The scrap of material dropped to the ground, leaving her completely bare to the elements. The fire's illumination spotlighted her.

He kicked off his shoes, stripped off his pants. Methodical. Brainless repetition, since the only thing on his mind was her. And not her body, but her soul.

"It's not just what I see that turns me on, Mel." Naked, Derrick stepped onto the blanket, his erection slapping his belly. He cupped her face in his hands. "It's what's inside that makes me crazy about you."

If it were possible, the light in her eyes grew even brighter.

He made love to her, the warmth of their bodies forcing back the cooling night air. Even the fire's heat faded as he touched her, stroked her to a higher pitch. Licking and sucking, caressing her breasts, the smooth slope of her belly. Priming and readying her for when he could wait no longer. They slipped together in one blissfully perfect moment, him surrounded, her accepting. The fire crackled and snapped as she moaned out her pleasure, calling louder on each progressive thrust. Melanie lifted her heels, dug them into his ass to help slam him into her core until there was no hope of retreat and only an explosion to experience.

Derrick stared into her eyes as she came, bliss causing her focus to blur. Then she shoved him over the edge as well, her sheath constricting around him so hard his climax ripped loose. Pulse after pulse of pleasure beat through him. Nothing remained but the connection between them that stole his ability to think. He clung to his sanity long enough to lower himself beside her instead of crushing her under his weight. Still connected, still intimately joined, he stroked her skin as she smiled sweetly at him. It took a long time for their breathing to return to normal as their bodies came down off the incredible high of passion.

But one thing was never going back to the way it had been before. Derrick wondered if the fact he'd fallen in love would be written on his every move from this moment forward.

Chapter Nine

Choss: Rotten rock—looks solid and safe, but is actually brittle and dangerous.

Melanie pulled up to the front of her rental, confused by the sight of her big brother Kane's truck parked outside.

"Do you want us to wait here?" Derrick asked.

"No, you may as well help me carry my gear inside before we nab some supper. There's no way I'm cooking, and I don't think there's much in the fridge anyway."

Nathan grabbed her duffle bag off the backseat and winked at her. "Dinner's on me."

She returned his smile easily. There was nothing awkward between them, and she was so thankful. Even Saturday night, after she and Derrick had basically stripped and gone for it in front of the man, she'd experienced no discomfort. Sharing the tent with the three of them, breakfast and the hike out—all of it companionable and relaxed, and it was due to Nathan's easygoing attitude. She knew it, Derrick knew it. Nathan was there, a part of their time, but not a challenge to their relationship, and grateful seemed an understatement for what Melanie felt.

It wasn't just the ease between the three of them that made

her giddy. They'd stopped to fill her car, and she'd suddenly become aware she was chatting to Derrick out the window as he pumped gas, her bare arm resting in plain sight on the open window ledge.

Someone had wandered past en route to paying at the kiosk, glanced at her and continued without another look.

There were no words to describe what a rush that was—to not have panic hit. To not want to hide.

She was still grinning from ear to ear when she opened her front door and ushered the guys into her small rental house. Kane rose from her couch, his face a storm ready to happen.

"Hey you, what you doing?" Melanie dropped her climbing bag on the countertop and headed to give him a hug.

"Waiting. I didn't think you were going to be this late." He nodded curtly at Derrick, eyed Nathan with suspicion. "You guys have good climbing conditions?"

"It was great. We got the pictures we needed for the article as well." And she had slept fantastic after all the attention, sexual and otherwise, but she wasn't about to tell her brother that part.

Kane glared at Nathan but spoke to her. "Did you sign anything? Do you have to let him keep the pictures?"

A small bubble of her happiness burst. His unexpected and harsh tone confused her. "Why are you asking that? What's wrong?"

"What's wrong is that Mr. Big Shot Photographer over there has been feeding you a line, and I'm worried."

"Nathan? He's working for *Rave*—"

"Right. A 'where are they now' update to show how far people have come since their tragedies. Well, the first story in the series was in this weekend's magazine and it's nowhere near the inspirational thing you told me Nathan was looking for."

Nathan stepped forward. "What are you accusing me of?"

"I don't know, maybe setting my sister up?" Kane snapped. "The article was supposed to be something Melanie could be proud to be involved with. If this is your idea of good publicity, then you're going to be in a great deal of pain when I'm done with you."

Holy shit. Melanie stepped between her brother and Nathan. "Kane, stop. What are you talking about?"

He slapped a magazine into her hand. It was folded open to a page with bold pictures. The photos were gorgeous, a celebration of light and shadow. She recognized Nathan's work from the test shots he'd done for her.

Nathan moved to her side. "What's wrong? My photos are good."

"The pictures are great, the story is crap," Kane growled. "It's dark and bitter, and more like a *National Enquirer* or a scandal sheet than anything else. The man was supposed to be making a comeback from a drunk-driving accident—turns out he's the one who was drunk, and the article shows he's even more of a loser than before the incident."

"Oh, come on, so just because someone else in the series hasn't done as well as Melanie, that's my fault? My byline is on the photos, not the story."

"Yeah, but it seems that you'd be in on the whole series concept. What do they intend to write about Mel?"

Nathan shook his head. "What I shared was what I was told—it's all supposed to be positive stuff. I had no information about the guy in this article other than clicking the shots, so don't make me out to be some kind of evil villain."

Melanie had had enough. She swung to Nathan's defense. "Kane, stop it. Stop it right now. I trust Nathan. We not only go way back, but we've talked a ton over the past couple days, and I know he'd never do anything to hurt me."

Kane glared at Nathan for another moment before turning on Derrick. "And you—I thought you were my friend until I had an eye-opening conversation with Jack. How the hell could you think taking another guy into her bed would be a good thing for Melanie? What kind of asshole are you?"

She couldn't believe what she was hearing. She held out a hand to stop Derrick from answering. "Oh my God, Kane, you did not just say that. How dare you stick your nose into my personal life?"

"It's true though, isn't it? You fooled around with them both this weekend."

The fact she hadn't actually slept with Nathan was none of Kane's business. "Derrick's number-one focus has always been what's best for me."

"Letting another guy into your relationship? That's not how a man who cares about you acts, Mel."

The implied insult that she wasn't capable of making her own decisions was more than enough to ignite Melanie's temper. "Oh, like you're the one to give me shit. You're sleeping with Dara, and so is Jack. How it that any better? In fact, if anything it's even weirder because you and Jack are like best friends. Don't be a bloody hypocrite."

"We both had a long-term relationship with Dara before we stepped into anything physical. You've only been with Derrick for a couple months, and he's already inviting another guy into the action? When you don't know how long the dude will stick around or what his real motivations are? It's not the same."

"Butt the hell out, big brother."

"I *am* your big brother. I care about you and I don't want to see you hurt."

"This isn't about you. Holy *crap*, you have no idea, do you?" Melanie shook her hands in his face before stepping back. Nathan had retreated slightly, standing uneasily by the edge of the living room. Derrick waited at her side, a dark tower of barely contained simmering rage. She crossed her arms over her chest and glared at her brother. An emotional explosion trembled on the horizon. She lowered her volume to emphasize her words. "You have no idea how much pain I've been in over the past couple years. Not physical, but mental. How I could barely make it out of bed some mornings because I was sure someone would find a way to remind me I wasn't what I used to be. That I was lacking."

Kane's face had gone pale under his summer tan. "I didn't know it had been so bad."

She hadn't finished. Slowly over the past week all her burdens had come unraveled, been lifted from her, and being able to vocalize what a relief she experienced made her voice tremble. Melanie lifted her chin defiantly, directing a fierce look in his direction. "Well, after this weekend *I* know I'm not less of a woman than I was before the accident. I had two gorgeous guys lavish attention on me, and it felt damn good. They gave me physical proof that not only was I strong and brave, and all those things, I was desired. Lusted after, even, and *by God,* it was amazing."

All Kane's bluster disappeared, and he seemed to struggle to get the words out. "I...I don't know what to say."

Guilt radiated from him, but that wasn't enough to wipe away his interference or the other hurt his words had caused. She turned her back on him for a moment to lay a calming hand on Derrick's arm and speak quietly. "Thank you for letting me deal with this."

Derrick nodded, the tension in his body relaxing a notch. "Your battle, but let me know when you need backup. By the way..." He leaned in closer. "You're spectacular when you're pissed."

Oh God. The flash of amusement his words caused smothered a huge section of anger still burning inside her. Impulsively, she wrapped her arms around his broad chest to hug him tight. How did he do that? Offer exactly what she needed to hear? "You are so perfect."

He rested his chin on the top of her head for a moment as he squeezed. Derrick was a rock, her rock. Solid, and completely there for her. Not to take over her life, but to provide a firm place to stand while she took back control.

She was falling in love harder by the minute.

Melanie turned to face her brother. He'd meant well—she needed to remember that—but it was well-meaning friends and family who had caused a lot of her pain. "There's nothing else to say, Kane. There was nothing you could do to fix it, so I kept it to myself."

Kane looked wearily around the room as he dragged a hand through his hair. He took in Nathan, standing alone to the side. His gaze lingered on Derrick and the way he held her close. "Okay. You're right. You're right, and I need to butt out. But Mel...if you do need me in the future, tell me. Please."

She sniffed, her throat tight with emotion. "I will."

He glanced again at Nathan. "Anything, including shit like breaking knees. I know how to make someone disappear so they'll never find the body."

Yup, that sounded like her family. She forced out a laugh. "Have shovel, will use it? Kane. It's going to be okay. I really do trust Nathan."

"I'm looking out for her too. Stop being an ass toward both your sister and me. Damn idiot." Derrick's deep rumble made Melanie hide a smile.

"Yeah, well, I'm still not sure I approve of you dating her, so don't push it, spider-boy." Kane hesitated then held out his arms. Melanie slipped from Derrick's embrace to give her brother a quick hug.

Kane took his leave with only a few more suspicious glances directed Nathan's way.

And then, they were alone.

Melanie made herself busy, unpacking and tucking her camping gear into the storage chest in the corner. Some of her bright happiness had disappeared, clouded by Kane's accusations, but she figured it would pass. She just needed a few minutes to get her brain back on target and remember the past thirty-six hours.

An incredible thirty-six hours. It seemed too short a time for the changes she felt inside to have occurred.

"I swear, Mel, I knew nothing about this." Nathan had the article in hand and a huge frown marring his face.

Shit. She hurried to his side and tugged the magazine from his fingers, tossing it to the couch. "I said I believed you. Nate— you've never been the kind of guy to go around hurting others. I don't think you're going to start with me."

"But what if—"

"What if *what*? What could they print that could possibly hurt me anymore?" A huge sweep of emotions rushed her again. Incredible gratitude was the most prevalent, and that's what made the words easy to say. "'On the outside, Melanie Dixon appears to have healed, but in reality, she's still a mess of scars.' Nathan, if they had done this article even a few months ago that would have been true."

"Oh, Mel."

The late-afternoon sun shone in the windows, lighting the tiny living room. Derrick sat on her well-worn couch, his dark eyes watching her intently, his body poised and alert. As if ready to leap to her side on a moment's notice, to either guard and protect, or to care for her more intimately. Nathan's eyes revealed his deep desire to provide her the assurances he thought she still needed.

What she needed now was not what she'd required a day ago. Healing had arrived and it felt incredible.

"But, guys, it's not a few months ago. It's not even yesterday. It's today, and right here and right now, I'm not the same woman. Because of both of you."

She'd been turned inside out over the past two days. Stripped bare, in more than one way. Discovering she'd fallen in love with Derrick had filled her heart to the top with hope and happiness. Yet somehow, Nathan had done the impossible. He'd made the scars fade more than she ever thought possible.

The two of them had done it—Derrick by being willing to ask, Nathan by giving unselfishly. She couldn't let things end this way. She wanted to give back to them both, the two men she'd come to care for so deeply.

Empty Chinese food containers littered the floor around them. Contentment and warmth filled him as Derrick watched Melanie pull another laugh from Nathan.

When she'd made them grab takeout instead of eating at the restaurant, he'd wondered what was going on. Then she'd sweet-talked him into opening the gym so they could haul out mats and set up their own private smorgasbord, and it had made even less sense.

Until she'd started provoking Nathan. There was no way the man could continue to be gloomy over Kane's accusations, not with Melanie applying her full power to teasing him.

She was a live wire—sheer vitality radiated from her every move. Not sexual in nature, but simple all-out energy.

He was going to explode with happiness. Seeing the woman he'd always knew she was emerge—it was a miracle, and he'd gotten to watch it occur. The barriers and walls were gone, her liveliness turned way up past high.

Melanie Dixon was a power to be reckoned with, and he was madly in love with every enthusiastic inch.

Derrick leaned on an elbow and enjoyed the interplay snapping between the other two.

"Like that's a threat, monkey girl."

"Oh yeah? You're a good one to talk. Couldn't even finish a basic 5.5 route."

Nathan sniffed. "I'm an *artiste*, not a jock."

Melanie tackled him back to the mat and tickled him.

"Stop it, not on a full stomach. I call *deliberate cruelty*. Derrick, make your woman stop picking on me."

Derrick wasn't getting in the middle of this fight. "Hey, if she's happy, who am I to hold her back?"

Melanie nodded curtly, a smug expression on her face as she straddled Nathan's chest. "See? If I'm happy, then all is good with the world."

She swung off Nathan and plopped to her butt next to him on the mat before turning to face Derrick and winking.

His face ached from smiling so much. "Okay, sweetheart. What do you have next on the agenda? I can't believe you wanted to eat here for the incredible ambiance."

"Hey, I like ropes."

Derrick managed to not choke on his own spit. Oh, the images in his brain.

She knelt, the tip of her pink tongue poking out to wet her lips for an instant as she glanced between them. "I meant it, guys. What I told Kane. You've made a huge difference in my life."

It wasn't what she said, but how she said it that made Derrick's pulse pick up. The light-hearted teasing was gone, replaced by a thoughtful, contemplative tone.

"We care about you." This wasn't the time for confessions of love.

Melanie twisted to press both hands to his knee. "I care about you as well."

The short silence that followed felt relaxed. Comfortable.

Until she turned to face Nathan. "And you—I still can't believe you. You're like a saint to put up with all the teasing I did this weekend."

"Saint Nathan." He seemed to consider it seriously for a moment before reaching to tweak her nose. "Don't think it fits. It's okay, monkey, I survived."

Her expression was unreadable. "Surviving isn't always enough, Nate. I've learned that the hard way."

Derrick stroked a hand down her arm. There were no words.

She turned to face him, whispering for his ears alone. "I want to prove to Nathan that I trust him. I want to thank him for being there."

Derrick didn't think she was talking about a store-bought gift. "He doesn't need anything. Caring for you doesn't require payment."

She straightened, anger flashing. "Caring for me also

shouldn't require him to put up with being insulted."

Ahhh. "Kane thought he was looking out for you."

"Unintentional pain still hurts like hell, Derrick."

They stared into each other's eyes. She gripped his forearms tightly, clinging to him. There was something in her face that made him pause. Longing was there, but also an incredible strength.

It took all his strength to ask the question. "What do you want?"

"To finish what you offered me in the mountains. What I was barely able to accept, but the acceptance changed my life. To be with two men I trust explicitly."

His blood pressure shot skyward, pulse pounding. Without intending to, his volume rose as well. "Be with us how? Sex?"

"Melanie, what the hell are you talking about?" Nathan roared. Derrick snapped his head up, ready to protect her. Guard her if necessary. But the other man was shaking his head, hands raised in protest as he rolled to his knees. "Damn it, this isn't something to joke about. Don't go screwing things up with Derrick. Not for some kind of cheap thrill."

Melanie scrambled upright, her petite body seeming to tower over them as he and Nathan remained sprawled on the safety mats. "I'll have you know I don't consider anything about you *cheap.*"

"Mel—"

"I *trust* you." Melanie touched Nathan's cheek. "You and Derrick. Completely."

Derrick's confusion and momentary sense of betrayal morphed into understanding. She wasn't asking on a whim, or out of a misplaced sense of obligation.

If her self-esteem had been tied up in the aftermath of her

fall, Nathan's was connected with his photography. Kane's accusations could have hit hard. She had assumed Nate needed her as much as she'd turned out to need him. Wanted to wash away a little of the hurt Nathan had experienced in exchange for the gift he'd given her.

Nathan caught her hand where it lay against his cheek, kissing her palm softly before pulling her close and enveloping her in an enormous bear hug. He gazed over her shoulder at Derrick, shaking his head slightly as he stroked her hair.

"Oh, monkey. I think I'm a little bit in love with you right now. You've got a heart that simply refuses to stop giving, and I'm honoured beyond belief that you'd offer yourself like that. But I have to say no." Melanie protested, and Nathan pulled away and stuck a finger in her face. "I am first, and foremost, your friend. Getting a chance to prove that you're an extremely attractive woman was a wonderful experience, but I'm bowing out of anything else. Unless…"

Derrick froze.

She straightened. "Unless what?"

There was a moment of hesitation before Nathan spoke, and then he stared at Derrick, as if asking his permission. "I want to watch again."

Melanie took in a rapid breath and Derrick tucked her back against him as she swayed off balance.

Nathan chuckled. "Does that surprise you? It did me, a little. Seems I've got a kink I wasn't aware of before."

"Watch? You want to watch…what?"

Nathan stood and paced toward the wall, turning slowly to face them, one brow quirked upward. "You two make love. Maybe take a few more pictures." He shrugged lightly. "If the answer is no, I'm fine—"

"Yes." Melanie sat upright, then stiffened, twisting to face Derrick. Her mouth hung open in a perfect O as she stared for a second. A blush raced over her cheeks and she lowered her eyes. "I mean, if it's okay with you."

He pulled her against his chest, breathing in her scent and feeling the tension in her body as she leaned in tighter. He spoke softly, just for her ears. "I understand why you suggested this."

She tilted her head back to stare at him. "It's important to me, Derrick. To be sure Nathan knows how *much* I trust him, but not if you don't want to. I'm sorry I sprang this on you without asking first. That was wrong of me."

There was no way he could remain angry, not when the expression on Melanie's face so clearly showed her heart.

She knew what she wanted, and why, and damned if he wasn't going to give it to her. Didn't stop possessiveness from rising up and flooding him as well. They could give reassurance to Nathan, but at the end, everyone would know who belonged with who.

Chapter Ten

Hangdog: A climber who hangs from the rope on a route.

Derrick delicately brushed a knuckle along her jaw as he admired her dark beauty. The way her eyes flashed, mouth twisted into a smile that was one hundred percent trouble, her chin rising in challenge. He slid his fingers around the back of her neck, teasing as he leaned in to kiss her. She grabbed his head and gave back as good as she got, a heated exchange, all teeth and tongues. They scrambled each other's brains as the air between them evaporated.

That wasn't the only thing that had vanished. Derrick dragged his hands down her shoulders to discover she'd been busy. Her clothing had disappeared, and all he touched was sweet, hot flesh.

His knees shook with anticipation. Then she slipped out of his arms as mysteriously as her clothing, only for him to feel a tug on his zipper and his jeans being peeled off his hips.

"Holy hell." Derrick focused downward to find Melanie kneeling before him. She was stark naked, big brown eyes staring at him as she wiggled his pants lower then leaned in to nuzzle his groin.

He was going to die, but he'd die happy.

Melanie caressed a hand over his erection, palm curving around his shaft as she dragged her fingernails over the fabric constraining his cock. When she finished by cupping his balls, stars blurred his vision.

Stripping off the final barrier between them was the work of a moment, and he didn't feel any remorse when she wrapped her fingers around his shaft and held him tight. She wanted to give Nathan a show? He'd accept the challenge and revel in every moment.

The touch of her tongue made his spine straighten, but it was the moist heat of her mouth enclosing his cock that turned his mind to mush.

Derrick watched, fixated, as she moved in an easy rhythm over him, saliva slicking his cock as she bobbed her head. Ball-breaking pleasure wrapped him tight as she sucked hard on each withdrawal. The urge to tangle his fingers in her hair and take control hit. He wanted to slam forward, feel the soft back of her throat against the crest of his cock. But even more, he wanted to switch positions and drive into her sex. Feel her tightness and heat until he had nothing left to do but give in to his release.

He closed his eyes and savoured her touch. Whatever she wanted—he'd do it. Willingly and completely. Which meant no matter how good this felt, he couldn't let her take him over the edge that approached at the speed of light.

He pulled from her mouth with a soft *pop*, the hard suction she gave at the final moment enough to make his eyes cross.

"Stand her up."

Nathan's gruff command brought Derrick back to reality—he stood naked in his climbing gym, as another man watched him play sexual games with Melanie. It shouldn't have turned him on as much as it did, seeing the hunger on Nathan's face that matched the desire in his own belly. He stooped and lifted Melanie to her feet. Their bare skin made contact, his erection trapped against her firm stomach. She wiggled, causing a fire of urgency to rain down.

It was time for him to take control. Because while Derrick's ardour was racing upward at the thought of how hot the situation was about to get, his heart could only handle sharing Melanie, even like this, one last time. From here on, he was going to make sure all her fantasies were two-person only, with him and her in the starring roles, no audiences. And no one else directing the action.

Derrick twirled her on the spot, leaning her naked body against him. That left them both facing Nathan. If the other man wanted to watch, Derrick would make their playtime something worth witnessing. Something to claim Melanie in an unmistakable manner. Fuck if that made him a possessive asshole—she was his.

He reached around to cup her breast, his palm covering the firm mound as he massaged and teased, his fingers plucking at her nipple until her head fell back against him and she whimpered.

"What do you want, Mel? My mouth? My tongue stabbing into you until you can't think?"

She squirmed, widening her stance. "Anything. Everything."

"Ropes?"

Utter silence greeted him. Then her breath quickened, and her chest heaved as she fought for control.

Yes.

He kissed her nape. Soft. Gentle. Made sure she was solid on her own before he released her and made his way to the baskets where they stored the climbing ropes. He ignored the thicker weight and reached for the softest one. Once he had it in his hand, he made eye contact with her and slowly pulled the length free. In all their escapades over the past months, he hadn't used ropes with her. One handful after another, the loops fell to the floor at his feet, their weight creating a hushed pulse with every new section. He let the strands slide through his fingers, enjoying the complete fascination he witnessed on her face. The trembling in her limbs.

He grabbed one more thing, then stooped and picked up the coil before returning to her side. His cock was so full it barely moved from its vertical position as he walked.

She flicked a glance at both his hands as he approached, examining the items he held. Her gaze landed on his groin, and she licked her lips. The tiny flash of pink tongue teased him. He wasn't going to be able to last long once they got going.

He stopped beside her, letting the rope hit the ground with another solid thump.

Goose bumps rose over her skin, and he smiled as he knelt at her feet.

"Step in."

Melanie raised a brow, but obediently lifted one foot at a time, resting one hand on his shoulder as he slipped a well-padded climbing harness onto her.

"Derrick? What are you doing?" Melanie brushed his fingers as he worked to close the buckle on the harness.

"You said you like ropes. So do I."

Her eyes went black, pupils so wide they blurred into her dark brown irises.

Derrick threaded one of the fixed climbing ropes through her harness loops, tying off the figure eight faster than he ever had in his life. Then he reached down and got ready for the best part.

"Back on your knees." Shit, was that his voice? He half expected her to run from the room screaming, the words burst out so gravely and harsh.

Instead, she smiled and fell gracefully to her knees. Only her gaze remained glued to the rope, and her breath hitched again.

He stepped behind her, leaning down to kiss her shoulder. He trailed the end of the rope over her back, and she arched in reaction, perfect breasts presented toward where their now-silent witness stood.

Derrick concentrated for a moment, gathering his own strength. Then he began.

Her arms he left hanging. The first loop of rope crossed her body from left to right, the strand passing between her breasts. The second loop he wound around her torso, then a mirror loop right to left, framing her torso into erotic art.

Every layer he added—slow, methodical—brought increasing noises of pleasure from her lips. Small moans and sighs. Tiny gasps as his knuckles brushed her skin. When he was finished, the waist belt he'd placed on her was covered, except for the traditional leg harnesses looped around each of her thighs. The attached belaying rope lay free, blossoming from the middle of her back.

Nothing guarded her sex. She was locked in place, unable to move her upper body, and yet her sex, her breasts—all bare for his pleasure.

And hers.

He knelt, raising her chin until he could stare into her eyes. Making sure she was fine, that she was still on board. From the happy sigh she gave him, the hint of glazing in her eyes, and the wetness painting her inner thighs, it was clear she was enjoying herself.

"Ready?"

She nodded. He touched her breast again, just passing a fingertip over the peak, and her eyes closed. "Hmmm."

"More?"

Derrick waited for her nod, then paced to the wall where the rope of her harness fed up to the ceiling carabiner. He lifted her skyward, only a couple feet, securing the loose end to the wall. He'd chosen a fixed rope that left Melanie suspended in the center of the room, free of any entanglements.

Derrick dropped to his knees and nestled his face against her, smelling her arousal, feeling the curls damp with moisture.

"Oh God. Derrick..."

He lifted her left leg over his shoulder, bringing her that much closer. One hand he slipped upward to open her, enjoying the way her cream glistened on her lips. Leaning in closer, he licked, her instant gasp of pleasure making him smile against her sex.

Then he gave up all restraint. Nibbles and long solid laves. A teasing caress around the heated nub of her clit. When that pulled a soft moan from her, he did it again, pausing to flick harder with the tip of his tongue. He'd barely gotten started when Melanie cried out, her fingers below the ropes clutching the straps of her leg harness as her body pulsed in climax.

It was only the beginning. He dipped in for another round.

Melanie still hung suspended in the air, shaking from yet another orgasm. "Enough, stop. Oh please, I need..."

She wasn't sure what she needed. Oxygen? It was hard to breathe, but that had nothing to do with the ropes enveloping her body. Everything to do with the man stalking her like a wild beast ready to take down his prey.

Never had any prey been as willing as she.

Derrick caught her against him, kissing her until the air thinned to the equivalent of a high mountaintop. When he finally let her go, she could have sworn the room was spinning.

"You ready?" Derrick snuck away for a moment, grabbing two more ropes from where they rested against the gym walls. Released from his hold, she twisted in an actual circle, her rope supporting her vertically, but not restricting the slow spiraling motion.

He knotted the new ropes together then passed the connected section around her upper torso. When he tugged, she tipped forward in slow motion, supported on the webbing in the middle.

The combination of ropes and harness put her on her belly in a flying position. Or, wrapped up as she was, like a fly in a spider's web.

She glanced over her shoulder. "Am I ready for what?"

Sex and fire shone in his eyes as he ran a hand over her rope-encased back, down her naked butt. "Anything I want."

There was possession in his tone. He opened her legs wide and stepped between them, and comprehension hit. "You made a sex sling."

"Hmm. I did." His cock nudged her core and she closed her eyes to concentrate fully as he pressed them together. Stretched wide, open to his invasion, his cock hot and hard as he filled her.

Each backward rock speared Derrick deeper. The sensation was physically powerful, and exactly what she wanted—to offer herself up and be unconditionally accepted. Not even once had she considered her body except for the pleasure she could give him. The bliss he was causing.

Not even once had she considered Nathan watched.

The shock that raced through her at the realization was startling in its intensity. She had offered herself to Nathan, wanting to give to him if he needed her, but it was the man she'd come to know in such an intimate manner over the past months who held her mesmerized. With his touch. His claiming.

It was impossible to feel guilt. This was what Nathan had asked for. It was what she needed.

Derrick clung tightly to her hips as he pounded into her, unrelenting strokes feeding the fires inside that were ready to burst again. Then, before she could come, he stopped the momentum of her swing. His harsh groans echoed off the walls, his body bent over her as he held himself deep. Melanie let her head hang and breathed through her nose, the smell of climbing chalk buried beneath the scent of sweat and sex on the air.

When he lifted his torso, it was to let his hands roam again. Stroking in sweeps over her bare cheeks, teasing her hips and inner thighs. He tugged her legs downward, then stroked his fingers over her hole, teasing the sensitive nerves.

"I'm going to fuck your ass."

It wasn't a question, but it was. He'd never taken what she wasn't ready for, or what she was unwilling to give. He stroked again. A slippery finger dipped into her passage, and she squirmed. Where he'd found the tube of lube—she didn't need to know.

"Oh yes. Do it."

He worked her in a rush, fingers scrambling on her hips. Soon it wasn't fingers touching her, but the hard and much larger tip of his cock.

Derrick pushed forward, opening her, and she squeezed her eyes tight. The fire she felt wasn't pain, wasn't pleasure. Somewhere between the two sensations she hovered, just as she floated off the floor of the gym. Between worlds, between realities.

With a final groan, Derrick brought his groin tight to her ass, and she sighed.

"So damn beautiful."

Then Derrick swung her away and let her weight in the sling and momentum drive her back on him. Melanie gasped, needy moans escaping as he speared her again and again. He wasn't gentle anymore, and she couldn't do anything but accept his need. The nearly violent pleasure he thrust upon her.

The burning in her ass was good. Dirty and hot, and just when she thought she'd explode, he dug his fingers into the softer flesh of her hip and froze, fighting for control. Melanie let out a little scream as he pulled her upright, the move burying his cock in her ass.

There was no room. No retreat. If before she'd been between worlds, she'd traveled light years farther into outer space.

He touched *her*, inside and out. Her body, her mind. Her soul.

And there were no more scars there.

Time blurred, sensations shot to a tantalizing edge before rocketing her off the cliffs and setting her into freefall. Her climax tore her apart and rebuilt her as her body squeezed tight around his shaft. Voices shouted in passion—hers? Derrick's? They were together and one. Melanie leaned back, letting Derrick support her as she gave way to complete boneless relaxation.

Oh God, that had felt good.

She couldn't open her eyes, she was so sated. He withdrew from her body, lowered her to a kneeling position. Even as the ropes fell from her limbs, even as the harness was removed, she drifted in some faraway place she had no intention of leaving anytime soon.

How Derrick found the strength to carry her, she had no idea—she couldn't peel her eyes open. Not when he laid her on the mat, not when a warm cloth touched her body.

And when his strong arms held her close as they lay back on the mats, Melanie gave a happy sigh and let sleep take her.

Nathan stared down from where he'd retreated to the upper galley for a better view. Melanie curled herself around Derrick, her hair strewn over his naked chest as she used him as a pillow. He wrapped an arm around her shoulders, their torsos touching, limbs tangled together. Light movements of their chests revealed the easy breathing of sleep overtaking them.

They looked good together. They were good together.

For the past week Nathan could have sworn he was riding a bloody roller coaster. Steamy sexual desire followed by intense frustration. Professional advancement and condemnation. Helping a friend tear down walls that had trapped her for years, then realizing friendship was all he could offer her—if he wasn't riding a high he'd been hitting a low, and the cumulative effect had come close to draining him of all common sense.

Kane's outburst had shocked him, but not because he didn't know deception occurred in his business. His intentions were clear as far as the magazine was concerned. It was the fact that for him being with Melanie *was* far more about sexual experimentation than long-term commitment. Kane had hit the nail on the head with that one, and guilt rode Nathan hard.

The only redeeming factor was his decision to not come

between Derrick and Melanie.

And then? When she said she wanted him? *Goddamn, fucking hell.*

Nathan had wanted her too, and it had taken all his strength to turn away. To walk out without one more taste of the paradise that was going to be Derrick's to enjoy for what looked to be forever.

He had watched, the burn of jealousy fading as he visually feasted on their lovemaking. It wasn't his turn for love like this, but seeing it? Knowing it could be real?

That was a gift he'd never expected to receive.

Nathan watched the lovers snuggle together on the mat, oblivious to his presence. This was as it should be, and only one thought repeated in his mind.

Time to move on.

It had been good to witness unconditional love. Someday he hoped to find for himself what was growing between Melanie and Derrick.

Nathan grabbed his camera bag and backpack, and silently slipped out the door.

Chapter Eleven

Red-Point: Lead climb from bottom to top without falling after rehearsing the moves.

Melanie wrinkled her nose in disgust. The only thing that made her read to the end was morbid curiosity. Kind of like slowing to check out a car accident. "This article isn't any better than the others."

"But at least it's not about you." Kane plucked the magazine from her fingers and tossed it in the trash.

"I feel damn sorry for the poor sod it is about." Derrick passed the popcorn bowl over, and Melanie mindlessly added butter and salt.

The second of *Rave*'s two September issues was out, without the article featuring her, and Melanie was both confused and relieved. Just as Kane feared, each new magazine release had proven the stories to be sensationalized garbage. Even knowing she wasn't yet the focus of negative attention didn't make Melanie's anxiety disappear. While she trusted Nathan, he had been clear the actual article was out of his control. She'd almost resigned herself to being center stage in a nasty exposé.

Still, there was something else wrong she couldn't put her finger on. She helped carry the snacks into the living room, distracted from her gloomy thoughts by the sight of her brother with his best friend Jack, their pregnant partner snuggled between them. Now that it was official the three of them were together on a permanent basis, Melanie got a huge kick out of teasing Kane.

Dara didn't seem to mind the banter—in fact, she aided and abetted every chance she got.

"You need anything, Dara?" Melanie plopped the popcorn bowl on the coffee table, moving aside beer bottles to make room.

Dara glanced on either side of her before turning back and raising a brow. "I have two guys at my beck and call. Trust me, if I want anything, they've got it covered."

Jack chucked a piece of popcorn at her. "Kane's on slave duty this week, woman."

Of course his instant capitulation two minutes later when she asked him for a glass of water proved her point, and Dara winked at Melanie from where she was curled up, nestled between her men.

Melanie crawled onto the love seat next to Derrick, and they all dove back into their movie.

By the time the DVD finished, Melanie had realized what was bugging her. She slipped back into the kitchen and was digging through the garbage when Dara wandered into the kitchen, Derrick on her heels.

"It's not Nathan." Melanie flipped the magazine open and scrambled through the pages.

"It's not Nathan what?" Dara asked.

"The pictures. Look, Derrick, those aren't his shots. That doesn't look at all like his work." A huge sigh of relief hit, even though now she was more confused than ever.

Dara made a disgusted sound. "Throw the magazine out again, Mel. There's nothing in that trash you need to see."

"But Nathan isn't listed in the credits anymore. Not for any of the shots. I wonder why?"

"When is the article on you supposed to be published?"

Melanie thought for a moment. "He said it would be fourth quarter, since he was taking the shots in August. But *none* of these pictures are his, and I know while he'd been assigned to get all the illustrations for that series of articles, he usually has other credits as well."

Dara leaned back on the kitchen counter, the front of her shirt hanging loose. "Maybe he switched jobs? Have you managed to get hold of him at all?"

"Just a couple emails. He said he was fine, things were okay. It was like talking to a total stranger. At least we know he's still alive, but that's about it."

"Then there's not much you can do but wait." A huge yawn escaped Dara. "I'm sorry, but I'm ready for bed."

A couple hearty laughs sounded as Jack and Kane joined them, carrying in the dirty dishes. Kane wiggled his brows at her. "No objections on my part with that suggestion."

Dara smacked him on the chest. "Behave. You two are the reason I'm totally exhausted at nine o'clock. Building a baby is hard work."

"So's starting one." Jack ducked under her swing then scooped her up in his arms, ignoring her protests. "Thanks for the evening's entertainment, guys. We'll see you in a few?"

Derrick leaned Melanie back against his chest, resting his chin on her shoulder. She savoured the warmth of his body as her brother and the others took their leave. When she really considered it, the article was an annoyance on the edge of all the good things she now had in her life. And Dara was right—there was nothing she could do anyway but wait.

"I'd better be getting home as well." She twisted in Derrick's arms to give him a good-night kiss.

He brushed their lips together and refused to let her escape. "Stay."

It wouldn't be the first time she'd slept over. In the month since Nathan had vanished, they'd spent more and more time together. She still hadn't gotten up the courage to actually confess her feelings in words, although they both seemed to have come to the conclusion they liked each other. A lot. Melanie opened her mouth to answer, and he kissed her again, stalling her response. She smiled against his lips, stroking her fingers over his broad shoulders. She loved being in his arms.

Derrick whispered against her cheek. "Stay with me forever."

A shiver raced up her spine. *What?* "Derrick?"

He held her chin delicately in his strong fingers. "I love you. I want this to be your home. With me."

Melanie's heart pounded, a flush of heat racing over her entire body. "You love me?"

He laughed, and the lightness of the sound broke into sparkling pieces and bounced off the walls of the room to fill her ears with joy and her heart with hope. "Damn it, Mel, you missed your cue. It's like climbing. You ask 'On belay?' and I respond 'Belay on.' So when I say 'I love you', you're supposed to say it back. I know it's taken me a damn long time to get up my courage to ask you. I was holding out, trying to figure out the exact right moment, but unless I've been totally misreading you for the last—"

She dragged their mouths together and kissed him senseless until there was no possible way he could be uncertain

291

of her response.

October

"Derrick, come look."

Melanie carried in the package she'd found on the front porch when she got back from her run. The parcel was well wrapped, and she brought it into the living room, excitement rushing her as she spotted the return address.

"What's up?" He wandered down the stairs, wearing nothing but his jeans and total distraction hit. Reaching with one hand, she touched his chest and let him draw her in for a long, slow kiss that made her toes curl.

She was the luckiest woman in the world. Melanie released him, sighing with sadness as he pulled on his shirt and covered up all that wide expanse of firm male chest. She couldn't get enough of him. Even having moved in together didn't give her enough time to fully appreciate not only his body, but his presence.

How he made her feel inside and out.

The leaves on the trees had completely changed colour in the past week, and they were well on their way into fall. Outdoor climbing was over for the season, but she'd been working hard in the gym whenever Derrick was scarce, getting ready to share her surprise with him.

She shook the box. "This was on the top of the steps. Look who it's from."

Derrick swore lightly. "Nathan. Bugger it. Go on, open it up. Let's see what he sent us."

He tugged her toward the couch, and they sat, sunshine falling over their shoulders as she worked the edges of the paper open.

The wrapping fell away to reveal a fabric-covered hardcover rectangle. Melanie grabbed the handwritten note taped to the front and leaned against Derrick to read it with him.

Hey, Monkey.

You've probably been wondering what the hell is up with the article, etc. When I got back and went digging I found a few things I didn't like. Kane wasn't far off in his accusations, and Rave did have an agenda. It wasn't mine, so I didn't deliver the pictures I took. That kind of put me in breach of contract, making it simpler to quit, and that's about all I have to say about that.

She'd have felt guiltier if they hadn't already discussed the likelihood. "Oh my God, he did quit."

Derrick squeezed her shoulders for a moment. "It was always a possibility. He's a big boy. Trust him, he knew what he was doing."

Melanie nodded, but she still felt remorse for having been a part of Nathan losing a prime position.

My private project, on the other hand, rocks. As promised, final decision is up to you. I've made a mockup—done in private, so no one but me has seen it. No one will see it unless you and Derrick give me the go-ahead.

If you approve, I'll work toward publication. If not, this book is for you to enjoy, my gift to you both in celebration of your courage.

I'm shooting freelance now and doing okay. I'll drop in when I'm in the neighbourhood. You're special people. Thanks for sharing your lives with me.

Derrick picked up the book and laid it across his knees, opening the front cover to reveal a full-page black-and-white photograph of Melanie. Shadow-draped, her naked body was silhouetted against a pale background. The strongest point of illumination highlighted her face and her eyes. Her attention was riveted on something before her, and the camera angle made it appear she looked directly at the viewer, demanding they see her absolute determination.

The title in plain font, black on white—*Rising, Freestyle.*

The dedication—*To Melanie, who ascended from darkness into the light never losing the beauty in her soul.*

Page after page of the most gorgeous and sensual pictures followed, tastefully done, but all downright erotic. Close-ups defining the detail of her neck, the curve of her buttock, the contrast of Derrick's heavy thigh muscle against Melanie's leaner limb. A loop of rope draped over her breast, the faintest shadow of the climbing wall with a marked route disappearing skyward in the background.

Derrick turned to each new offering with deliberate care. Reverence. Not only pictures, but simple one-line text accompanied the occasional shot, echoing the words Melanie had shared over the weekend away. Each one revealed a moment of pain, her struggles.

The need for time to bring healing.

The necessity of devoted friends.

The rediscovery of love—for herself and for another.

"This is incredible." Melanie ran a finger over a close-up image of Derrick kissing her back. Firelight glowed, the hints of reds and yellows creating a mystic world. His darkness was somehow made deeper, her body ethereal and angelic in comparison.

294

And in spite of her scars, stunning.

Derrick pressed his lips to her temple. "Because you are, and always have been, beautiful."

By the time they finished the book, tears threatened to fall as she appreciated Nathan's sublime skill with photography. Understood what a gift he'd given to her, not only when he was there, but now through his art.

She looked up to see Derrick ignoring the photo book and instead staring at her.

"Are you okay?"

Oh God. There was only one possible answer to that question. "I have never in my life been better. Derrick, if I said I wanted Nathan to go ahead and get this published, what would you think?"

He considered for a moment, his expression somber. "I don't know, there's a shot of my bare butt in there, you know."

She'd noticed. "That's my favourite. Think I'll ask Nathan if I can have a blowup for our bedroom."

Derrick grinned. "If I can ask for an extra of the shot of your boobs."

Melanie hit him before carefully placing the album aside and crawling up to straddle his lap. "Serious."

"I am serious."

She tugged his chin up and slowly lowered her head until their lips brushed. Familiar, yet magical. His kiss ignited flames inside and warmed her soul.

A solid knock on the front door was the only thing that stopped their caresses from carrying on to the next logical progression.

Melanie abandoned his lips with reluctance. "Save my seat."

"Permanently."

Images from the incredible offering Nathan had produced still flooded her mind. Somehow they would track him down and let him know their decision. Tell him to stop in and visit them soon.

Melanie swung open the door and stared into a familiar pair of blue eyes above a cocky smile.

A happy squeal escaped as she threw herself into Nathan's arms. Melanie clung to his neck with one arm, squeezing his neck tight as she laughed and cried and pounded on his shoulder with her free hand.

"It's you. It's you."

Nathan laughed and squeezed the air from her lungs with his hug. "It's me. Can I come in?"

He managed to place her feet back on the floor only a second before being caught in a hug by Derrick. Melanie couldn't stop her heart from racing. Nathan was back.

He'd left without saying a word.

She thumped him on the shoulder again for good measure. "You ass. What the hell were you thinking, running out on us?"

Nathan followed Derrick into the living room. "I was thinking you needed to move on, and so did I."

He had a point, but Melanie was still pissed. "You could have said something before you disappeared."

"And what's with the magical appearance right now?" Derrick asked. He pointed at the photo album on the coffee table. "Were you in the delivery truck with the packages?"

"Sort of." Nathan gave a sheepish smile. "I dropped off the book and I've been parked on the street up the road waiting until one of you picked it up. Felt like a complete ass every time one of your neighbours walked by and eyed me like I was a crook casing the joint."

Melanie checked him over. He looked good. Trim and strong, still as dashing as ever.

But he didn't make her body ache like he'd done before.

She glanced at Derrick. He smiled and held her hand, all warm and intimate in his. Both of them at ease. This was their home now, and Nathan was simply a good friend come to visit.

A deep sense of peace rolled over her. "Come on—I'll make us coffee."

Melanie led them into the kitchen and got the water going as conversation spilled around them. She had so many questions she wanted to ask, but in the end, it seemed most of them came down to one thing.

Were they all happy?

Nathan sipped from his cup before pointing between them. "So, what's up with you guys? One house, I hear."

Derrick beamed. "Melanie's moved in. I sacrificed my closet space to her shoe collection."

Yeah, right. "Damn, I forgot I was supposed to start leaving stockings on the shower rod."

They exchanged contented smiles before Melanie tore her gaze away and returned to Nathan. "And you? The note said you quit *Rave.*"

He nodded. "There was a little more involved than that, but it's okay. You don't have to worry about them including you in the series either—that was part of the deal with me leaving."

An icy cool wall of relief hit. "You're serious? How did you pull that off?"

He shrugged nonchalantly. "Part of my negotiations. I can't talk about the details, but I don't want you to fuss, okay?"

"Do you miss working for *Rave?*" She didn't want to have

ruined his career.

Nathan snorted. "Not at all. The freelance I'm doing pays just as well, and now that I've bought a camper, I'm mobile and can work anywhere. Amazing how being able to travel freely makes it easier to get some assignments."

"Sounds as if you're even more footloose and fancy-free than usual," Derrick teased. "Going to take advantage of better weather in the south and get away from the coming snow?"

Derrick continued to quiz Nathan on his plans, and Melanie simply soaked it in.

With her lover's arm around her, Melanie was anchored in the warmth of her surroundings. She enjoyed the chatter as Nathan filled in the missing gaps from the past months, and his optimistic hopes for the future. Knowing that Nathan was going to be okay, finding a place in Derrick's heart—her happiness was almost complete now.

There was only one more thing she wanted to accomplish, and it was time.

Somehow they ended up back at the gym, Chinese takeout boxes scattered again.

"Why do I feel like we've entered a time warp?" Derrick stroked her hair as Melanie leaned against his chest. He hoped she wasn't going to suggest another round of sex in front of Nathan. He wasn't willing to share her ever again, not even that way.

She giggled. "Sorry, no wild sexcapades this time."

"Well, damn," Nathan complained. "I had this new rope trick I wanted to show you."

She stuck out her tongue and he instantly clicked a

picture. "Will you stop that?" she demanded.

"Monkey."

"Jackass." Melanie scrambled to her feet. "I want to climb. Derrick, belay me?"

That wasn't what he expected. "Right now?"

She was already scrambling into her harness. "Now."

Derrick exchanged a confused shrug with Nathan, but went to grab his belt. Nathan gathered the remains of their dinner and cleared the floor, stepping out of the way to allow Melanie access to the wall.

She grabbed him by the arm on her return journey, hauling him close and hugging him fiercely. Nathan was stiff at first before returning the salute.

They were both grinning like fools when he stepped away.

Derrick was in the middle of checking the straps on her harness when Melanie caught him unaware. The gentle touch of her lips to his cheek was accompanied by her fingers tangling in his hair. She tugged until their lips connected, then continued the light blessing of their mouths together.

It would be easy to do this all night long.

When she pressed her hands to his chest, it was to both push them apart and to keep them together, her fingers clutching the front of his shirt. "I love you."

A rush of happiness hit like a rockslide, making his knees weak. "I love you too."

"On belay?"

Oh man. Would he ever get used to her high-energy mood swings? Derrick adjusted the rope, taking up the slack and pulling his head back into the game. "Belay on."

Melanie grabbed the wall, stepping up to lift both feet clear of the floor. "Climbing?"

He'd support her as high as she wanted to go. "Climb on."

One move followed another. Deliberate. Cautious, yet not. She tested her grip before releasing each previous hold, but she didn't take the simplest route up the wall. She reached and stretched, using her muscular legs and flexible core to attempt challenging holds.

Nathan stepped behind him and spoke quietly as if afraid to disturb her. "What's she doing?"

Derrick shrugged but kept his eyes locked on her rising body. "Proving something to us? Something to herself?"

"She doesn't have to prove anything to me."

Melanie didn't even hesitate as she passed the fifteen-foot marker, progressing one hold at a time. Pride swelled inside Derrick at her fearlessness. "I couldn't agree more."

Halfway up the wall she paused. "Take."

"Got. Fabulous work." The poise she showed highlighted how far she'd come in the past five months.

"Oh, I'm not done."

Derrick waited, watching her peer down at him from her perch. "What's up, sweetheart?"

She flashed a grin on them both. "Give me slack. I'm climbing the rest freestyle."

Shit. "Melanie…"

"Do it. I'm good. Really I am."

He paused. Assessing. Looking into her bright eyes, her confident face. It took a lot for him to release his own fears. "As you wish."

She blew him a kiss before facing the wall resolutely. "Climbing."

Derrick forced himself to obey her request—mostly. She

wouldn't get hurt. Worst-case scenario, if she did slip off a hold, the rope he still controlled would halt her before she'd fallen far. He wasn't strong enough to let her completely free, so he cheated, just a little. Gave her a loose rope, but took up the extra slack to make sure the most she could fall was less than five feet.

It wasn't a case of not trusting her skills, but loving her enough to care even when she didn't ask him to.

"She's beautiful when she's climbing." There was a note of awe in Nathan's voice.

"She's beautiful all the time," Derrick corrected.

And when Melanie reached the top of the wall and sounded the bicycle horn mounted on the ceiling, Derrick fought back tears.

"Take." Sheer delight tinged her voice as she called out.

Derrick tightened up the extra rope to secure her in position. "Got." *For now. Forever.*

Far above them, a loud shout echoed off the walls as Melanie cried out her victory, both hands raised over her head. She spun in a lazy circle as he lowered her to the ground and into his arms.

"I did it." The words brushed past his cheek as she whispered in his ear. "I really did it."

Derrick squeezed her close in spite of the ropes and harnesses tangled between them. She'd more than accomplished her goal. She'd risen above her fears, and he was going to enjoy every moment of watching her face the future.

Together, they could rise above any challenges that came their way.

About the Author

Vivian Arend has hiked, biked, skied and paddled her way around most of North America and parts of Europe. Throughout all the wandering in the wilderness, stories have been planted and they are bursting out in vivid colour. Paranormal, twisted fairytales, red-hot contemporaries—the genres are all over.

Between times of living with no running water, she home schools her teenaged children and tries to keep up with her husband—the instigator of most of the wilderness adventures.

She loves to hear from readers: vivarend@gmail.com. You can also drop by www.vivianarend.com for more information on what is coming next.

Play out the hand her way...or fold?

Raising the Stakes
© *2010 Jess Dee*
Three of a Kind, Book 2

After four years, Megan Loxley has given up waiting for her best friend, Desmond Reed, to realize she loves him. It's time to move on. When Des introduces her to his poker buddy, Alex Truman, the instantaneous sparks that flare between them signal her life is about to change forever.

Des could kick himself. How could he have failed to notice the perfect woman was by his side all this time? Now it's too damn late. And her innocent prodding about why he's suddenly so distant is only making his hunger for her worse. Then she gets one step too close—and his self-restraint snaps.

Stunned, bewildered, furious, Meg can't help but respond to the kisses for which she waited so long. God help her, she loves Des. And Alex, too. Immeasurably. Now what?

It may make her the greediest woman alive, but she's determined to win the next hand—even if she has to change the game a little. First step: state her wildly sexy proposition in a language both men will understand...and hope they'll stick around and play by her rules.

Warning, If you're looking for a cool game of poker, you won't find it here. This novella is so hot the cards are still smoking. The heroine may be new to the game, but she knows exactly how to play her two kings.

Available now in ebook from Samhain Publishing.

SAMHAIN

PUBLISHING

It's all about the story...

Romance

HORROR

www.samhainpublishing.com